T.L. BODINE

The Darkness of Dreamland

Previously published in an earlier version as Tagestraum in 2014

Second edition

ISBN: 978-1-7374650-0-3

Cover art by Claire Stewart

This book was professionally typeset on Reedsy.
Find out more at reedsy.com

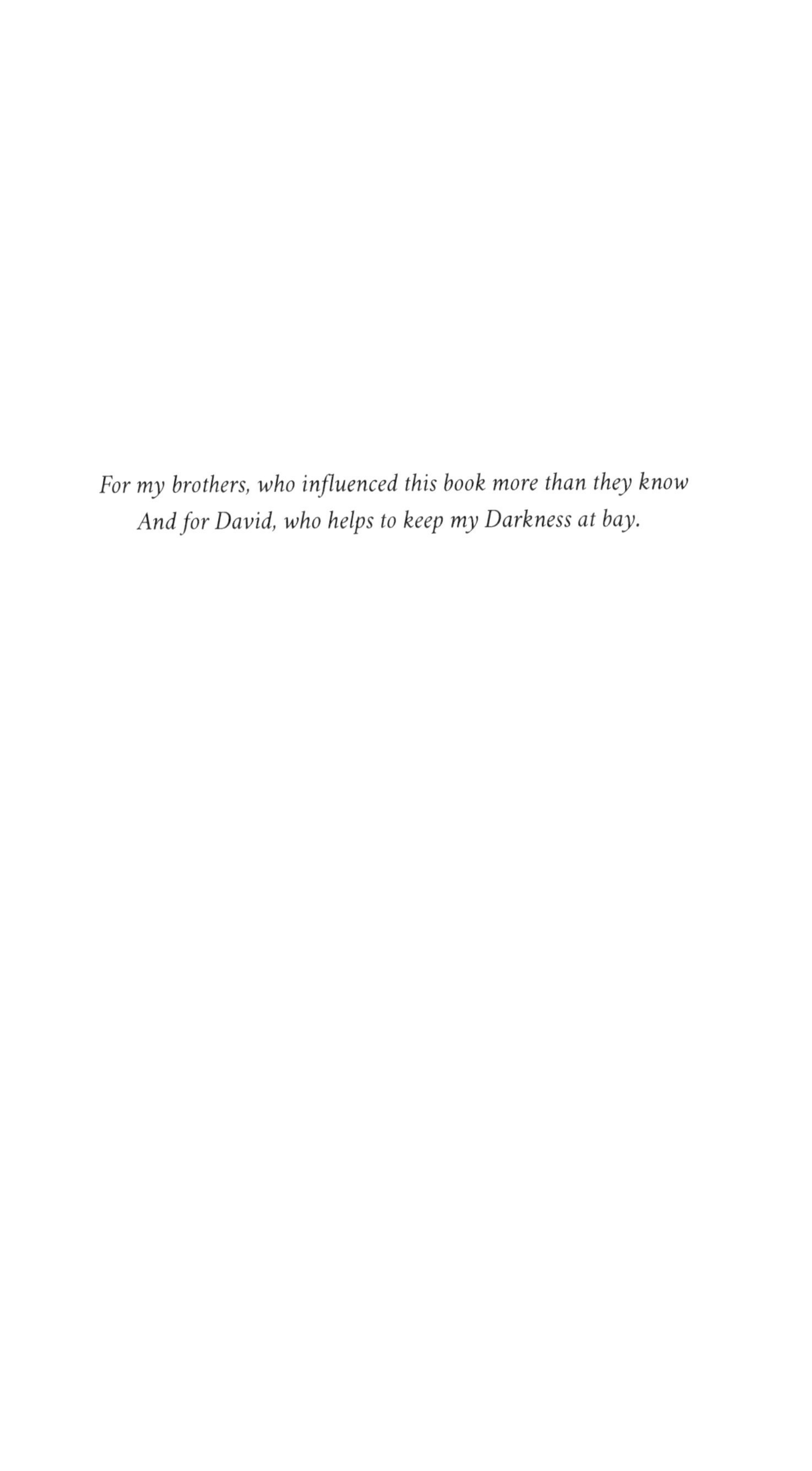

*For my brothers, who influenced this book more than they know
And for David, who helps to keep my Darkness at bay.*

Come away, O human child!
To the waters and the wild
With a faery, hand in hand,
For the world's more full of weeping
Than you can understand

—W.B. Yeats, "The Stolen Child"

Preface

In 2014, I released a novel called *Tagestraum.*

It suffered every problem you might expect from an inexperienced self-publisher: a badly designed cover, messy formatting, and a title that was both hard to pronounce and conveyed no information about the book. When I was first writing the story, the idea of naming my Dreamland something more foreign and exotic seemed appealing. But the problem with making a play on words in a language you don't speak is that it just doesn't work very well, as my German readers have kindly and gently pointed out.

But for all its flaws, I still believe very strongly in the story, and thought it deserved a second chance at finding its readership. The book you now hold in your hands is the result.

The Darkness of Dreamland is essentially the same as *Tagestraum.* It's been reformatted, copy-edited, and given a fresh cover. It's also had some factual inaccuracies cleared up and a few changes made to the first couple chapters. But heart and soul, it's the same book, and I'm excited to send it out in the world to find new readers…and perhaps make a few old fans happy to see fresh life breathed into this odd, dark, funny, horror-fantasy book.

Thank you for reading, and I hope you have as much fun visiting Dreamland as I had writing it!

THE NIGHTMARE MAN

The Nightmare Man came today.

Adrian could still hear the echo of Nathaniel's words in his mind — the words the boy had said when he'd first shown him the drawing. The sketch now stared up at him from the coffee table, crudely drawn in crayon but clear enough to recognize: A tall, cloaked man with a gaping mouth rimmed in teeth like the maw of some deep-sea fish.

The first time Nathaniel had shown him The Nightmare Man, months ago now, a cold chill had crept up Adrian's back, a sense of déjà vu that he could not entirely place. He didn't know why, but he was certain he'd seen the figure before, with its pale skin and bony hands. That first night, he'd searched online, pulled books off his bookshelf and flipped through them, certain he'd seen the creature somewhere. But he couldn't find a matching image in any book or movie or video game, and certainly in nothing that a seven-year-old would have seen.

It bothered him not being able to place it. Now, with Nathaniel missing and no leads on his disappearance, it bothered him a whole lot more.

The phone clicked in his ear as the voice mail picked up. Adrian waited for the beep, then said, "Hey, Detective Roark? It's Adrian Montgomery again, from Social Services, about the Weaver case? I'm not sure if my last call went through…you didn't call me back. I just wanted to —"

The phone beeped, and the call disconnected.

Adrian dialed again. It took longer to connect this time. Finally, the line picked up, and a woman's electronic monotone said, "We're sorry. The voice mailbox you are calling is full. Please try your call again later."

For good measure, he tried it one more time. When he got the same message, he rose from the couch and walked into the kitchen, depositing both his phone and the sketch into his pocket.

He opened his refrigerator. Light bathed the room, and he stood in the glow for a long time, staring at the mostly-bare shelves. After a minute, he closed the door and walked into his office, sitting down at the computer chair without bothering to turn on the light.

He pulled up the online Missing Children Registry, searching for familiar names. There were a few; Social Services and missing children tended to go together more often than he'd like. Not like Nathaniel, though. Kids were usually kidnapped by their estranged parents, or ran away from home. They didn't just vanish from their backyards in broad daylight, with no witnesses, no suspects, no evidence.

And they didn't tell their child welfare agent about The Nightmare Man.

Nathaniel wasn't the kind of kid to run away. Adrian was confident of that. He'd been working with the Weavers for nearly eight months — ever since Nathaniel's second grade teacher found out that the boy was staying by himself in a motel room while his mother worked two jobs as a maid and night greeter at Wal-Mart. Things had been bad, then, but they were better now. Angela Weaver had a decent new job, was renting half of a town house. Nathaniel's grades were improving. Adrian had seen all of it happen, coming as close to a happy ending as any case he'd ever worked on. It didn't make any sense for things to go wrong *now*.

Adrian reached the end of the missing person's registry. There was nothing new from the last time he'd checked that morning: no other disappearances from the area, no other vanishing children. He spent some time skimming the news, scrolling through Google looking for un-clicked links about the story. There were none. Several pages in, he felt his eyes slide out of focus, and found himself re-reading the same results several times without them sinking in. Realizing, as he noticed this, that he was exhausted, he pushed back his chair and shut down his computer.

He made his way across the room, unbuttoning his shirt as he padded down the hall into his bedroom, the silence of his house keeping him company.

His walls were bare. They always had been, even when he hadn't lived alone, although Jessica had pestered him about it when they'd moved in together.

"Most people keep photos of their family in the hall," she had said in her usual half-teasing, half-nagging way. *"You've got to have pictures of somebody."*

"We don't like family photos," he had told her. *"And besides, I don't like being watched by my walls."* Jessica had laughed. But it was true. Adrian didn't like photographs of people, and he never had. He didn't like the way they caught moments of time in stasis, the way that dead people could stare out of their frame with cheerful ignorance of their fate.

He gave a shuddering yawn, shrugged out of his shirt, and lay down on his bed, too tired to finish undressing. The bed seemed too big these days. He was accustomed to going to sleep in an empty bed, but knowing that he would wake up in one made it worse.

Adrian had practiced the same sleep ritual since he was a kid, so long that it had become essential. He'd tried to explain that many times to his wife, without much success. Jessica had always liked to talk in bed. She talked when they made love, and even afterward she would trace shapes onto his chest with her fingertips and ask what he was thinking. On nights they didn't have sex — which had become more and more frequent as the marriage wound its way towards the inevitable — she would lie beside him in stony silence, punctuated by the sort of questions that had no right answer and would invariably lead to a blazing argument that would carry long into the early hours of the morning. After that, sleeping was impossible, ritual or not.

To combat this, Adrian had started going to bed an hour earlier than she did, so he would have time for his sleep ritual. She had always taken this as a personal affront despite his continual, weary explanation that she really had absolutely nothing to do with anything that went on in his head. *It doesn't really matter now,* Adrian thought, taking another deep breath. *You've got all the time in the world to do whatever you like. Hope it was worth it.*

With his eyes closed, Adrian visualized the inside of his mind. He always imagined his mind as a cavernous room, like a chamber in a cathedral. The walls were lined, floor to ceiling, with file cabinets, each of them labeled.

Every night, before falling asleep, Adrian sorted through his thoughts from the day and filed them away safely into the appropriate place. He imagined himself labeling a fresh drawer with a sticker that said "missing children" and filed away everything away for the night. He would deal with all of it later.

He gathered up his sour memories and tangled longing and pointless arguments and put them into the "Jessica" cabinet. He hesitated a moment, then imagined himself locking the drawer.

Adrian's breath slowed. Darkness crept into his now-empty, peaceful mind. His body grew heavy, liquid, and then dissolved altogether as sleep overtook him and he fell clumsily into a dream. He'd had the dream before. Everything felt familiar, like re-watching an old movie that's since been forgotten. Adrian knew that he was asleep — knew that he was dreaming — but it didn't matter. The dream held him all the same.

He walked along a pathway: a long, straight road that stretched out forever into the horizon. At its end, the trees like tangled bones curved over it to form a roof. The further he traveled, the longer the path seemed to grow, the thatched tunnel ahead of him looming even further away, unavoidable but impossibly distant.

A figure stood in the mouth of the tunnel, silhouetted against the woods as though it had been cut out of the world with a knife. Adrian started running, wanting to catch the figure, wanting to get closer. No matter how quickly he ran he could not reach his goal, as though he were running the wrong way on a moving sidewalk. He wanted to call out but he had no voice; there was no sound here in this world of roads and trees and darkness.

The figure at the end of the road turned its face toward him.

It was incredibly tall, stretched long like a late-afternoon shadow. Its cloak fluttered and swirled around it as though made of something non-solid — liquid, or smoke, or darkness, maybe all three. The figure lowered its hood, revealing a skull tightly covered with pale grey flesh and empty white sockets for eyes, as though two windows to nothingness had opened within its face. It had no nose, and its mouth was perfectly round and rimmed in rows of tiny needle-sharp teeth that flashed and rotated in its lipless, gaping maw.

Its blank eyes locked on Adrian, the figure raised its hand. Long, spindling fingertips like claws appeared from within the rippling folds of its cloak, and it beckoned to him.

* * *

Adrian awoke with a jolt, his skin tingling with cold sweat, his heart thudding in his throat. He clung to his sheets, blankets twisted around his legs, pale sunlight bathing his room, and forgot what it was that had made him so afraid.

He realized after a moment, as his senses came back to him, that his phone was going off. It buzzed insistently against his leg, and he struggled with his blankets and pants to free it from his pocket. He read the caller ID with a groan. Why in the hell was his mother calling him at 5:59 a.m.? A myriad of frightening possibilities blossomed into his mind simultaneously: someone had died; someone was in the hospital; someone was in town and wanted to visit. Hastily, he turned off his alarm clock before it could have the chance to go off at six, and answered his phone. "Hello?"

"Sorry. You were asleep."

"No, Mom…no, it's fine." He yawned and sat up; through the curtains of his window, he could make out the pale haze of the newly-risen sun. "What's up?"

"I woke you up. Here, go back to bed sweetie, I didn't…" She trailed off. Adrian tried to remember when she had started calling him 'sweetie.' "I just figured you always used to be a morning person, and I was up early, and got to thinking…."

"No, it's really okay. What's up?"

"I just haven't talked to you for a while. Is everything okay?"

That was an interesting question. He paused to think it over, not sure quite how to answer it. It was more complicated than he was comfortable with. No — who was he kidding. It was a conversational landmine. He thought about Jessica, and the haunting emptiness of his house without her; he thought about Nathaniel Weaver; and he thought about the Nightmare

Man, and how ridiculous he felt for being scared of a child's drawing. "Yeah, I'm fine. Mom, is everything okay?"

"Yes. Everything's going great up here." There was an uneasy pause. "Do you and Jessica have any plans for Thanksgiving?"

Adrian's stomach rolled over uneasily, and he wondered how it was that, somehow, in three months, he hadn't mentioned to his mother that he was getting a divorce. Had he really not spoken with her in all that time? "No, not really."

"I was just thinking…it would be nice, wouldn't it?" His mother's voice sounded hopeful, pregnant with the whispers of passive aggression that had been a staple of his childhood. "To have a Thanksgiving together as a family again? Like we did before…" She trailed off.

"Um, sure. Yeah, it'll be fun. I can take the weekend off and everything." He could, too, if he wanted; he could have taken off the whole month, with all the stockpiled vacation time and sick leave he had never used. "Jessica might not make it," he added, and wondered why he was even bothering to lie — especially when being caught was inevitable. "But I'll see what I can do."

"Oh, Adrian, that would be wonderful! You don't know much Dad and I —" She stopped dead, as though catching herself saying something profane, and her voice creaked a little from trying to suck the words back into her mouth before they got away.

All these years later, it still bothered him to hear his step-father referred to as "Dad." It bothered him that Evan's name seemed to have been permanently changed, that "Dad" was a proper noun, even though the only person who ever called him that was Adrian's mother. No one should ever call the person they slept with "Dad," especially not in polite company, especially not in the company of adult children who didn't share any chromosomes with "Dad."

And most especially not when Adrian's own father had never been called "Dad"; he had been "Daddy" when Adrian was little, and then he had become "Your Father," another proper noun, a title or maybe a pejorative. "Your Father" was spoken with implicit accusation. "Your Father" meant that ownership of him had passed hands, that he might belong to Adrian but he certainly didn't belong to the rest of the family.

She was silent a moment, and then, briskly, "Well, I guess I'll let you get going. I'm sure you have to get ready for work and everything. Talk to you soon." And she hung up, sparing him the awkwardness of a sentimental farewell. If she was calling him "sweetie" now then she might start saying "I love you," and Adrian wasn't sure he could actually say that out loud to his mother. Not because he didn't love her — he did — but because it seemed a little late in their relationship to be trying new things.

He cast a glance at his alarm clock. Exhausted, feeling the grit of tiredness in his eyes and the low dull pain of a headache starting behind his right temple, he rolled the alarm forward an hour and went back to sleep. He'd forgo his morning run in favor of a little shut-eye, he decided.

This proved to be the wrong choice.

His alarm woke him from a hazy half-daze an hour later, and he opened his eyes even more wearily than the first time. It threw the rest of his morning off, no matter how hard he tried to follow his normal routine. He couldn't get his shower at the right temperature. He had no clean pants and had to put yesterday's pair back on. The toaster burned his wheat toast, leaving deep, ashy singe marks in the bread. By the time he finished getting dressed for work, he wanted nothing more than to crawl back into bed and start all over, like he could just keep hitting 'reset' until the day felt right.

But there was no time for that now. If anything, he was running late.

He checked his phone as he started out the door. He hoped that Detective Roark would have returned his message while he was getting ready, but there was no missed call from him. There was a call from Angela Weaver, though, and he listened to the message as he made his way out into the driveway.

"Hey, um, Adrian. I mean, Mr. Montgomery. It's Angela. Listen, I was wondering…this is so weird, I don't even know what to do, but I got this call last night from this guy. He said he was a psychic and he knew where Nathaniel was. And…shit, I don't know, I don't want to talk to the cops about it because they'll think I'm nuts, and I probably am nuts, but what if he knows something? I can't just….well, anyway. Give me a call, if you're not too busy, I want to know what you think. He said he was going to come by this afternoon. Thanks."

He placed the phone back in his pocket, writing himself a mental sticky-note to call Angela back when he got a minute, and climbed into his car to drive to work. His eyes burned with sleepiness and that low, pulsing ache had spread to both temples. He felt an odd detachment, as though part of him were still asleep. Going back to bed was looking more and more appealing with every minute he stayed awake.

He thought he saw things moving in the shadows along the sidewalk: hulking creatures, bony creatures, wide-eyed creatures, giant fluttering creatures made out of smoke and darkness. But when he looked again they were gone, leaving just trees and trash cans and stray cats behind. After a while he forced himself to stop looking for them, though his eyes did stray to the rearview mirror more often than necessary. *Sleep-deprivation induced hallucinations*, he thought. *Your eyes playing tricks on you. There is nothing following you, so stop it.*

He arrived at the office, half-expecting there to be a monster lurking there, but none appeared. He settled down for his day's work in relative peace aside from the lingering feeling of unease. The fluorescent lights cast no shadows for monsters to skulk in. He emptied his pockets onto his desk, putting everything in its proper place for the day — wallet and keys in the locked drawer, cell phone on the table. His fingertips brushed a paper in his pocket — the sketch of The Nightmare Man — and he hesitantly laid it out on his desk, tucking it under his day planner.

Adrian glanced up, once he had gotten settled, and his gaze traveled without his permission to a desk across the room, landing upon the lines and curves of the woman he had spent seven years with. He knew those curves by touch, could still feel them under his fingertips. He watched her, and crossed his hands on his desk and fiddled with his stapler so he would forget how her skin felt on his.

Jessica didn't notice his eyes burning into her back and carried on working, apparently unbothered by his proximity. He lowered his eyes and set down the stapler — it was smeared with sweat and tumbled from his hands with an audible thud — and he stared down at the papers on his desk with the steady intensity of someone trying to fight off a wave of nausea.

She'd asked him, once, to come to therapy with her, and she'd taken his staunch refusal as the final sign that he had given up trying on their relationship. He wished he could have found the words to explain how far from the truth that was; the fact was that he simply despised therapists. He hadn't seen a therapist since the grief counselor he had met with for a few sessions as a kid, and he had every intention of never seeing one again. They had the tendency to pry places, to try and open doors in his mind that he kept shut for a reason.

He looked back up at Jessica, boring his eyes into the back of her skull, before reaching for his telephone. Still focusing on her back, the gentle curve of her shoulders, the tumbling waves of auburn hair, he dialed Angela's number.

"Hello?"

"Hey Angela, it's Adrian. I just got your message." Out of habit, he picked up a ballpoint pen and fidgeted with it, as though intending to take notes. He watched as Jessica stood, tossing her hair, and, carrying a stack of papers, made her way toward the hall to the fax machine. He looked down, hurriedly, at the notes he wasn't taking.

"Oh, hi. I wasn't expecting you to call me back so fast. It's been crazy here, between the cops and the search teams and all the people trying to give me casseroles." He could hear her smiling on the line, and was astounded, as he always was, at how cheerful she could manage to be in the face of total life crisis. He'd never had that skill. He was lucky to be cheerful on a good day. "But...yeah. This psychic guy called, just out of the blue. Said he saw the Amber Alert and the picture matched a vision he'd had...really freaky stuff."

"I wouldn't get my hopes up, too much," Adrian said, as gently as he could. "From what I hear, these types are all quacks just trying to get some attention or make a buck off of some person's tragedy."

"You're probably right. Still, I just...I want to give it a shot. Just in case. I won't pay him anything," she added, quickly, as if this was the key point — as if Adrian's opinion on the matter of her finances counted for anything. "He just...he knew things, Adrian. Knew things about you. He knew you worked with…with us. He knew what you looked like and everything. I mean…the whole thing was just very strange. If it's too much to ask, I get that, I don't want to get you into trouble or anything, but…" He heard a hint of heartbreaking desperation in her voice. "Not as a social worker. But as a friend…can you come, tonight, and talk to him?"

He couldn't really say no; now that he had heard the desperation and fear in her voice, he didn't want to deny her what may have been her only hope. "Of course," he said, after just a moment of hesitation. "Here," he pushed the papers on his desk away and opened his appointment book. "My last appointment of the day is on that side of town, anyway. It won't even be out of my way."

"Thank you…I really appreciate this…it means a lot to me…thank you." He could hear the smile again, through the phone, and he couldn't help responding in kind. "I don't know what I would have done if all this had happened and I didn't have you to help me get through it. Nathaniel will be so happy to hear about how much you've helped us. He really looks up to you."

"I'm just doing my job, Angela," he said, and knew perfectly well he wasn't.

She laughed, maybe a little nervously. "Yeah. Well, okay. I'll see you tonight, then."

"Sure thing. Take care." He hung up, and then glanced back down at his appointment book to check and see if his last appointment of the day really was on the same side of town. He was relieved to note that it was.

"You're looking quite pleased with yourself." Jessica was standing behind him. He could feel her looming over his shoulder, and the tone in her voice had an undercurrent of steel that, in their married years, would have caused him to cower. "Did I overhear that right? You're doing some extracurriculars with Angela Weaver?"

He wondered just how long Jessica had been standing there, listening in — and why she would bother. Was that jealousy in her voice?

"She needs some help dealing with one of those quack psychic detectives. I'm just stepping in to make sure she doesn't get taken advantage of, that's all. You know how those guys are."

"Right. Playing the white knight, like always." Her brows raised, and she shifted her weight from one hip to the other, crossing her arms neatly beneath the swell of her breasts. "No leads, I take it?"

He shook his head.

"Well. It's only, what, day two of the search? There might still be a happy ending." They both knew perfectly well that, when kids are concerned especially, being found safe and sound became less and less likely with each passing hour. "They're sure it's not the dad?"

"His dad's on house arrest fifty miles away." It had been sixteen hours, in fact. It would be twenty-six by the time he got to Angela's house tonight. And, he remembered, Detective Roark had *still* not called him back.

Jessica's eyes landed on the folded piece of paper on his desk. She reached out a hand to touch it, but Adrian snatched it away hurriedly and tucked the drawing away in the back of his appointment book. He noticed the pale line of untanned skin where her wedding band had been.

She shrugged. "Well, hopefully he'll turn up. It's a duplex, right? Did anybody check the other apartment?"

"Why do you care?" He said, more sharply than he'd intended. He knew perfectly well that Nathaniel wasn't in the next door apartment, because he'd searched it himself. Angela, panicking, had called him first, and together they'd searched the whole house, the woods nearby, knocked on neighbor's doors, asked the gas station attendant. Then the police had arrived and done all the same things. "You've got other things to do, I'm sure."

Her lip curled. "Fine." And then, because Jessica had never been able to back away from a fight in seven years of marriage, "Just…keep your nose out of places it doesn't belong, all right? Do your job, and let the cops do *their* job. You're going to get yourself in a world of trouble with your damn hero complex."

"I do not have —"

"I know how you are. And I know how you feel about her."

How he felt about her? There it was, again, that undercurrent of jealousy, and Adrian was steamrolled; how was it, in the eight months he had been working with Angela Weaver, that Jessica had never shown any signs of jealousy or concern, and now that they were all but divorced…

"You like taking on projects, Adrian. It's not my place to tell you what to do, but…"

"So don't tell me what to do," he cut in. Confusion, surprise, and hurt mixed uncomfortably in his mind and his already-pounding head started to pound harder. *Hey Jessica*, he thought, crazily, *Mom wants you to come over for Thanksgiving. I forgot to tell her we're separated. You're cool with coming, right?*

She sighed, and her expression softened. "You just want to help. I know you do." She drew her lower lip between her teeth, biting it thoughtfully like she always did when nervous about something. She'd looked at him that way just before she'd mentioned the divorce the first time; she'd looked at him with genuine fear in her eyes, like she was expecting him to hit her. But — no. That wasn't right. She was afraid that he would hurt himself. The only thing that had kept her around, that look said, was the fear that he might find some pills or a gun or car exhaust and off himself after she walked out the door. "Just be careful. Please."

She turned and left, without further word, and Adrian watched her go, feeling the confusion and the hurt battle for their position at the top of his emotional totem pole.

Baffled, and more than a little aggravated by this sudden intrusion of unwelcome uncertainties in a day that had already reached its intrusion quota, he pulled away from his desk, carefully packed his briefcase, and set out for his morning appointments, purposely putting thoughts about Jessica back in her filing cabinet. He'd have to dream up a stronger lock.

ALONE IN A ROOM

Nathaniel Weaver was certain of two things: First, that he wasn't playing make-believe anymore; second, that he wanted to go home now. At first, things hadn't been so bad. The Nightmare Man looked scary, but he hadn't hurt him. Instead he had taken him here, to this little room, and fed him cake. The cake had tasted good, but the frosting was too sweet; after a few bites Nathaniel's mouth was dry and sticky, and whenever he burped it tasted like sugar and butter. He asked for a glass of water.

The Nightmare Man left, then, and hadn't come back.

Nathaniel hadn't been scared at first. He sat patiently at the small table, humming a little song to himself, and waited for the dream to be over with. But he knew, deep inside, that he wasn't dreaming, and as time wore on and no one came with his glass of water, that realization became more and more real and more and more frightening. So he had started to cry. He cried for at least ten minutes, big loud temper-tantrum sobs like he hadn't done since he was in training pants. No one came. His sobs died away and his chest heaved with big, miserable gasps as tears trickled from his eyes and snot dripped from his nose and he wiped away the snot with the back of his hand and slept for a little while.

He woke up on the floor, curled in a little ball. His shoulder hurt from being hunched up.

He was still in the room, and there was still no glass of water.

Nathaniel almost started crying again, but he didn't. It wouldn't help anything. That was the thought he had: It won't help anything. This struck him as a frighteningly grown-up thought, and that more than anything cemented the severity of this situation into his mind. *Crying won't help. Mommy's not here. Nobody will help you.*

His heart jumped up into his throat and he climbed up to his feet and ran around the room like a mouse caught in a shoebox. *There has to be a door,* he thought. *The Nightmare Man left through a door. I can, too.* But after he'd run around the room twice, he knew that wasn't true. The Nightmare Man was fully capable of appearing and disappearing wherever he liked, with or without a door.

Nathaniel Weaver sat down heavily and hugged his knees to his chest.

There were no doors in the room. What was in the room: a small, Nathaniel-sized table and matching chair; a plate of half-eaten cake with blue too-sweet frosting; a half-deflated beach ball; and a pair of rollerblades with their laces tied into a knot. These last items were in the corner of the room — which, now that he had stopped running around, seemed to have grown smaller — and Nathaniel stared at them moodily. They made him angry. He wasn't sure why they should, but they did. He wished that they weren't here. He stared at them hard and pretended that they disappeared.

They didn't budge.

Sighing, he curled up on the floor again and tried to sleep.

Nathaniel had first seen The Nightmare Man eight months ago, a little bit after Daddy Did The Bad Thing And Went Away For Awhile. He was living in a motel room with his mommy, but he didn't like it there. They only had one bed and she cried at night and it woke him up a lot. Also, the blanket was scratchy and smelled like cigarette smoke. One day Nathaniel had been taken aside by his teacher at school and she had asked him some things, and then the next day someone had come to his motel room — Mr. Montgomery, but he didn't know his name at the time. He looked a little bit like Daddy, because he had red hair — hair just like Nathaniel's — but nothing else about him was like Daddy at all. Eventually Nathaniel realized that he really liked Mr. Montgomery, but at the time he had started crying and gone to hide in the bathroom when he came inside. Everything was really scary at first. Nathaniel was afraid that maybe Mommy was going to

Go Away For Awhile, too.

That's when the Nightmare Man had first started visiting.

At first he came at night. Whenever a bad dream woke him, he would be there — just standing at the bedside, staring down at him with those big white eyes. At first Nathaniel would scream and his mother would jolt awake and grab him and they would hold each other in the dark until they both fell back asleep. But after a few visits, when Nathaniel realized that the person in his bedroom didn't seem to want to hurt him, he had stopped screaming, and then he started seeing him more and more often. He showed up at school. He walked Nathaniel home, stayed with him when he was alone. He was almost like a friend.

Nathaniel started to fall asleep. He had always been very good at falling asleep, no matter what. When he was a baby, his parents hadn't needed to do any of the usual tricks like driving around the neighborhood or rocking him for hours. He had always been able to switch off immediately. His Daddy used to joke that he felt more at-home in dreamland than in the real world, and it was partially true. Nathaniel had always had particularly vivid dreams.

The dream he had now wasn't like the usual kind, however. It was a memory. In it, he was sitting on his Daddy's shoulders at the beach. He had a beach ball in his arms. His arms almost didn't fit around it and he hugged it as tight as he could because the wind was blowing. That was it — the whole memory. Beach ball. Beach. Shoulders. Wind. This repeated as though it was a movie being played in every room of a house and Nathaniel was walking from room to room, watching it start and play at different spots.

Then the dream began to change, but it was all wrong. The memory didn't make sense anymore. They were still on the beach — the gulls cried overhead, the waves lapped at the shore — but it was raining. No, snowing? No. Leaves were falling. That was it. Red and gold and brown leaves fell around him like confetti and faraway he heard someone crying. It wasn't him. It was a grown-up. He knew the way that grown-ups cried, because Mommy did it so much.

The realization that this was no longer Nathaniel's memory made him realize this was no longer his dream, either, and he woke up in a slow, hazy confusion. In the small, blank room he sat in there was no way of knowing how long he had slept.

But there was a glass of water beside him when he awoke.

DOWN THE RABBIT HOLE

The drive out to the Weaver's house was a familiar one, considering how many times Adrian had been there on welfare visits, but it felt strange now that he was making it after hours. He thought he should call Angela, but then stopped himself. What would he say to her? Double-check that she had, in fact, invited him? That was ridiculous — of course she had asked him to come, or he wouldn't have considered it, whatever Jessica might think to the contrary.

It seemed like the only thing to do, now that he had agreed, and it was too late to turn back, so he kept his eyes ahead of him on the quiet, empty old country highway, and drove. Shadows flickered in his peripheral vision. He ignored them.

The townhouse itself was beautiful and tired. It had chipped white paneling and large, four-pane glass windows with green shutters that had been nailed to the outer walls to keep them from clapping in the wind. The upstairs, from where the home had been converted into a duplex and currently stood vacant, was dark and empty, but Angela's downstairs apartment was clearly lived in. A bright red child's bicycle leaned against the porch; a deflated soccer ball sat in a puddle in the yard, which had faded from overgrown summer weeds to wet, muddy autumn dirt.

Adrian parked on the street at the end of the long driveway and started up the walkway with a blanket of white noise in his head. It sounded like the crackle of rice cereal and it ebbed and flowed in time with the pounding in his skull. Angela's car was parked in the driveway; behind it, an unfamiliar, flashy black sports car of the kind generally purchased by insecure balding men on the precipice of their middle age.

He lingered at the base of the driveway a moment longer before making his way up the white gravel walkway to the house and up the wooden porch. It creaked a little under his weight, and the house seemed to groan as he crossed the deck to the front door, opened the screen door, and knocked.

"Coming."

He heard her voice from the depths of the house, and he looked around, feeling exceedingly nervous, as though he weren't supposed to be here — as though, if the neighbors were watching, they would be making snide remarks against his character. Which was ridiculous. There would have been people coming and going all day, between cops and media and search party volunteers. He wondered how long the psychic had been here.

Angela Weaver looked like someone who hadn't slept or looked in a mirror for a couple of days. Her hair, a strawberry blonde with coppery highlights, fell loosely around her shoulders, damply curled and, although she was only in her late twenties, graying around the roots. Her eyes were the same size and color as Nathaniel's, with worry-lines around the edges. A half-smoked cigarette smoldered between her forefingers.

"Oh, sorry," she said, stepping back from the door and looking guiltily at her cigarette, which was flaking ash out onto the tile of the doorway. "Forgot you don't like smoke."

"It's alright," he said, following her inside, glancing around at the familiar interior; it was decorated in the spirit of white trash and tourism, and somehow it always made him smile, if only because it had so much character. The real fireplace had been replaced with an electric one, and the mantle over it bore a singing mechanical trout. As he passed, the fish jerked its head toward him and demanded, somewhat desperately and a little off-key, that someone take it to a river.

"We were waiting for you to get here, before we get started," Angela said, stepping over a small collection of Matchbox cars that had taken over the hallway into the kitchen. "You just missed the last search party of the night. They had dogs and everything."

"I'm sorry."

"They're going to find him."

"I'm absolutely sure you're right." He wasn't.

Someone Adrian assumed must be the psychic was sitting at the kitchen table, a cup of coffee between his hands. He stared rather intently at the coffee, as though searching for answers in the bottom of the cup. Adrian felt an immediate and irrational dislike for him, this parasite preying on a mother's tragedy.

"Isn't it tea leaves that tell the future?" Adrian asked, pulling out a chair opposite him. "Not coffee dregs?"

The man didn't respond, but simply continued to stare into the depths of his mug. His eyes were small and squinted, as though he had spent too much time staring at the sun, and his face had a drawn, weathered look. He looked as though he had been homeless at one time, or addicted to drugs — some hardship that had abnormally stripped him of his extra flesh and left him looking gaunt and withered.

"Zachariah, this is Adrian."

"Adrian Montgomery, Social Services," he clarified, offering his hand.

The psychic looked up, small eyes narrowed further in suspicion or examination, and after a moment he took his hand, giving it a weak pump before withdrawing. He handed him a business card, and Adrian took it reflexively.

Zachariah Moses, Psychic Detective
Let Me Solve Your Unsolved Mysteries

Zachariah's head tilted and he looked down at his own hand contemplatively. "…Leaves," he murmured, under his breath, the way someone says something they've just remembered but don't fully understand.

Adrian ignored it. "So. You know where Nathaniel is, then?"

"No," Zachariah said, simply. "Not exactly. But I've seen him."

"When? Before or after the Amber Alert yesterday?"

"Before," he replied, sounding annoyed. "I saw his photograph and recognized him from my vision."

Angela lit another cigarette and stared out the sliding glass door into the backyard.

Adrian looked back to Zachariah. "Okay. So what did you see, if you don't know where he is?"

"Skepticism is the first barrier to destroy on the path of enlightenment," Zachariah returned, looking sour; Adrian guessed that the psychic probably had not been keen on Angela's insistence for a neutral party's involvement. "I saw him in a cave — deep underground. He is being held there against his will, and there's a little girl with him. Younger than he is." He hesitated here, a moment, as though he planned to say something further, but he stopped before saying anything more.

"I see. And you have no idea where this cave is, or who's holding him there, or why?"

Zachariah shook his head, and his weather-beaten face looked crestfallen; there was something hungry and desperate about it. "You look remarkably like him," he said.

Angela had once pointed out the same thing. "It's the hair," Adrian said, as he had when Angela had first mentioned it. "You don't see a lot of kids with really dark red hair like this."

"You're the only one in your family," Zachariah said. "Your brother has dark hair. Your sister's is curly like yours, but blonde."

"I don't have a sister," he said, automatically, but something tightened in his chest. "Stop changing the subject."

Zachariah cast him a long, thoughtful look, and said nothing. He glanced toward Angela, who stood with her back toward them, shoulders held high and tense as she smoked. She dropped ash onto the floor by the sliding door. "I have to see the place where he disappeared. I have to find the path," he said, finally. He looked back to Adrian. "It sounds insane to you, and I understand why you must think that. But if I can just find the path, I'll know who took him."

Something in his tone made Adrian uneasy. It felt as though his small, narrow eyes were boring into him. "Fine. Let's go look, right now." He cast Angela a questioning look; she avoided his eyes, and stamped out the last of her cigarette in an empty Diet Pepsi can. "I don't know what you're planning to find that a professional search party missed, but I hope for Nathaniel's case you're right."

"I'm not looking for something that the mundane eye can see," Zachariah said. He rose from his chair and swept past Angela without a word, heading out onto the porch.

"You all won't mind if I stay in here?" Angela asked, in a quiet, timid voice that didn't suit her at all. "I've just…I don't know if I have it in me to go out there again right now."

"Of course," Adrian said. He hesitated beside her, before laying a hand tentatively on her shoulder. "Hey. He'll turn up. The police are looking everywhere."

"Do you have a sister?"

"What?"

"A sister. Do you have one?" Her eyes caught his. "Like Zachariah said?"

"I said I didn't," Adrian said, and glanced at the porch, where the psychic stood. He gave Angela's shoulder a little squeeze. "Try not to worry too much. It'll just be a couple minutes, then we can get rid of this guy."

She said something noncommittal, and he opened the door out onto the porch and into the backyard which separated the house from the empty wooded lot behind it.

A small corner of the fence had been pulled clear, leaving a triangular crawlspace by the post; this had been Nathaniel's access point to the wild place beyond his own yard, his favorite, secret place — if a secret place could truly exist when all the other kids in the neighborhood kept their secret place there, too.

"This is it?" Zachariah stood beside him, following his gaze to the hole in the fence. "He was back there, when he was taken?"

"You're the psychic. You tell me," Adrian muttered, and shrugged. "What makes you say he was taken?"

"Someone is holding him there, I told you. In the cave. Someone you know." He glanced over at Adrian. "It's no coincidence that you, of all people, are here with me."

"That doesn't make any sense." Someone you know. A real someone? Or an imaginary someone?

That doesn't make any sense, either, Adrian, he thought. *Imaginary people can't kidnap kids. Jesus, you need a good night's sleep.*

Adrian stared into the depths of the small wood. The trees, huddled in a conspiratorial circle, refused to give up their secrets; he leaned forward, almost expectantly, and was rewarded only with silence. Slowly, without realizing what he was doing, or why, he walked to the fence line, rested his hands atop it, and peered into the stand of trees. It was darker there than it was in the sunny backyard; the aged trees wove their branches together, the sun filtered by bony, tangled limbs and the remains of dying leaves. Leaves carpeted the ground, crunchy and broken or else slimy and warm with decomposition. Adrian could smell them from where he stood, warm and nauseating; he had always hated the smell of old leaves.

"Can you feel it?" Zachariah asked, breathlessly, beside him. "The energy here? It's thick with…memory."

"Memory?" Adrian asked, absently, too distracted by his own half-formed thoughts to put much heart in his disdain. "What's memory feel like, exactly?" But, even as he asked it, he realized that he already knew. He vaulted with small effort over the short, bedraggled fence, walking into the woods with a sense of purpose as though he were being tugged forward.

"Well?" he asked, his voice hushed despite himself; he cleared his throat and, with a concentrated effort at bravado, "See anything?"

"It wouldn't be something I saw," Zachariah said, pulling away almost reluctantly as he moved between trees, reaching out with his hands, his thumb rubbing his fingertips as though running fine silk between his fingers. "At least, I don't think so. It would be…something else." He stopped, and stared with interest at a place a few feet away, where there was nothing to look at.

Adrian scoffed, and shook his head, turning his attentions elsewhere, intent upon focusing on something other than what the psychic was doing. He turned, slowly, on the spot; nothing was out of place. He wondered what Nathaniel did here; there was no sign of a fort, no shelters pieced together from fallen branches and leaves, no discarded rough-hewn spears, or mud-pies, or half-buried toys. Indeed, if Adrian hadn't known better, he would have thought he had chosen the wrong patch of overgrown vacant lot — there was no evidence here of any childhood fantasies being played out, or any childhood at all.

"It's here," he heard Zachariah say, mutedly, as though whispering across a football field. "Can't you feel it?" Again, that hungry desperation had awoken in his voice; it was joined by something that sounded like fear. "It's not…not normal here. I don't like this."

Adrian was going to respond with something catty, but couldn't find the proper jab; he felt something here as well, but he couldn't quite describe it. It didn't seem like a bad feeling, exactly, but one that he had certainly not felt since he was a child; it took him back, uncomfortably, to a time when he was young, and innocent, and he was teaching his baby sister to play hide and seek…

Something moved, in the corner of his eye, and he turned to look. The air in front of him seemed, almost, to shimmer, as though a heat wave was rising up from the earth, as though the air had become liquid rippled by a slight breeze. He looked away, then looked back. The shimmer remained. His brow furrowed and he moved forward, but the closer he got, the further the ripple seemed to be, always in front of him, unreachable.

He wondered if perhaps there was something wrong with his eyes, and raised his hands to rub them; when he lowered his knuckles, he blinked, rapidly, because he didn't understand what had materialized in front of him at all. He looked back, over his shoulder, trying to find Zachariah, to prove for certain whether he was going insane — but the psychic had disappeared from view, and Adrian was forced to return his gaze to the impossible sight before him.

The trees, in the seconds his eyes had been closed, had huddled together and bowed, forming a tunnel that looked unnervingly familiar — a long, straight, thatched-roofed-tunnel of tangled tree limbs that led indefinitely into nothingness. Adrian stared at it and stepped forward, waiting for something else — waiting for a tall, skeletal figure robed in shadow to stand in the archway, and beckon.

No one materialized. Adrian was alone.

His fingertips brushed the rough bark of one of the trees — and the ground beneath his feet grew slick and tilted forward as though a chute of ice had developed beneath him. He plummeted, blindingly fast, into infinite darkness. He would have screamed, if the suddenness of his unsettled feet had not torn the breath from his lungs; instead, soundless, he hurtled through a passage of displaced earth and space.

The passageway, which had been a black void from the outside, exploded around him in brilliant, swirling colors, flashing and bursting around him like fireworks, swimming in his vision and rotating over every wall. There was no sound in the tunnel, but the void of sound was palpable, as though one need only release a mute button and the world would erupt in screaming. He tried to reach out, to grab hold of something, to steady himself, but felt nothing when he threw out his hands. It was as though the tunnel was made only of light, as though his body had been replaced by air.

When Adrian was a child, he had a kaleidoscope; he couldn't remember where he had gotten it, or precisely when — as a gift, perhaps, from his grandmother, or picked up on a whim from the dollar store. He remembered lying back on his bed, staring through his kaleidoscope at the slowly rotating shapes and colors, and pretending that he was looking through a spyglass into another world — a world that only he could see, made of color and magic. The game had been short-lived; he had grown bored of it, progressed on to cooler, more interesting or more high-tech toys, and the kaleidoscope and all its magical properties had been discarded and forgotten. But now, falling indefinitely through space, it came again to his mind, because he felt now as though he were falling through the world's largest kaleidoscope, a rabbit-hole dug by acid-tripping rabbits.

Somewhere — in the recesses of his mind, or from further down the tunnel, both were the same — he could hear voices. He couldn't make out the words, but he recognized the people speaking, aural snapshots of his childhood, the times of which he couldn't pinpoint, but the emotion was burned so deeply into him that he recognized it immediately. He heard sounds of arguing, of the bitter hurt that could only manifest itself in violence. He heard sobs, and cries, and desperation and misery, the sounds of hearts breaking.

Somewhere, he heard a laugh, a familiar, haunting laugh, one he hadn't heard for nearly twenty-five years, and it would have brought tears to his eyes if he had eyes to cry with. He could see her, almost, the innocent gleam in her eyes, the beaming smile, and that laugh, the bright, babbling laugh of a child who would never grow to adulthood. He looked at her, without eyes, and reached out for her, without arms, and yearned desperately to be close to her.

But she faded away from him, as he knew she would, and he urged himself forward, wanting, more than he had ever wanted anything, to see her for just a moment longer — but, as though the tunnel had read his mind and responded in sadistic kind, she disappeared entirely from his view.

Samantha? He called, his non-voice deafening in his thoughts but dying in his throat. *Samantha, come back, please.*

The words echoed in his thoughts, surrounded him, reverberated, soaked into whatever was left of his self, and consumed him. He was aware only in a peripheral way of the rapidly approaching ground, and the realization that if this was a falling dream, he should be waking up by now.

DREAMLAND

Adrian had been hung over once, and only once, in his life. On his twenty-first birthday, his friends had kidnapped him from his dorm room, threatening to burn the essay he was writing if he didn't come out drinking with them that night. He had agreed, and, with each successive round, as the room became dimmer and noises more muted, he had grown fonder of everyone around him until his memories faded entirely. He had awoken the next morning facedown on the tile of a bathroom that wasn't his, naked except for his socks and his watch, with complete certainty that his eyeballs would explode from their sockets at any moment.

He felt exactly like that now.

He realized, as his body began to regain some sense of feeling aside from pain, that he must be outside — at least, he could feel dewy grass, the moisture soaking through his shirt and up into his skin, permeating his pores. He could feel the earth, moist and soft but not quite muddy, beneath him, and felt as if he could sink down into it and disappear entirely. Grass tickled his nose, and he smelled and tasted earth with each inhalation. He wanted to roll over or stand up, but his body wouldn't cooperate, as if he were a puppet and someone had cut all of the strings.

He could hear quiet animal noises, though he wasn't sure what kind — a gentle sniffling, the sounds of heavy breath and heavier footfalls, and he felt the nearness of something, the warmth of it invading his space. *A stray dog,* he thought, vaguely. A raccoon. A bear. Something.

The animal let out a low, snuffling grunt. A large furry muzzle jabbed into Adrian's ribs, hitting him with enough force to rock him onto his side before he rolled again to his stomach, feeling nauseous.

He groaned, feeling the creature nose into his side again, bruising his ribs with its enthusiastic prodding.

Early in their marriage, Jessica had convinced him to get a dog, the only dog he had ever owned. It had been a big, hulking, shaggy thing, with a cold nose and sad brown eyes hidden under a tangle of untidy white and grey hair. It had loved Adrian with a sadistic intensity that rivaled only the intensity of Adrian's immense dislike of the creature.

It had the habit, every morning, of worming its way into the bed that he and Jessica had shared, settling itself between them and then pushing, slowly and insistently, until they were separated by the full length of the vast animal between them. Or, when Adrian had been in his office, reading over his papers for work the next morning, the dog would pad into the room and, with a determined expression on its otherwise dopey face, would jab its nose into Adrian's hand, forcing him to scratch behind the long bedraggled ears until the dog had had its fill.

The dog died two years after they got him; he had gotten loose from the yard and, dodging and weaving through traffic, misjudged the distance and met a grisly end beneath the tires of a Dodge Ram. Adrian had been uncharacteristically moved by the loss and Jessica, who had never been able to succeed in probing the deeper complexities of Adrian's well-guarded psyche, never quite understood why he had been so shaken by the death of the dog he had hated. Adrian had never been able to explain. They never got another dog.

"Get off," he muttered. His voice was hoarse and muffled by the ground. He wasn't sure the creature had heard him, as it responded with another heavy jab. A long, warm, wet tongue went up his neck and cheek. Adrian heaved himself onto his back, although every muscle screamed in pain from the exertion. He rested for a few seconds, panting, and waited for the pain to subside. Slowly, he opened his eyes, then let out a cry and closed them again. It felt like his brain would explode from the sudden burst of dazzling light that invaded his senses.

But the pain and the dazzling light hadn't been enough to block his vision entirely, and, standing alongside the burst of color in his mind, there was the retinal burn of something else, something he could make no sense of. He forced his eyes to crack open again.

Through his narrowed eyes, he could barely make out the shape of a vast, white beast that seemed hazy around the edges. It felt too bright to look at, and Adrian winced, wanting to turn away but wanting, just as badly, to see it clearly. Slowly, his eyes adjusted to the light and he stared blearily at the creature, which stood a few feet from him and stared back at him, quizzically, with large pale blue eyes.

It was, without doubt, a unicorn.

A slender white horse, its pelt the color of the core of the sun, a whiteness that flashed and dazzled and was impossible to gaze upon without going blind. It glowed like the sun, too, a brilliant ring of white-gold fading into a pale haze, shifting and shimmering around the horse's flanks as though the creature itself were made of light, or of heat, or a combination of the two. It had a long, golden mane that fell forward into its expressive blue eyes, and its spun-gold tail streamed behind. A horn, at least a foot long, woven from a substance that looked remarkably like diamond, rose between the eyes in a gentle upward curve. Adrian blinked. The unicorn continued to stare at him.

Adrian started to laugh, then, unsteady laughter that rocked his body and bubbled out of him uncontrollably. Tears streamed down his cheeks. He laughed, and sobbed, and hiccupped, and his whole body shook. The unicorn tilted its head.

"Oh, this is rich," he said, addressing the unicorn between hiccupping sobs of laughter. "A unicorn." A desperate giggle leaked out of his throat again, then he fell silent, his sides hurting worse than they had ever hurt, a lifetime worth of laughter spent, depleted, indefinitely. "The psychic's going to love this."

And still, the unicorn stubbornly refused to disappear.

Adrian, emptied of laughter, felt the beginning of fear clench uncomfortably in his gut. "Where the hell am I?" He asked, his eyes going unfocused as he attempted to look at the unicorn without being dazzled by its beautiful white-hot visage. If he expected the unicorn to respond, he was disappointed; it only gazed back at him, quiet and curious, and whatever was left of Adrian's sanity rushed out of him like air escaping a balloon.

Distantly, he heard music, a lyrical, beautiful, wild noise. The way Apollo's lyre must have sounded, the way whale-song must sound at the bottom of the sea. The unicorn's ears perked up and its head rose, whipping around to look over its shoulder. Adrian struggled to his elbows. The sound came nearer, drawing closer and louder, and he could make out words, although they made no sense; perhaps, he thought, they were being sung in another language, or maybe they weren't even words at all, but a series of strung-together sounds, beautiful without meaning. Whatever they were, they filled him, and he felt a sense of peace, of quietude.

He caught a glimpse of the figure: small-statured, and feminine in its silhouette. It drew near, and the unicorn rose to block his view, and Adrian collapsed back against the earth in exhaustion. He closed his eyes and silently urged the music to clear away the awful, resounding pain in his skull and body. And perhaps the music heard his plea, because sleep — true, deep, peaceful sleep — overtook his him, and for the first time in the months since Jessica had walked out of his life, he felt utterly still as sleep washed over him.

* * *

He was no longer outside; he could feel the softness of a bed beneath him, and felt a stillness around him that suggested that there were walls. *I'm back in my bed*, he thought, relieved; *I'm back in my own, warm bed, and I'll open my eyes and realize that I just had a long, crazy dream and then I'll get up and go to work and won't have to worry about anything anymore.*

He smelled something, a delicious smell that was simultaneously intensely familiar and totally exotic, and as he became aware of the odor his stomach became aware of its hunger and gave a loud rumble of protest at its mistreatment.

This wasn't his house. Nothing that smelled that good had ever been made in his house.

He struggled to pry his eyes open. He lay in one corner of a single-room cottage on a soft bed made up of burlap bags stitched together. A lumpy pile of rags was piled in one corner atop another burlap mattress. Shelves lined the walls. Some of these held pots and pans. Others were filled with jars of all different sizes and shapes that seemed to be filled with different colors of smoke.

There was something cooking in a large black kettle in the fireplace, and something else — from this distance, Adrian couldn't make out precisely what — baking among the coals. A single window, little more than a hole in the wall, peered out across a patch of garden. In the distance, among the trees, he could barely make out the shimmering pale form of an incandescent unicorn.

Well, so much for it all being a dream, he thought, and closed his eyes again. *Unless maybe I'm still asleep. Or possibly crazy.* The smell from whatever was cooking in the fireplace swelled and consumed the room, filling his nostrils and causing his stomach to ache in desire for whatever it was that could imbue a room with such a tantalizing odor.

He struggled to sit up, his arms shaking as he pushed himself. He heard the door open, but he couldn't see it from where he lay.

"I wouldn't do that, if I were you."

Adrian collapsed back onto his bed, his trembling arms giving out. He searched out the source of the voice, and his eyes landed upon what was, without question, the most beautiful woman he had ever seen in his life.

She was intensely familiar, although he could say with absolute certainty that he'd never seen her before in his life. At certain angles, she looked identical to people he'd known before, as if someone had pieced her together from snapshots of his memories. Short and wide-hipped, like his first highschool girlfriend. Her lips pouted just like the girl he'd lost his virginity to. And she had Jessica's eyes — large, expressive, and brilliant green.

But a pair of pale gossamer wings rose from her shoulder blades, and her hair was a short shock of bright violet.

"Do what?" Adrian managed to gasp, as a delayed reaction, his voice rasping hoarsely from a throat that felt as though he had been screaming for hours. Perhaps he had.

"What you just did," the woman replied, and turned from him to make her way to the hearth. She unloaded the small bundle of firewood she carried onto the floor and dusted herself off, carefully picking splinters from her scant clothing. "You'll be wanting some more rest. It's harder to fall through when you're, well…" she trailed off, and there was a tension in her shoulders that betrayed a degree of discomfort; it also caused her wings to stand up at a rather awkward angle.

"Fall through…?" He coughed, and felt a horrible burning in his throat, the soreness of over-used vocal cords mingling with the sting of bile.

"Yes. Through the portal." Then, with more curiosity than concern the woman asked, "How are you feeling?"

"Like shit," he replied and attempted, again, to rise. He managed to make a seated position by leaning heavily against the wall, and stared across the room at the purple-haired, gossamer-winged woman. "Where am I? And who are you?"

"I'm Sonia." The tension in her wings seemed to relax, slightly; at least, they drooped a bit and folded over each other a little. "And this is, obviously, my house."

She busied herself by stirring the kettle, periodically lifting a massive ladle to sip, then lowering it, apparently satisfied with the taste because she never added anything — but she did not back away from her position at the fireplace. Adrian got the distinct impression that she was trying to avoid staring at him. He wondered how alien he must look to her, and how pathetic — with his hair unkempt, his suit jacket missing, his trousers torn and his eyes almost certainly bloodshot and dulled by exhaustion. Then again, she was the one with the wings and the unicorn, so he didn't feel too bad for staring.

"Adrian," he offered, feeling like that would be the polite thing to do.

She looked over her shoulder, only for a fleeting moment, her emerald eyes glimmering with an emotion Adrian couldn't identify. It made him sad, somehow, and he wasn't sure why. "You remember. That's good."

"Remember?" He blinked at her. "Remember what?"

"Your name." She pulled away from the kettle to make her way to a neighboring wall, where a tall cabinet filled with pots, pans, and dishes stood; she pulled a small, lopsided clay bowl from the cabinet, carried it back to the kettle, and filled it. "That's good," she repeated, as she handed him the half-full bowl of soup.

It was heavier than he had expected, the solid clay bowl contributing heftily to the bulk of his dinner. The soup itself was as good as its odor had promised; the broth was thick with simmered tomato and onion, and there were large chunks of vegetables that Adrian couldn't identify. It was hearty, and slightly spicy, but in a way that warmed rather than burned.

He drank it in long, hungry gulps, and felt strength flow into him, warm and comforting. Silence passed between them as he ate. Sonia sat at the thick-legged oak table by the hearth, elbows rested on the knobby surface and chin laid on her interlaced fingers, and watched him with rapt emerald-eyed attention. Adrian consumed his soup with the desperate appreciation of a starving man, and the silence stretched until he had finished the last of the dregs from the bowl.

"Glad you liked it," Sonia said, her voice even, and he looked up, unable to tell if she was serious or mocking him; perhaps both were the case. "Feel better?"

"A thousand times over," he said, reluctantly setting his bowl down next to him and feeling that the silence, now that he had finished the soup, was rather awkward. He wanted to ask about where he was, and what was going on, and how he had gotten here, and what would happen now — but he found that the questions died before making it to his throat. Instead, he watched Sonia with the same rapt attention she had given to him, and felt his mind become surprisingly blank. Was this real? Maybe it wasn't, but it seemed safest to act like it was, at least until it was all over. As mental breakdowns went, this didn't seem so bad.

"If you want to sleep some more..." Sonia offered, and Adrian interrupted her.

"No. No, I've slept enough, and the headache's just started to go away."

And it had. "I…I'm very confused."

His eyes caught sight, again, of a dark, lumpy figure across the room — something he had seen, on his initial visual sweep of the room, but not registered as anything worthy of his notice. Now that his eyes could focus properly and the pounding had receded from his brain, he could make out the shape of another person, dressed in tatters and hidden under layers of ragged blankets. It was quiet and still, and Adrian felt a sudden sense of foreboding.

"Is that…?" He waved his hand, vaguely, toward the pile of rags.

Sonia nodded. "The person who came through with you? Yes."

"Is he okay?"

"Well, he's alive," Sonia said, and crossed the room; she had an uneasy, nervous air about her, as though she were used to perpetual motion and confinement was causing her undue worry. "He doesn't remember, though, like you."

"Remember…what?" He tried to catch the faerie's eyes and found instead only her constantly shifting wings, the tension lines in her back, the occasional flash of purple hair or glimpse of a frown as she paced before him restlessly. "His name?"

"Yes, precisely," she said, and stopped to give him an endearing, quietly patronizing, smile. "You're doing very well. You might even make it into tomorrow."

He stared up at her, feeling disconcerted and more than a little baffled. "Make it? Where…I don't…" He sighed, raising a hand to rub his temples; the horrible, throbbing pain in his head had receded, but it was replaced now by the subtle but persistent ache of befuddlement. "None of this is making any sense."

She knelt at the hearth, digging among the ashes before the fire with a pair of long tongs; she withdrew something, tightly wrapped in paper, and blew away the ashes and embers. She deliberated over the parcel for a moment, carefully unwrapping it, and set it down on a platter before reaching back into the ash again with her tongs.

Adrian watched her, entranced, and caught a whiff of a new odor, warm and yeasty, unmistakably the smell of fresh-baked bread; it sent him back to Thanksgiving morning in the depths of his childhood, and for a moment he was thoroughly transported back to a suspended moment in time. *His mother was standing at the counter, kneading bread, her hands buried to the knuckles in dough, the bulge of her stomach visible beneath her apron. He looked at her and wondered if she would still love him when the baby came.*

"Here."

He looked up, shaken from his memory, and realized that Sonia was standing before him, again offering food; now it was one of the loaves that she had pulled from the ashes, and he took it, looking it over in his hands. It was small and round; the crust was charred in places, golden in others, and pale tendrils of steam rose from it.

"Eat it. It'll help."

He wanted to ask, *help with what?* but he knew better than to expect a straight answer. He nibbled, curiously, at the crust of bread, and his senses were assaulted by a surprising array of flavor and texture. It tasted the way angel food cake would taste if it were really made by angels.

He finished in a few bites and tried to remember what he had planned to ask before he had been waylaid by the overwhelming power of sensation; his eyes followed Sonia again, almost out of habit now, as she paced the room like a tiger in a zoo. "You said…you said I might 'make it' until tomorrow?" He pressed, at length, gingerly. "What did you mean by that? Am I in danger?"

She paused, and shifted a little uncomfortably, avoiding his eyes. "I…you should be, yes," she said, with the air of someone caught in the uncomfortable position of explaining something inappropriate to a small child. "But as I say, you are doing very well. Maybe you'll be all right."

"…Okay." That hadn't helped; that hadn't done anything at all, except for bring a feeling of panic to the forefront of his mind. He pushed that away forcefully and carried on. "But if I'm not all right…what…?" He couldn't quite form words to explain his fear, because he wasn't entirely sure what he was afraid of. His eyes wandered to Zachariah, asleep or worse in the corner, and his brow furrowed. He tried a different tact. "What's wrong with him, exactly?"

Sonia bit her lower lip in a way that forcefully reminded him of Jessica. The wings on her back fluttered rapidly, buzzing faintly like the hum of a bumblebee. She didn't answer him, and looked away awkwardly; she cast a look around the room, as though searching for some other morsel of food she could distract him with and finding nothing.

Adrian pushed himself off of the cot. Every inch of him ached, but the pain wasn't unbearable, and he tentatively stood for a moment on the hard dirt floor. He wrapped his arms around himself, protectively, and then, with effort, headed across the room to Zachariah. If Sonia wouldn't tell him what was going on, he would find out for himself.

The faerie didn't stop him, and he crossed the room in a half-dozen small steps. A jar of colored smoke sat on the floor beside the cot. The contents were gray-blue and moved with the languid churning of a lava lamp. He watched the smoke — or was it some kind of liquid? — for a moment before searching the lumpy bundle of blankets for Zachariah.

The psychic's weather-worn features were peaceful; he was deep in slumber, apparently untroubled, dirtier than he had been but otherwise unscathed. "He looks okay," he said, uncertainly, examining his features with interest. If anything, he looked more peaceful than he should, as though in his sleep he had lost all the hard years that had etched into his face. "What's… what's wrong with him?"

Sonia sighed, her wings sagging, and she looked at him sidelong. "I'm…I don't do this, much," she admitted, finally, resignedly. "I'm kind of nervous, actually."

"Nervous?" He blinked and looked up, startled.

"I don't…I don't know how to explain," she said, her hands behind her back, staring at the floor. "I'm…I mean, I don't know…it doesn't happen like this, you know."

He smiled a little; now that he looked at her, she seemed quite young — little more than a teenager. He gave her an encouraging nod, and remained silent; asking questions seemed to make her more uneasy, judging from the way her wings would sag or flutter and her eyes would dart around to avoid him.

She seemed to recognize the encouragement in his eyes, and smiled back at him. "I'm not sure where to start." She bounced on the balls of her feet, her hands rolled into fists, swinging at her sides. "Here…are you steady enough to come outside with me? I think it would be easier if I could show you, rather than try to explain. And," her eyes strayed to Zachariah on the floor, "he's not going anywhere."

He nodded, perhaps a little too enthusiastically, realizing as he did so that he was intensely curious to see the outside world. Part of him thought that, maybe, he would walk outside and the illusion would shatter, and he could go back to a mundane world where he was just crazy. He knew most of the people who worked at the mental hospital. They'd be kind to him there.

Outside, the world was wild and strange; not so different from any other forest, in appearance, but the feeling of it was different — hyper-real, as though it had been painted in watercolors. The trees were regular trees, in the regular colors, and the sky was the same shade of blue as skies everywhere, but there was a quiet humming energy to the place, a subtle vibration of strangeness. Adrian's brain may have tried to make sense of the things he saw, to catalog them as normal — but there was nothing normal here.

Overhead, clouds slowly drifted over the sky. They didn't just resemble different shapes — they actually took form, fluffy artist renditions of ducks and palm trees and airplanes that scooted across the sky and twisted and formed new shapes before they disappeared over the horizon. In the distance, a low mountain range broke over the tree line. Beyond this a single purple peak rose into the sky, looking out-of-place and self-conscious. The birds in the trees sang and chirped as he walked past, and when he caught glimpses of them they were oddly shaped and improbably colored, as though they were made by someone who had molded them out of clay using a single reference photo and a whole lot of imagination.

He waited for her to start talking, but her eyes had wandered away again to watch the clouds overhead — which, at the moment, had taken the shape of a pair of kittens that raced and gamboled around in the sky. "Where am I?" he asked when he realized she wasn't going to speak without prompting.

"Dreamland," she said. "It's…it's a place where people come, when the real world doesn't want them anymore." She looked back at him, her face obscured by the translucent gossamer of her wing. "And where children visit, when they're still young enough to find their way here. And, of course, it's where faeries live."

He wasn't sure where to start with the questions. "What happens to them, then? When they get here?"

"Adrian…" she stopped, suddenly, and looked at him with eyes large and gleaming with emotion that threatened to burst out of her. "I like you, a lot. You're different from who normally comes here."

Adrian, flattered but confused, couldn't find words to answer, and she pressed on.

"So I can't tell you. Just…here. Come see the world, while it's still light out, and if…I'll explain it to you in the morning, if you still want to know."

He couldn't find it in his heart to argue with her; he had never seen anyone's expression so earnest, so desperate, and certainly never poised on him with such innocent concern. She tugged his hand and led him out into her yard, and together they walked along the tree line.

Through the trees, he could make out a vague shimmering that he thought must surely be the unicorn. Butterflies as large as his palm fluttered between multi-colored wildflowers growing in patches between trees, and the air was sweet and unpolluted. Ahead, between the trees, he caught sight of a twisted, multi-hued shimmer that coiled on the horizon like a maelstrom made of rainbows.

Together, they completed a slow revolution around Sonia's cottage, past the trees and the garden, and back up to the doorway. Sonia kept a tight grip on his hand, perhaps afraid that he might try to run if she gave him the chance.

"Night is falling. We'd best be back inside," Sonia said as she ushered him back through the door.

"Already?" Adrian wondered, aloud, and glanced up at the sun. He must have slept most of his day away, he thought. There was no other explanation for how quickly the sun had moved across the sky. But, hadn't it been lighter just a few minutes ago?

Sonia's hand pressed against the small of his back, gently shoving him back into the cottage.

Inside, Zachariah was awake; he sat up, clutching his blankets to his chest, his eyes wide and blank, his expression slack. He stared vacantly at the wall across from him, and looked as though his mind had been thoroughly broken. That peaceful, unbothered expression was still on his face. It had been reassuring — even sweet — when he slept, but it looked wrong on his features now. His short-cropped hair stood up on one side of his skull, and, despite the warmth of the fire spreading through the small house and the blankets he was bundled in, he shivered slightly. "The cat's got loose," he said, his voice unsteady but quiet, muttering to himself. "Better run, kitty. There's too many mice here for you to eat. They could eat you back." He shuddered violently, his body giving a sort of sideways jerk, and fell silent.

"You can't help," Sonia murmured, and wrapped her hands around Adrian's arm. "It's always like this. He'll suffer just a little longer, but then…well, he'll stop suffering. It's okay."

"He'll…are you saying he's going to die?"

Her smile wavered a little, and she pushed him down onto his cot, holding either shoulder with her delicate hands, her face inches from his; he almost expected her to kiss him goodnight, but she withdrew. "He's…" Her brow furrowed. "When people come through the portal — people like you and him — grown-ups, I mean." She looked relieved, as though it had taken great effort to articulate this much, and carried on, "When grown-ups come through the portal, it does things to them. Like that." She pointed at Zachariah, who was rocking slightly, arms wrapped around his knees, muttering to himself again. Sonia looked back at Adrian, hesitantly. "Dreamland…isn't really made for grown-ups."

"I'm all right," Adrian said, almost defensively.

"Well, yes, you seem to be…" Sonia looked uncertain. "That's enough, for tonight. I told you…I'll explain it all, as best I can, tomorrow. For now, let's just…" she trailed off, looking uncomfortable. After a moment, she looked up, her eyes hopeful, gently curious. "What's it like? Where you're from?"

He stared back at her, wondering why she was so desperate to change the subject, and decided pressing the issue would be unwise, as much as he wanted to. Instead, he leaned back against the wall, closing his eyes, and considered her question. "Well…I live in the suburbs," he started, unable to think of any better place to begin. "So it's not…there's a lot of people, and buildings are closer together, and there's pollution…" He wondered if he'd have to explain about pollution, but Sonia made no gesture of confusion so he carried on. "And there's…technology. Cars, and computers, and airplanes…" He stopped, because he met her eyes and recognized the expression of someone whose question had not been answered the way she had intended it to be, and he fell silent, awkwardly.

"You. What are *you* like where you're from?"

"Oh." He considered this. "Well, I work with families who need help. Kids. Like if they're being mistreated, or their family's having trouble, I help them. I have a wife…well, I mean, an ex-wife. Sort of. So I live by myself now."

Sonia nodded encouragingly, watching him with liquid eyes.

"And…" Emboldened, he pressed on. "Every morning, I go running, and after I shower I drink a protein shake and sometimes eat a piece of wheat toast. Then I go to work, and when I come home I eat a TV-dinner because… well, actually, I don't really know how to cook, and if I eat a TV-dinner all the nutritional information is on the box." He felt himself blush; somehow, in light of the strange and alluring food he had eaten since arriving here, admitting he ate TV-dinners seemed really pathetic. Actually, when stated so baldly, all of his life seemed pretty pathetic. He looked up, eager to change the subject. "How about you? What do *you* do?"

"This," she said, and then, brow furrowed, "…Well, not this, exactly. *That*, actually." She pointed at Zachariah. "That's more like what I do."

"I don't understand?" He was starting to feel like a broken record.

"The portal," she said, patiently. "It opens onto my land. I'm sure you must have seen it out there. I…find people who have fallen through, and I tend to them until…well…until they don't need me."

From across the room, Zachariah looked up, for a moment, and said clearly, "No, mother, I will NOT." He looked defiant, and for a moment appeared ready to stand; then he collapsed back into his bed and resumed nonsensical muttering.

Adrian looked back at Sonia. "So it's the fall through the portal that does….that?"

She nodded. "It shows up differently, in different people. Sometimes it's very fast. Sometimes they seem just fine, and then…." She trailed off, looking at Adrian sadly. "Although, there's some who think it's not the portal that makes them crazy. That they find the portal because they're *already* crazy. But either way…that's how they end up, eventually."

Silence descended between them, and after a moment she glanced up, over her shoulder, at the darkness falling outside. Her wings, which had been fluttering gently, stood stiff and upright, like the hair of a frightened cat. "It's coming," she whispered, breathless. Her green eyes locked on his. "Listen. You seem strong. You remember. Maybe…maybe you have a chance." She reached out, touched Adrian's shoulder, and his flesh erupted into goosebumps beneath her fingertips. "Stay away from the floor. And don't let them see that you're afraid."

"Don't…"

She touched a finger to his lips to silence him. "There's no time for questions. I'll explain everything, in the morning, if you make it through the night." With that bit of unnerving, obscure advice, she moved away from him, across the room to Zachariah.

What she did after that, Adrian had no idea — because, before he could react, before he could think, the world was immersed completely in darkness.

THE DARKNESS

Total blackness enveloped the cottage as though someone had thrown a blanket over the house, blocking out all hints that there had ever been light. Suddenly blinded, Adrian cried out, groping around himself for his bed, the wall, anything to give him a sense of place in the void. Where the overwhelming color of the tunnel had been disorienting, nauseating, this was worse — it felt like drowning, as though the darkness was a tangible substance pressed down on him, smothering him.

Claustrophobia, he thought, desperately; *fear of being buried alive, fear of being consumed, deepest terrors of the human psyche.*

Zachariah shrieked. Adrian heard him thrashing, struggling, his legs tangled in the blankets like an insect caught in a spider's web. "Oh my god the cave the fucking cave please don't make me —"

He stopped abruptly, as though someone had hit the 'mute' button.

In the darkness, Adrian heard whispers, scuffling, the movement of dark crawling things that breed in the night. The noise made him think of spiders, long-furred spindling legs carrying them across the floor; he thought of bats, the silken whisper of their wings on the night air; he thought of rats, chittering and scuffling quietly in the black. He pulled his blanket close to him, drawing it to his chin like a child. He huddled against the wall and felt himself tremble, feeling the brush of terrible creatures moving around him in the dark.

When he was a young child, before he had started his sleep ritual, Adrian would draw himself into his blankets each night. The posters around him would watch him with black, vacant eyes, and the branch outside his window would tap and scratch at the glass. He would wrestle, each night, with the certainty that something terrible lurked just beyond, in the utter darkness of sleep — something that wished to do him grievous harm.

He felt that now, the certainty, the terror. Something warm and oozing moved across his hand, and he let out a cry that was stifled by the blanketing dark.

He squeezed his eyes tightly against the darkness, as though he could block out the night with further dark — and then realized, as his eyelids slid closed, that he was no longer in the dark, but in the brightly-lit theater of his own mind. Feeling a sense of unease, he tried to open his eyes again, to escape the vision he had found himself within — but it was no use; his mind had surrendered the use of his body, and he was paralyzed, trapped within the familiar room he had built in his thoughts.

His thoughts traveled, against his will, to a door, which opened and swallowed him into the space he had always imagined as his mental panic room. This was the place where he kept things he had no intention of ever thinking about again. He had always imagined that the room was fitted with a large, steel safe, the kind with the big round wheel for a handle, and now he saw that with astonishing clarity as though he were really standing in a room that existed somewhere other than his own mind.

Realizing that, panic rose up in him, and he tried to think of something else — tried to envision something else. He tried to think of an elephant. It didn't work. He tried *not* to think of an elephant, and that didn't work either. Trapped in a room of his own making inside of his brain, Adrian glanced around uneasily at the things he had stored here, and found himself plunged suddenly into a memory.

He was four years old, and his mother had come home with the new baby, a little girl they had named Samantha. She was beautiful, and perfect in every way, with rounded, cherubic features and soft, downy blonde hair and huge green eyes.

Adrian hated her.

William had encouraged this hatred, had fostered it with careful jabs at Adrian's meager sense of self. "Mommy won't love you anymore, now that you're not the baby." That's what William said. "I'm the oldest, so mommy will always love me, but now there's a new baby, so she's the youngest and you're not *anything*. Just watch — mommy and daddy are going to forget all about you, and you'll have to move out in the garage like a dog."

It was cruelty of the kind only young children can wreak upon each other, and rooted only in William's insecurity and desire for whatever power he could have. Adrian recognized that now, understood that, even forgave it — but some wounds cut too deep to ever heal, and Adrian could still feel the scar as it was laid open by the vision before him.

He had woken in the middle of the night and crept soundlessly into his parent's bedroom to peer into his sister's crib, to get a good look at her face-to-face, look his demon in the eye. He had slept in his parent's bed until a few weeks ago, when they knew the baby would be coming any day; then he had been unceremoniously dumped in the terrifying darkness of his own bedroom, alone and scared, his position of honor usurped by the tiny being now before him, sleeping so soundly in her crib.

He looked down at her, and hated her, and wanted her gone from his life forever.

Consciousness touched the edges of his mind, and he realized that he again had feeling, control over his body, and he reached out in the dark, groping for something, anything, to reassure him of the reality around him, to reassure him that there was something outside of his mind. His hand brushed the rough wood grain of the wall, and slowly the world around him faded back into being.

It was dark, but not preternaturally so; he could see, in the gloom, the vague hint of the sunrise in the distance, lingering beneath the horizon. Sweat clung to his pores like the after-effects of a nightmare. His heart thudded in his chest, up in his throat, and there was another feeling, deep in his gut, a feeling of burning shame. Terrible guilt, intense and unshakable, wracked him, and he trembled; because a part of him had never stopped hating his sister, had never stopped resenting her…and it made it all his fault, what came next. He braced himself for it, but no further visions came, and he fell back against his bed, shivering and sweating.

Desperately, he fought to reconstruct the careful walls in his consciousness, the mental barriers that contained his demons. His mother had taught him, when he was very young, how to contain his emotion — she had explained to him how, when things became overwhelming he could put everything that he was unable to deal with into a box in his mind, seal the box and shut it up in a closet to deal with later. He found, in later years, that it was most effective if he locked the closet and never opened the boxes again. He'd imagined a bigger room, to contain all the boxes he needed. Eventually, when thoughts began to overflow the boxes, he had imagined file-cabinets; then he imagined the panic room, and the industrial-strength safe in the corner, and the padlocks on the door.

He felt tears on his cheeks, and total, complete exhaustion. His head lolled to the side, his muscles too weary to control it, and his eyes fell on Sonia, who was sitting up in a rocking chair, her legs folded beneath her, her chin in her hands, staring across the room at him with intense, blazing curiosity. He attempted to make some sign to her, to call out, to speak, but he was too tired; she said nothing, made no movement towards him. Slowly, uncontrollably, Adrian felt himself slipping off to sleep.

* * *

When he awoke again, the sun was streaming, bright and aggravatingly happy, through the window and over his face. He felt the warmth burning against his eyes and stared, a moment, at the red backs of his eyelids, and tried to remember why he was hurting so badly, and why his insides were trembling.

He sat up, slowly, tenderly, and cast a look around the room. He expected it to have been ransacked by those creatures last night — to have been torn apart by skittering claws, or stained by crawling ooze. It hadn't been, and everything was as it was, where it should be. The fire smoldered low in the embers at the hearth, and Sonia dozed in her rocking chair, her knees pulled up to her chest and face buried in her knees, curled up like a wild mouse. Adrian's eyes wandered to the corner, to Zachariah's pile of rags, and found that they were empty — Zachariah was gone.

Intrigued, he rose from his cot, casting a furtive glance at Sonia's sleeping figure, and crept forward to examine the rags and blankets. Perhaps Zachariah had risen from his sleep and wandered off, he thought; maybe he had crept away in the darkness. Or maybe the darkness crept off with him.

He had just started to convince himself that the whispers in the dark had been no more than a dream, an unpleasant hallucination created by darkness and exhaustion. There had been no real threat, he thought — not really, just smoke and mirrors and unpleasant childhood memories, that was all.

And yet, he thought, looking down at the nest Zachariah had slept in. He looked back up at the door, still bolted from the inside — and then down, again, his eyes sliding into focus on something which had not registered for him before, something impossible and horrifying.

He was staring down at Zachariah — or, at least, at what was left of him.

When Adrian was eight, he had spent a few weeks of the summer at a youth camp up in the mountains. He hadn't realized it at the time, but he and William had both been shipped away for large chunks of that summer to allow time for their parents to negotiate the divorce — to scream, and sling accusations, and wallow in guilt and drink too much, to threaten and make up and tear each other apart from every angle until they were certain, beyond doubt, that the only solution was to leave each other.

But he had enjoyed summer camp, while it lasted.

One day, he had met with a forest ranger who told them about all manner of interesting things — radio tracking collars, tranquilizer darts, bear cages, relocating animals by helicopter. Then she had passed around a number of items for them to hold: a coyote skull, a huge pair of elk antlers, a bear claw, and, the most fascinating and disturbing to Adrian, the skin of a badger. He had held it far longer than anything else, running his hands over the rough pelt, the smooth line connecting the white and black markings. The eyes were two partially-opened slits, and there was a hole where its nose would have been. It still had its claws, long, heavy, vicious things, but otherwise it was completely flat, and heavier than it looked like it should be.

Looking down at Zachariah's remains, Adrian remembered the badger skin.

Zachariah looked as though he had been gutted, deflated like a balloon. His skin, unblemished, was folded up within the blankets, ashy pale and bloodless. His face, misshapen and deformed without a skull to hold it up, was contorted further with terror; his nose was sunken into his face; his mouth hung slack into a wide, toothless gap, and his eyes were gone from behind the fleshy slits of his eyelids.

Adrian screamed.

A long, loud, primal cry of terror tore from his throat and carried across the room with a force of its own propulsion, hanging on the air and resounding as one endless note. He scrambled to get away, all coordination lost in his blind fear, and he fell over himself, landing hard on the swept dirt floor and clawing into the strata, crawling on all fours to escape.

The scream woke Sonia, and in a single, deft movement she leaped from her rocking chair and dove across the room, wings fluttering. She landed deftly, like a cat, beside Adrian and swept him into her arms, holding him to her chest, cradling his head to her bosom like the mother of a terrified child. "Shh," she whispered, holding him, rocking gently back and forth, the fluttering of her wings creating a quiet breeze against his face. "Shh. It's okay. It's okay."

He felt himself quiet, after a moment, his body too exhausted to maintain the horror; he felt his heart slow down as the painful thudding subsided to a more manageable beat. He took a long, deep breath, and, suddenly aware of his proximity to Sonia's warm, supple body and the sweet, flowery smell of her, he pulled away.

"What...what the hell...."

"The Darkness," Sonia said.

He struggled to stand, and realized he couldn't, and resigned himself to leaning back on his hands. He gaped at her. She smiled, if shakily.

"I told you yesterday," she began, folding her legs beneath her, arranging herself comfortably on the dusty floor, "that if you survived the night, I would explain. So...I guess I have a lot of explaining to do."

IRRATIONAL BEINGS

"You might have heard stories of changelings," Sonia began, watching him with uneasy eyes, as though afraid he might lash out at her. "Of children, stolen by the faeries, taken away and replaced with faerie children in their place."

"...Okay." He cast a nervous glance at the corner, where Zachariah's deflated body was lurking, just out of sight among the blankets, and shivered. "Go on."

"Oh. Here." She stood and moved to stand over Zachariah's remains. She ran a hand over one wing, and Adrian realized that the wings had a fine dusting of some odd, glittering substance, like the dust of moth wings. She gathered this in her palm, held it over the blankets, and muttered an incantation in a language Adrian didn't recognize — the same language she had been singing in, in the woods — and sprinkled the wing-dust over the body.

Adrian expected the body to disappear.

It didn't.

Nothing happened, actually; at least, not as far as Adrian could see. Sonia stood over the body a moment, head bowed as if in prayer. Then she bent down, lifted the body in her arms — it flopped, uselessly, awkwardly, like a partially-deflated blow-up doll — unbolted the door, and, with a clumsy heave, flung Zachariah's rubbery remains out onto her door step. She whistled, a long, low note, and a unicorn stepped from between the trees. Gleaming with all the brilliance of the sun, it lowered its head over the deflated corpse, and opened its mouth.

Sonia closed the door, rather hurriedly, and dusted off her hands on her short skirt.

"Unicorns eat dead bodies?"

"Well, yes," she said, a little uncomfortably; her wings fluttered, humming quietly in what Adrian now recognized as extreme unease. "What else would they eat?"

Around the cracks of the door, Adrian could see a faint, multi-hued glow — the brilliant, gleaming white of the unicorn, but other colors as well, greens and pinks and blues, all of them star-bright and mingling in blinding, prismatic brilliance outside, suggesting that other unicorns had come out to join in the feast. He could just make out the faint sound of many creatures breathing and shifting outside the cottage, and, beneath that, a very quiet, wet noise, much like a hungry dog hurriedly slurping up table scraps.

Anxious to cover the noise, he turned back to Sonia. "Right. Anyway. Changelings. Go on."

"Well," she continued, a little uncertainly, looking at him with concern as though not entirely sure if she should comfort him or ignore his distress, "The stories were sort of true. Faeries have always lived in a world parallel to human kind, beside it and just touching, but never overlapping. And sometimes, faeries would steal children away, although they wouldn't normally trade them out for anything. Just take them."

"Why?"

"Faeries have a particularly dear relationship with children. We need them."

He looked uneasily at the door, beyond which the unicorns seemed to have ceased feasting; at least, they sounded as though they were moving away, their hoofbeats quiet on the earth.

"Not to eat," she said, with a twinge of impatience. "Listen. We are Irrational Beings." The way she said it suggested capitalization, as though *Irrational Beings* was a taxonomic definition. "Like the unicorns, outside, like dragons and trolls and all that. We cannot live in a world governed by logic and reason — there is no room for us, there."

"Dragons and trolls," he echoed, but there wasn't much left in him that could still be surprised.

"When humans were young and superstitious, and all the mysteries of the earth were unsolved, our worlds were closer, and we could travel freely between them. Then, as humans became more industrious, as they learned science and technology and abandoned their own faith and superstition, they started to pull away from us. There weren't as many wild places, where things were still unknown, that Irrational Beings could use as doorways. Our world became smaller. And darker." She stood, fidgeting, and again Adrian was struck by her need for constant motion, the way she grew uneasy when left stationary for too long; she turned to the hearth, and busied herself with re-building the fire, her back to him.

He watched the glittering, constant motion of her wings for a moment, thoughtfully, before he asked, "Darker. Like…last night?"

She nodded. "Irrational Beings are, by their nature, chaotic and prone to self-destruction," she said, and her voice was tinged with sadness. "We do better when closer to the mundane world. It has a calming effect. And the same is true in reverse — without our presence, the human world becomes too introspective and takes itself too seriously." She glanced over her shoulder. "Depression, I think you call it."

He considered this, and nodded.

"Anyway. As I'm sure you've figured out already, Irrational Beings have a particular love of children because they are endowed with this fantastic, beautiful capacity for accepting all sorts of unreality as truth. They are the last safe haven of nonsense in a logical world, and we need them in order to flourish, and keep our world close to the human world, maintain as many open doors as we can. They…help provide the light of our world. So faeries take a particular interest in the safety and well-being of children." She smiled, turning away from the fire, which was now alive and crackling merrily. "From what you told me, you do, too. So this should be something you can understand"

He nodded again, and began to think he understood where this was going. "So you kidnap children who are unhappy," he said, slowly. "And bring them here, where you can keep them safe."

"The children come when they need us, and they leave when they're ready. We don't force them into anything. We just show them the door." She shifted her eyes as she said this, carefully avoiding his gaze, and the thought crept into Adrian's mind that she might be lying — about any of it, or all of it, there was no way for him to know.

"But what the hell are you thinking, bringing children here, with that… that…those things that came last night?"

She shook her head. "You misunderstand me, Adrian. Listen." She held up a hand, to silence him. "I'm not explaining this right. The Darkness… they're not…Dreamland isn't built for grown-ups!"

"So whenever an adult comes here, you kill them to get them out of the way?" He regretted it, as soon as the words left his mouth.

Sonia looked at him, coldly, her eyes narrowed, a deeply wounded expression forming on her beautiful face. "After everything you have seen," she said, with a voice like cold steel, "you can ask me that? After I brought you into my home, and fed you, and held you when you sobbed like a terrified child — you have the nerve to ask me that?"

"No — no, I didn't mean — "

She continued, in a cold, curt tone. "No. It's not Dreamland that has a problem with adults. It's the adults who can't handle Dreamland. It does things to them. You saw, with your friend, what it does — before the Darkness even came. You felt it, the fall through the portal, and again last night. The rational mind reacts badly to this place, and tears itself apart, like…like a violent allergic reaction." She shivered, and again Adrian caught a flicker of something in her expression, something she wasn't telling him.

"So…it drives people mad?"

She shrugged. "For the most part, they're already insane when they get here, so I couldn't tell you for sure. You're the first I've ever been able to have a real conversation with."

He wondered what it was that she was hiding from him, but he knew *why* she was hiding it. She was trying to protect him in some twisted, overbearing way. That much was obvious from the way she looked at him: she thought he was safest not knowing the whole truth. He recognized the look. It was the look Jessica had given him so often when they tried to talk about the problems with their relationship

"The theory — although, as I say, I've never been able to prove this — is that they can only become aware of the portal when their minds have become suitably irrational. And, unfortunately for adults in your world…a suitable degree of irrationality seems to be the defining symptom of insanity. Once they've found the portal, and fallen through, and been subjected to the chaotic fabric out of which Dreamland was woven…well, it usually breaks them completely."

"And eats their guts out," Adrian muttered, unable to contain himself.

"Well, yes, sometimes." Her brow furrowed. "But it's not…it's not what you think. Things work differently here, that's what I've been trying to explain to you. Dreamland, it's…"

"Chaotic?" he suggested.

"…Very literal," she finished, violet brow furrowed. "Imagination is very, very real here. Metaphors aren't just words. Feelings are reality. The world is always changing and adapting because it gets created whenever anyone interacts with it." She looked around the room, a little desperately. "Have you ever felt…empty inside? Completely spent, and hollow, like nothing mattered and you didn't even really exist? Like you were…uh…deflated?"

He nodded.

"Well, there you go."

"Ew."

"Yeah." Behind her, the fire had died down to a hot, clear flame over the glowing embers, and she replaced the cauldron on its hook above the flames to warm it for breakfast. "Anyway. That's everything, then — I told you I'd tell you everything in the morning, and now I have." There was a subtle note of defensiveness in her voice.

"…That's *not* everything," he replied. "I mean, don't get me wrong, I appreciate the info but…I don't understand…." He wanted to understand; in fact, he wanted rather desperately to understand, because it suddenly seemed of utmost importance. A thousand questions came up at once, each seeming equally important, but what made it out of his mouth was an indignant statement instead. "I'm not crazy."

He almost didn't want to admit it. Being crazy — believing that everything he was seeing was a hallucination — seemed like a much cozier explanation. But he felt in his heart that it wasn't true.

"Well, no…you seem to be doing very well."

He shook his head, and heaved himself to his feet, finally trusting his legs to hold him upright. "That's not…no. I mean, that's not why I fell through the portal, or whatever. I'm not some lunatic who lost his grip on reality and started seeing faeries. No offense."

"None taken."

"So…what the hell am I doing here?"

She looked up from the cupboard, her arms full of fresh vegetables, and shrugged. "I don't know, Adrian. I don't know why you could see the portal, and I don't know why your friend came with you."

"Well, *he* might have been crazy," Adrian said, reasonably, and then shook his head violently before he had the chance to think about Zachariah's remains. "But *I'm* not. I've been…Sonia, I've seen that place before. The portal, or whatever. I've dreamed about it."

She didn't say anything, but seemed to consider this, biting her lower lip in that way that reminded him so forcibly and so painfully of Jessica. Her wings hummed.

"I don't usually remember my dreams — but when I saw it, I knew I'd seen it in a dream. Only when I dream about it, I think there's someone standing inside, and he's waving…no, beckoning. He's asking me to come with him. And…Nathaniel saw him, too, before he disappeared — *the Nightmare Man*."

The realization was sudden and powerful. Maybe the psychic had been onto something after all — or maybe his presence had just been a coincidence, and the doorway had been here all the time. Adrian turned his eyes hopefully toward Sonia.

"There's this man — or monster, or maybe he's a faerie — but he's tall, and he wears a cloak. And his eyes are big white empty sockets and he has a round mouth full of teeth." He looked up at her expectantly. "Have you seen him? Or maybe a little boy, about this tall, red hair like mine.."

"Adrian — "

"He's wearing these Spiderman sneakers, and his name is Nathaniel —"

"*Adrian!*"

He stopped, startled by the exasperation in her voice.

"I don't have any idea what you're talking about."

He opened his mouth to try and explain again, but she shook her head and held up a hand for him to be quiet.

"Every morning, I go outside and check the woods around my house for some poor lost soul who's wandered into my life, and I nurse them and I care for them and I ease the last hours of their suffering. And when they die, I say a little prayer and dispose of their body and I wait, wait, wait for the next one. That's it. *That's* what I do." The cold, hard gleam had returned to her eyes, and her voice lowered in volume but rose in intensity. "First you start accusing me, now you're asking me about things I can't possibly know. What do you want from me?"

He shivered, and shook his head, his eyes downcast, unable to answer her. It hadn't occurred to him that she might be lying to him because she, herself, didn't know the answers to his questions.

"Then don't start accusing me, or threatening me, or acting like you're entitled to answers that I don't have. I can't help you, Adrian. I don't know anything. I'm a nobody. And the only thing I'm good for is keeping you happy until your last waking hour, and hoping the Darkness takes you away in your sleep to some place happier than here."

"I didn't mean…I don't…I'm sorry." He looked up, seeking out her eyes and her forgiveness.

She glowered. There were tears in her eyes.

Tentatively, afraid to upset her further, Adrian ventured, "But…I mean, of course you couldn't know for sure, but…Sonia, I'm kind of scared." The temporary gust of excitement about the portal and The Nightmare Man was long gone, replaced with the terrible memory of Zachariah's limp remains and Sonia's desperate outburst. "What's going to happen to me?"

She shook her head; the tears in her eyes shimmered. "I don't know," she said, and sighed. "I've had…I mean, sometimes people last the night. A few days. Sometimes they're okay, at first, before…"

She looked down, whatever she had been cooking utterly forgotten on the fire, and said nothing for a while. When she spoke again, it was very quiet.

"Whatever happened last night, in your head — that'll keep happening. Every night, when the Darkness comes, that's where you'll go."

He shuddered at the thought. He didn't want the Darkness shoving him back into the panic room in his mind any more than he wanted those creatures to eat him away from the inside. "There has to be a way out," he said. "I mean…no offense, you've been very kind to me, I like you a lot actually. I just…"

"No, stop. I understand." She glanced at her forgotten stewpot of vegetables and wrinkled her nose. "I want you out of here too. This place will destroy you." She paused, a moment, thoughtful, and then looked up at him, with a sudden light in her eyes. "The Gatekeeper."

"What?" Startled, he looked around, as if expecting someone to have appeared suddenly behind him.

"The Gatekeeper," she repeated, looking excited. "On the mountain. He'd know how to get you out!" Her wings flitted rapidly, buzzing like a swarm of bees at her back. "He knows everything. He has doors to everywhere, even the human world. My mother told me all about him…"

"Well, all right. So we go talk to the Gatekeeper. And maybe…" he felt, somehow, as though he were gearing up for a starring role in a *Wizard of Oz* television remake, and grimaced. *What is it you're looking for, Adrian? A brain? A heart? No — courage. Definitely courage.* "…Can you afford to come with me, though? I mean…in case someone comes through the portal…I wouldn't want to make you leave your job…."

She drooped a little; her wings lay, perfectly still, for just a moment at her back, and Adrian hadn't realized how much he had grown accustomed to the buzzing until they fell silent. She looked at the ground, thoughtfully, clearly having not considered this problem.

"I can go by myself," he offered, tentatively, not wanting to face whatever insanity lived outside alone but wanting — at least, in theory — to ease her of his burdens. "If I can find the way."

"Don't be stupid, you can't go by yourself," she snapped, and shook her head. "No, don't…don't worry about it." Her eyes met his. "I…this is important. Maybe more important than anything I've ever done in my life. The crazy people aren't going to really miss me."

His cheeks burned a little. He wasn't sure how he felt about being the Most Important Thing in someone's life, especially a someone he had only met the day before.

She ignored him. "Yes. Of course. Here — let me just send a message, and then…" she trailed off, opening the door and standing in the doorway, letting out another low, long whistled note.

There was no trace of Zachariah — no stray bits of flesh or hair, no bodiless fingernails — and Adrian breathed a sigh of relief. A new unicorn, one that gleamed a brilliant, pale pink, like sunlight through rose petals, broke through the trees. The fur was still glossy white, but the mane and tail were a bright, rosy pink, and it glowed in the doorway, brighter than the sun, casting everything in the room in a reddish hue. Sonia whispered insistent directions to it, in that strange language Adrian didn't understand, and then turned back to him with a smile. "As luck would have it," she said, closing the door behind her as the unicorn took off at a slow, easy canter. "I get a visitor tomorrow. Hopefully the unicorn arrives in time so we can journey back with her."

"A visitor?"

Sonia made her way back across the room and to the shelf of glass jars, counting them. Her brow furrowed in concentration. "Yes. A merchant, actually. Stops off to trade with me, give me supplies. I don't make my way into the main village very often. I'm…I'm actually not allowed to."

"…Not allowed…?"

She shook her head. "It's kind of complicated. And not really important. Don't worry about it, okay? Here…" she dug around on a low shelf — one that didn't have any glass jars on it — and tossed him a satchel. "Start packing."

LORELAI

That night, Adrian knew what to expect, and tried to brace himself. His stomach full with Sonia's cooking, the blankets pulled tight around his body, he waited for night to fall. Tonight he would be prepared. Tonight, he would —

The Darkness came suddenly and without warning, flooding into the cottage, oozing into every corner and blotting out all light, all warmth, all reality. Adrian was, once more, utterly alone, and a shiver passed through him. Something slithered past his bed; he heard it, the dry scratch of swept dirt sliding across something's belly — something slimy and scaly and unpleasant. He reached out for the wall, to steady himself, and found that the wall was gone, replaced with a seething warmth, a furry, pulsating *something* that moved over his hand, enveloping it.

In the darkness, someone screamed.

It was Adrian.

It's not real, he told himself, and found that he could not speak the words aloud. He jerked his hand back from the furry thing in the wall and buried his hands beneath his blanket. *It's not real, it's a hallucination, a reaction to stress and fear and it's going to climb inside and tear me apart and eat me away from the inside just like Zachariah, oh god oh god oh —*

He screamed again, and heard a sob in his voice, and forced himself deep inside his thoughts once more to escape the terrible dark. He locked himself into the panic room in his mind and barricaded himself against invaders.

Adrian was nine years old. His father was gone, out of the picture nearly a year now, and William had gone cold and untouchable, an irritable ball of rage that Adrian grew to fear even as he continued to love him. William didn't hurt Adrian, didn't touch him — didn't touch anyone, actually, and that was the problem.

Nine-year-old Adrian opened his eyes into his world, crafted from the fabric of memory. It was dark here, but not so dark as the reality outside, and so he stayed here, and wandered the halls of his childhood home.

Where's Mom? Young Adrian wondered, padding down the long hallway between his bedroom and the family room, his footsteps muted on the carpet. He was wearing his Spiderman pajamas. Adrian had always liked superheroes; he had a whole closet full of costumes and toys and action figures.

"Mom?" he called out, but voiceless in the way of dreams. "Mommy?"

She was home, at least in some literal sense; she was on the couch, vulnerable and asleep. Her shirt lay crumpled on the floor. She still wore a camisole, but it fell loose of one shoulder, and there were dark marks like bruises along her neck and breasts.

Nine-year-old Adrian smiled at the man who sat on the floor, one beefy arm resting on the couch beside Adrian's mother, a rough hand buried between her thighs. He wore blue plaid boxers that were too loose and showed too much; he smoked a cigarette with his free hand and smiled. "Hey little guy," he said, with a flash of too many teeth. "Mommy's still sleeping. Clear out, would ya?"

"No!" Adrian heard the words burst from his throat and they jolted him awake — or aware, he wasn't sure if he had been dreaming or merely remembering. He shivered, and noticed that the Darkness had lifted. Outside, the first tendrils of gray had touched the black sky, and he fell back against his pillow, sweaty and cold, but alive. Whole.

Across the room, in her rocking chair, Sonia's green eyes flashed in the semi-dark, and she smiled encouragingly. His eyes slid closed again.

* * *

The fire at the hearth died down to embers. Sonia knew that the coals were hot, even though she couldn't see them through the thick blanket of Darkness that had fallen over the cabin. She felt the shimmer of warmth and heard the low hiss of steam escaping the wood as it burned. The room was warm, but she shivered, and pulled her knees to her chest. Across the room, she could hear Adrian's breath. In a few hours, when the Darkness lifted, she would be able to see him: the rumpled auburn hair, the worry lines at the corners of his mouth, the furrows of his brow. But now, she knew he was there only by the sound of his voice.

He was crying. She heard the low moans, his voice choking around the sobs in his throat. She knew, when the Darkness lifted, that his cheeks would be damp with tears and his brow moist with sweat. That's how it had been the first night and she suspected it would be the same every night that he stayed here. Whatever he saw, it was terrible. Whatever humans saw was always terrible. How many times had she sat here, shivering against the Darkness that lay over her world like a blanket, and listened to the screams of humans going mad from their thoughts? Every time. Or, anyway, every time that they survived the night.

So why was *he* still here, then? That was the question that burned in her mind hotter than the coals in the fireplace. Of all the dozens of humans who had passed through the portal on her watch, no one had retained their lucidity the way Adrian had. At first, she had thought perhaps he was immune. She'd heard stories of faerie men who had slipped away to the human world and fathered half-faerie sons who found their way back to Dreamland. Maybe he was one of these, she'd thought; maybe the Darkness can't reach him because of faerie blood.

But that obviously wasn't true.

His dreams shimmered around him like aurora borealis. She saw them, when the Darkness lifted, curling out of his breath like so much steam in cold air. They were human dreams. Weak, incorporeal dreams…but undeniably human. And, besides, if he were immune then he wouldn't cry out into the night the way that he did.

No. The first night that he had come here, two things had become extremely clear to Sonia: he was special, possibly even unique, and she needed to protect him at all costs.

Through the windows, the first pale glow of light struggled to break through the shroud of Darkness. The Darkness resisted, but it trembled, and the light broke through its viscous surface like the thrust of a knife. Light tore through the curtain and the Darkness receded, fading through the window in smoky tendrils.

In the pale light of the pre-dawn — the sun would not rise for an hour, at least — Adrian looked pale and vulnerable. Sweat stood out on his forehead. His eyelids fluttered, and he sank down into his pillow. One eye opened, stared unseeingly across the room at Sonia, and then slid closed as he drifted back into untroubled sleep. His dreams crept cautiously from his nostrils and his gently-parted mouth. They moved slowly and gingerly, like uneasy rabbits peering from their homes for a hawk to swoop down onto them.

"Don't worry," Sonia said, in a murmur. "I won't take you."

The dreams shimmered, flickered, and hung still in the air, suspended like so much gleaming smoke. After a moment of hesitation, they fell back against his body and swept back into him with his next intake of breath.

Sonia smiled a little to herself. *They're shy,* she thought, and then corrected herself firmly: *No. They're afraid.* She looked guiltily to the floor. Adrian's steady sleeping breath had been overtaken by a snore. *It doesn't matter. You're going to keep him safe.*

Her own eyelids drooped and her wings lay flat against her shoulder blades. A last, sleepy thought whispered: *He'll forgive you for the lies, once he knows why.*

* * *

When Adrian's eyes opened again, the sun was high and bright. A small dish of porridge sat steaming at his bedside, and the scent wafted into thoughts before his brain had a chance to fully awaken. For a moment, he clung to the coattails of sleep, and he dreamed a jumbled nonsensical dream about porridge: creamy grains with fresh milk and butter and honey. His eyes slid open and he blinked himself awake. Drool gathered in the corners of his lips and he wiped it away with a furtive look at Sonia.

If she noticed the drool, she ignored it. "Good, you're up." Her shoulders were tight and her wings stuck up at an awkward angle. She paced the room, her hands balling into small fists at her side. Occasionally she would stop and crane her neck to peer out the cabin's one window, or open the door a crack to peek outside.

Adrian chuckled, despite himself. "Waiting on your in-laws?"

"What?" She closed the door behind herself and made an inarticulate noise in the back of her throat.

"Whenever my in-laws used to come visit, I'd do what you're doing now." *Although you look a little more tense than I was*, he thought. *And that's saying something.*

"What's an in-law?"

"My wife's parents," he said, and then, mechanically, "Ex-wife. So I guess now they're my ex-in-laws. Not that I have to worry about them dropping by anymore." *Especially now that I'm trapped in in some crazy faerie-land,* he thought. He drew himself upright in his bundle of blankets and held the bowl of porridge close to his chest. "What I mean is — you seem nervous."

"Oh. Well. I guess I am, a little." She frowned. She opened the door again and peeked out. "She'll be here any minute. I think I'll go out and meet her up the path, actually."

"Who?"

"Lorelai," she said. "The merchant. I...I should go warn her about you. You'll be a bit of a shock." She bit her lower lip. "Here. Get ready."

Without clarifying what he was getting ready for, she swept outside, wings buzzing like hornets. The door swung closed behind her and he watched her receding form with curiosity as he worked on his porridge. He wondered how Sonia could know whether the merchant — Lorelai — was on time or not. He hadn't seen any sort of clocks or time-pieces since he arrived, and with the sun's ambivalent tendency to rise and set whenever it pleased, he couldn't imagine any reliable method of time-keeping. Maybe he'd ask when she got back.

Except none of it's going to matter, he thought. *You're leaving soon, remember?*

He finished his porridge and rose, setting the bowl down on the hearth.

He hesitated a moment before getting dressed. Sonia had provided him with a neat stack of potential clothing he could change into. Most of it seemed to have been scavenged from people who had passed through the portal in varying stages of disarray. He held up a pair of trousers and noted a stain down one leg that looked suspiciously like urine. He set these down. In the pile, thrown haphazardly on top as though added as an afterthought, Sonia had provided some hand-sewn pants and a shapeless white shirt. Both seemed to have been made from some secondhand fabric — flour sacks, maybe, or old sheets — but they were clean, and fit surprisingly well. The pants ended a few inches above his ankles and the sleeves of the shirt hung nearly to his fingertips, but it felt right somehow that they should. He stared down at himself and felt like a pirate. Or a hobo. Maybe both.

He glanced at the window. The path leading into the woods was empty. Adrian looked back at the cabin and debated what he should do next. Finish packing? Yes — that seemed right. They had started packing already but hadn't gotten very far. Sonia had worked out a rough list with him of the items they might need for their trip to visit the Gatekeeper in the mountains, but she wasn't as much help in this as Adrian would have hoped. She had never gone on a journey without her family and hadn't left her own land at all since she came of age, so Adrian had taken over the preparations entirely, feeling — quite justifiably, he thought — that he was more experienced in the matter and, after all, this was one occasion when a rational mind would prove quite useful.

He looked at the satchels she had provided for him, and wondered — not for the first time — if he would be able to fit everything they needed in them. He had asked Sonia, hopefully, if they were some magical bags of holding, bottomless packs which could expand as much as necessary to fit their contents. She had looked at him as though he were insane, and he took that as a disappointing indication that they were only regular travel satchels.

After a moment of consideration, he started packing one bag with food: cakes that Sonia had prepared in extra quantities to set aside for the travel, blocks of hard cheese that he found in her pantry, fruit — fresh and dried — and potatoes. He found some seasonings that he didn't recognize but which looked useful, so he packed them as well.

In the other pack, he loaded in dishes and pans — Sonia had few of the latter, preferring to do most of her cooking directly on the fire, so this made for quick packing. He added blankets — a few extra, as he assumed mountains would be cold and they would, most likely, be sleeping outside — and then looked down at his packing job, feeling a little inferior. He tried to think of what he would take on a camping trip, and remembered he hadn't gone camping since he was at summer camp, and that hadn't quite counted since he had been in a warm bunk bed in an imitation-log cabin on a site with running water.

Outside, a glimmer of pink passed by the window, and Adrian glanced up. The pink-aura unicorn stood on the front steps and pawed at the stoop, tossing her head impatiently. Her horn scraped the door. She's back with the response to Sonia's message, he thought. "I don't know what you're saying," he said, loudly, to the window.

The unicorn stamped.

Adrian thought about opening the door, but he could only think of the wet crunch-slurp noise of the unicorns disposing of Zachariah's body. He imagined the unicorn impaling him on her thin woven-diamond horn. Stamping him to death under her hooves. Tearing into his flesh with rows of sharp gnashing teeth. "I'm not letting you in," he said, petulantly. He felt like a child home alone trying to fend off a visitor when his parents weren't supposed to be away. "Sonia's not home."

The unicorn made a low, obstinate sound and scraped her horn against the door again. She stamped her hoof and the door rattled a little on its hinges. Adrian's heart leaped in his throat and he was certain at any moment that the unicorn would break in and tear him apart.

He opened his mouth — maybe to admonish the unicorn, maybe to scream — but closed it again quickly. He heard Sonia's voice coming up the path: "Hepzibah, get down from there. You know better." The unicorn made a quiet sound. Sonia responded in whatever that language was that she spoke. The unicorn tossed her head and trotted away from the door, snorting in what Adrian couldn't help but feel was a very derisive manner.

Condescended by a unicorn. Add that to his list of firsts since arriving.

The door opened. Sonia started to walk inside but was pushed roughly aside by another woman of similar stature and with thin, veined wings like those of a hornet. She seemed to Adrian both very old and completely ageless. Her silver-gray hair hung in a thick, straight curtain to her knees and her eyes had a shrewd, world-weary look, but her skin was tight and unblemished and she moved with grace that seemed nearly preternatural. She swept into the room and was at Adrian's side within seconds, catching his chin in her hand and squeezing a little as she turned his face towards her. Her fingertips were warm and dry but her neatly-trimmed nails bit at the flesh of his cheeks.

"He's a grown-up, alright," she said. "No doubt about it. You sure you're not interested in selling, Sonia? You could make a pretty penny off 'im. Enough to leave this dump, anyway."

"Thank you, Lorelai," Sonia said, voice low and cold, "but as I told you, I'm not selling."

Adrian pulled away from her hand and stared down at her, feeling an immediate and intense dislike sweep over him. "Nobody's selling me to anybody," he said. He cast Sonia a pleading look. "…What would you want to buy me for, anyway?"

"Never mind," Sonia said, moving to stand between the two of them. She laid a hand on Lorelai's shoulder, just above where the wing sprouted. "Pick out the ones you want and let's get moving."

"I'll need twice as much as I usually get," Lorelai said. A sulky look stole over her beautiful, ageless features. "To cover for the cost of transport."

"Yes, yes, whatever." Sonia made a shooing gesture toward the wall of shelves. "Take whatever you think is fair. Only let's hurry up and get going. I don't want to be caught on the road when it gets dark."

"Nor do I," Lorelai said, and smiled in a cold, humorless way. Adrian's immediate dislike strengthened. She took a tentative step forward, turning her shrewd eyes to the shelves with their rows of irregularly-sized jars. She pulled one down and squinted at the slow-drifting smoke inside, pursing her lips critically. She gave it a little shake. "Weak stuff," she muttered. "How crazy was this one? It's barely holding together, it's so incoherent."

Sonia let out a quiet noise and crossed her arms over her chest — as though holding her hands hostage in her armpits before they had the chance to do something she'd regret, like beat the silver-haired faerie over the head with one of those jugs. Her wings buzzed so quickly that they were little more than a gossamer blur. "It's what I have."

Lorelai cradled the jug in the crook of an arm and worked at the cork with her neatly-manicured fingers. After a moment it gave way with a muted *pop!* and a little of the smoke escaped. It hung in the air over the mouth of the jug and Adrian saw the smoke itself shimmered, as though minute specks of glitter were suspended with it. The smoke curled in on itself like a snail. Rather than dissipate, it compacted itself and quivered as though held together by surface tension or viscosity. Lorelai prodded at the curled ball of smoke — or whatever it was, the more Adrian watched the more he realized that it was definitely not smoke — and it shivered as if it were alive. Then it ducked back into the jar.

"Well, it's not very high quality, but it'll have to do." Lorelai replaced the cork. "Time is, as you say, of the essence. Here, come help me load these up. Five jugs should be sufficient, I think."

"Five — " Sonia quailed.

"...Oh, you're right!" An unctuous smile spread over her lips. "I forgot — the human is coming along as well. Best make it ten, to compensate for the danger."

"*Ten!*"

Lorelai's eyes flashed. "Weren't you just telling me to take whatever I thought was fair? Forgive me — I must have misunderstood your instructions." Her eyes flashed back to Adrian. The tip of her tongue ran over her lips. "I could knock it down to two if — "

"Ten is fine," Sonia said, with some effort. "Gather them up and let's go." She looked back to Adrian, and set a hand on his chest. Green eyes met his. "Go pack up the wagon, would you? I need to...finish some business...with Lorelai."

"What —"

"I'll explain later."

He shut his mouth. He felt Lorelai's eyes on him and the gaze was hungry, like a cat watching a mouse just outside of its reach. He shivered and went to grab the satchels, careful to give Lorelai a wide berth. He glanced nervously at the door, made certain that the unicorn was nowhere in sight, and edged past the faeries and out into the yard.

He'd only been here for a couple of days, but he had spent enough time at Sonia's cottage to know what everything was supposed to look like. He knew, for example, that the straw-thatched roof had a nest of small, brightly-colored birds in it. He knew that chickens occasionally wandered freely over the yard, scratching and pecking at the dirt. And he also knew that the wagon — Lorelai's wagon — didn't belong here.

Where it *did* belong was in one of those creepy fairytale comic books he used to see in the convenience store, back when you could still buy comics at the check-out. The carriage was made of some kind of polished dark wood. It curved on all sides, coming up to a dome in the back, where the seating cabin was closed off with two doors on each side. The doors had windows with curtains drawn across them. At the front of the dark hump was the bench for the driver; the seat was covered in white fabric that might have been velour. It was discolored and worn bald in patches from heavy use. There were no shafts for a horse — and no horse, for that matter. It also had no wheels. Instead, eight spindly legs grew from the sides of the carriage. It looked like an enormous black spider crouched on the lawn.

Adrian backed away from it, finding his back to the door of the cottage. The bags slipped in his hand, which had grown damp with sweat. The carriage waved its two front-most legs at him. He tightened his grip on the bags, as much to tether him to something as to make sure he didn't drop them, and took a hesitant step forward. "Nice carriage…" he said, sidling up to it the way someone might approach a panicking horse or some dangerous, wounded animal. "Easy, now…"

The carriage had no eyes or ears, so he couldn't tell if it was paying attention to him, but it remained still as he approached. Its feet — if they could be called feet — were firmly planted into the soft dirt, each one tapered off like a spear. Adrian crept forward, clutching the bags to his chest like a protective shield, clinging to them like a child might cling to his favorite teddy-bear. The carriage doors swung open. A small, half-choked scream caught in Adrian's throat but he forced it down before it could escape. His sense of shame for cowardice still outweighed his fear of this incomprehensible faerie technology…barely.

The inside of the carriage was substantially more inviting than the outside. Where the front seat was worn and stained, the interior was bright and fresh as though it was rarely used. The overstuffed seats were covered in tooled white leather and the curtains hanging over the wide picture windows were velour. It was also roomier inside than it looked like it should be: Adrian realized he could easily lay lengthwise across the bench seat. The walls, too, were upholstered. It looked soundproof, private, and extremely cozy.

"Glad to see you're getting along," Lorelai remarked, emerging from the cabin. She carried two large jugs with her, one in each hand. She brushed past him and climbed into the front seat of the carriage, sweeping her skirt deftly to the side as she slid into place. She carefully laid the jugs beside her, one to each side, and held them in place with her elbows. "I thought you said he was smart." She met Sonia's eyes for a moment, challenging, and then turned back toward the road, the lines of her jaw taut.

"I said he *remembers*," Sonia replied. She carried four jugs — in each hand and in the crook of each arm — and she nudged Adrian with her shoulder as she walked up to the carriage and climbed confidently inside. *I guess she talked her down to six,* he thought, watching her. She set the smoke-filled jugs on the seat, set herself down on the bench opposite it, and patted the upholstered seat beside her. "Come on — she won't wait up for you much longer."

He glanced at one long, spindly leg and had a sudden fierce vision of Lorelai running him over, of the carriage trampling him and the spear-like points of the legs jamming themselves into his chest. He shuddered and climbed inside, the bags in his lap, reluctant to set them down.

The doors folded shut.

Darkness — not the preternatural, terror-breeding kind, but the regular, cozy absence-of-light sort — consumed the carriage and Adrian blinked rapidly trying to adjust his eyes. The smoke in the jugs glowed faintly, shimmering and flickering like lightning bugs caught in thick fog. He watched it, transfixed by the color and motion. He had never paid much attention to them in the cabin, but here in close quarters they seemed suddenly fascinating, especially now that he knew that Lorelai at least regarded them as valuable.

"What are those, anyway?" He asked, keeping his voice low although he suspected the carriage was soundproof.

She made no response; maybe she hadn't heard. "Want me to open the window?" Sonia asked, suddenly, leaning across him toward the curtain.

He caught her wrist in her hand. "No, it's alright. I get motion sickness." He smiled sheepishly. "It's bad in cars and planes, I bet it'll be even worse on this thing, with all the legs. I'll do better if I don't have to see outside."

Most people with motion sickness relish having a window to look out of, but Adrian was quite the opposite. It wasn't the movement that bothered him so much as the constant barrage of images, the world whipping by as though projected onto a screen. Besides, the glow of the smoke-jars was comforting somehow, like large nightlights.

Sonia slumped back in her seat. She rubbed her wrist with the fingers of her other hand, a vague frown on her face.

"…Sorry if I hurt you," Adrian said, glancing down at her wrist in the dim light. He didn't know how delicate faeries were. Maybe their bones were hollow, like birds.

"Huh? Oh! No, no." She smiled, vaguely, and clasped her hands in her lap. Her thumb occasionally strayed upward to brush her skin where he had touched her. "I'm alright."

But she didn't seem alright. She seemed shaken, actually. He opened his mouth to point this out, but a distant creaking sound caught his ears: a terrible wrenching noise like the sound of metal being torn, the sort of noise a car bumper makes when it's pulled from the car. He winced. If it was this loud through the padded walls, he could only imagine how deafening it must be outside. How had he not heard Lorelai's carriage coming from a mile away?

The carriage gave a shudder, as though it was shaking itself awake, and then it was moving. It undulated and skittered and wandered in drunken zigzags, like a crab trying but failing to walk in a straight line. The carriage rose and fell with each step, but also moved side to side, giving the whole thing a swinging circular motion. The metallic shriek of the legs faded, somewhat, as they moved, and fell into a rhythmic sort of tapping and creaking — the sound of a very old rocking chair.

Adrian clung to the satchels in his lap and doubled over, holding his head with both hands and willed himself not to vomit.

Sonia touched him gingerly on the shoulder, a mere brush of fingertips, but the touch was telling — full of uneasy concern. "Are *you* alright?"

"Fine," he managed. His head swam a little. He remembered a time when he and William had gone to a carnival at the local fairgrounds; he was eleven, and William was thirteen. This was years after their father left, and their mom was out with whatever suitor she'd picked for the week. Evan was a long time coming still. William was supposed to be watching Adrian, and they were both supposed to do their homework, order a pizza with the money she'd left for them, watch one of the videos she'd rented, and be in bed by ten. Instead they'd snuck out of the house — William's idea — and with their pooled allowance-and-pizza money they'd managed to stuff their faces with funnel cake and pink sticky cotton candy and still had plenty left over for the rides. Adrian had waited patiently in line at the ferris wheel and, when he got to the top, he stared down at the ant-like people in the fair, the twinkling dazzling lights of the city. The seat of the ferris wheel swayed a little, back and forth, and Adrian's sweets-filled stomach convulsed and he had puked all over himself and everybody beneath him in a wide arc.

"You're so stupid!" William had yelled at him. "You can't even go on a baby ride, you stupid sissy."

And Adrian, who was old enough to feel shame but not quite old enough to hold the emotion back, had started crying, which only set William off more.

"...Adrian?"

Sonia's hand squeezed his shoulder, drawing him out of the memory. His stomach did a lazy roll and he thought he might throw up after all — but then the sensation passed and he took a few deep gulping breaths. Cautiously, he lifted his head. The carriage trundled on. The luminescent smoke in the jars traced patterns of multi-colored light over the ceiling.

"I'm alright," he said, running one sweaty hand back through his hair, making it stand up in clumps along one side of his scalp. He felt the all-too-familiar sensation of pressure just behind his ear, gathering in his jaw, and he swallowed hard and tried to think of something other than the rickety sway of the carriage. "Just feeling a little sick. It'll pass." He leaned back against the seat and slid his eyes closed again. "I think I'll try and sleep until we get there. That always used to work in the car."

"Good idea," Sonia said. Her hand withdrew from his shoulder and settled into her lap. "It's not a very long journey. I'll wake you up when we get close."

He had expected it to be difficult to sleep, but he found that once he surrendered his mind to it that his body was more than willing to follow. He focused on his breathing and the inside of his eyelids. The carriage shuddered and jostled and trembled, but as Adrian retracted further into the comforting turtle-shell of his thoughts he noticed it less and less until he was oblivious to everything.

* * *

Nathaniel Weaver dozed, for a while. When he slept, he kept returning to the same place over and over, as though someone were rewinding a tape and playing it back repeatedly. He saw the beach, heard the gulls, held the beach ball in his arms. Autumn leaves fell around him. Someone, somewhere, cried. Always, when the sobbing started, he woke.

He wasn't sure how long he had been here, in this blank white room. Whenever he slept, it felt as though no time passed at all, but once he awoke it seemed that great long days had elapsed. When he woke, he would sometimes find that food or water had been left out for him — but not always. Other times he would awaken to the rumbling of his stomach or the dry, cracked feeling in his throat that made him think he wouldn't be able to talk, if he even had someone to talk to.

But, of course, there was no one to talk to. He wished the Nightmare Man would come back, just so he could have a little company.

Once he woke up and realized he desperately needed to go to the bathroom. He curled himself into a ball, as though squeezing his body into the most compact shape possible would forestall the inevitable. He hadn't wet the bed in years. The prospect of doing it now was too terrible and humiliating to consider. If he peed himself now, he would be stuck wearing the same wet, stinking pants, or else go without anything at all. He didn't know why, but being naked here in this blank, cold room terrified him.

He squeezed his eyes shut, trying to will his bladder into submission.

When this failed, he opened his eyes and realized that a toilet had appeared in the corner of the room. Curious and afraid, but overcome with necessity, he crept across the room, carrying himself gingerly to the foot of the newly-arrived, sparkling porcelain toilet. He looked around, assuring that he was alone. He fleetingly wished that whoever had put the toilet here would have had the decency to have included a wall, or at least some curtains.

No sooner had he thought this, than the air around him shimmered as though in a mirage and solidified, gaining color and weight. He stared, openly shocked, at the purple curtains that had drawn themselves around him. They hung from nothing, suspended in mid-air as though held up by invisible string from the ceiling.

He did his business, humming tunelessly to himself

When he was finished, he backed out of the curtains — he had a terrible, fleeting thought that they might close in around him, strangling him, but they allowed him to pass without challenge — and peered hopefully around the room. He wondered if maybe a sink would appear, so he could wash his hands, but none did. Suddenly very glad that Mommy wasn't here to see, he allowed his hands to drop to his sides.

"Bubba?"

The voice came from directly beside Nathaniel, and he jumped and wheeled around. Standing beside him was a little girl, no older than three. She wore denim overalls with pink flowers for buttons, and an embroidered butterfly on the pocket over her chest. Her hair fell around her shoulders in a mad tangle of golden curls, and she blinked up at him with wide eyes. Her nose wrinkled.

"You not my bubba." She crossed her arms over her chest.

Nathaniel wondered what a bubba was. He shook his head. "No. I'm Nathaniel. Who are you?" He looked around, his heart thudding in his chest. They were alone.

She didn't answer his question. "Play with me?" She tilted her head, looking up at him.

"Um…" He trailed off, noticing that the room had shifted around them. Where before there had been only plain white walls and a single white table, now there was a large doll house built to look like a castle. It was nearly as tall as the little girl, who went now to stand at it. Nathaniel followed.

She picked up a white plastic horse and made it gallop along the outer wall of the castle, making clip-clop noises with her tongue.

"Where did you come from?" Nathaniel asked. "Are you lost, like me?"

She shook her head, and held out the white horse. "Play with me," she repeated, more emphatically. "You be horsey."

Reluctantly, he accepted the horse. The little girl's fingertips brushed his, and his skin tingled as though he had been shocked by electricity. Now that he stood close to her, he could see that she flickered and glowed around the edges, the way Christmas lights did. He wondered if she was a ghost.

She bent down and pulled a figurine from inside the castle. It was the size of a large action figure, dressed in a full suit of armor. She picked up another doll, this one dressed in a long flowing gown and wearing a small silver circlet on top of her raven-black hair. The little girl glanced up at Nathaniel, who was still holding the white horse somewhat awkwardly in his hands, and huffed in impatience.

"I don't really play dolls," Nathaniel said. "Can I be the knight instead?"

She held the knight to her chest and glowered at him. "Be horsey."

Nathaniel looked around the room one last time, before settling down to his knees across from her. He set the horse back on the wall of the pink castle, and began to play.

CROSSROADS

Sonia hadn't been to Crossroads since she was a little girl. She had been born there, raised among the fields with the other faerie children, but she had been taken to the cabin at the foot of the portal when she was still very young in order to train for the family trade. "You have to start early," her mother had explained to her. "Because you won't be able to last very long. You'll age fast and die young. That's just the way these things go."

This hadn't been the most encouraging pep-talk, but then, Sonia's mother wasn't a particularly encouraging woman. She had sad eyes and heavy wings and she touched the humans as though they might be riddled with disease — as though they had fleas, maybe, or leprosy. She rarely talked and after she left the farm to retire in Crossroads, Sonia didn't miss her company. Somehow, the cabin had seemed less sad and lonely without her there.

Sonia's eyes ticked over to Adrian. He was slumped over in his seat, head leaning against the door frame of the carriage, clutching his satchel to his chest like a beloved toy. His jaw hung slightly open, but no dreams flickered on his breath. For the best, probably. It wouldn't do for Lorelai to throw open the carriage door and see the passenger cabin filled up with dreamlight. Not when she'd already bargained the price of their journey as far as she possibly could.

The shivering, creaky stride of the carriage slowed. The curtains were drawn, but Sonia felt like they must be close. The carriage still swayed up and down, side-to-side, but the motion felt more stable now as though the terrain had evened out — the roads in the heart of the village were better-maintained than those wandering through the wilderness.

"Adrian," she said, softly, leaning across the bench to prod his shoulder. "Wake up. We're nearly there."

He muttered something and shifted away from her.

"You won't want to miss this," she said. She shook him slightly. "And if you wake up we can get out of the carriage and walk a little. You'd like that, right?"

He grunted, but one eye opened. It stared out at her, closed, and then opened again. He struggled to sit upright and winced when he straightened his head. Pain throbbed in his neck, where it joined the shoulder. "Are we there yet?" he murmured, sleepily, like a child.

"Nearly," she said. "If you want, we can open up the curtains now. The road's a little more even."

"Alright," he agreed, hesitantly.

She leaned over him — she smelled like lilacs and he was suddenly self-conscious of his own odor, and that he had not showered in days — and slid open the curtains.

Light flooded into the carriage in a warm wash of gold. The sun was low in the sky, a fat lazy mid-afternoon sun that cast deep shadows over the fields. The fields seemed normal enough — puffy white sheep wandered over pastures like low-lying clouds, stacks of hay stood waited to be baled, vegetables grew in tidy green rows in rich brown soil — but the buildings were all strange. Some of them seemed to have been tossed together out of unlikely materials, while others were built haphazardly around the natural features of the land. One house had been carved into the side of a hill, with grass growing over the curve of the roof. Another was built among the branches of an enormous tree, the structure itself mostly hidden by leaves. Beyond that was a house that most closely resembled a beaver dam: a pile of scrap lumber interspersed with rocks and mud, with one large and very stately wooden door standing incongruously in the center.

"Where are we?"

"Crossroads," Sonia replied. "It's a faerie city. Most of the roads this far out pass through here, so you can't really get anywhere without traveling through."

He nodded. He leaned forward in his seat, craning his neck to peek out at the buildings. The farmland fell away, slowly, as the buildings grew closer together. He guessed they were reaching the center of town. "This far out?" He echoed.

"From the center," she said. "Before the mountains, there's the Center Kingdom. The further you go from the kingdom, the wilder it gets. Crossroads is pretty much the farthest south anybody will go, if they can help it."

"Oh. And I guess the road to the Gatekeeper crosses through here?"

She nodded. "Yes."

Peering outside, Adrian could easily see why they called the town "Crossroads". The carriage jangled forward toward the intersection of at least a half-dozen streets that all ran together like the hub of some very large, crooked wheel — streets that crossed over each other as though they had been designed by a child scribbling out a maze onto a piece of paper. He guessed that Irrational Beings probably didn't have a lot of social engineers to build their towns.

"Well...we're nearly there." Sonia's voice sounded a little strained. She fidgeted in her seat. "Adrian..." she began, in the tone of someone who has been putting off bad news as long as possible, "This might be...difficult...for you."

He blinked, caught off-guard. "What do you mean?"

"The...faeries...that live in Crossroads...well, they're perfectly nice people, and I'm sure we won't have any problems, but..." She bit her lower lip. "I don't know how they'll react to you."

"You don't think they'll like me?"

"No, it's not that. They're..." Sonia trailed off, realizing that Adrian wasn't listening. All motion sickness forgotten, he had pressed his nose against the glass of the carriage window and was staring out at the village center as it unfolded. His jaw hung open, slightly, although he was unaware of it.

Where the farmlands had seemed mostly deserted for the evening, the village center was alive with activity. A tremendous building that looked to be made from salvaged bits of enormous clockwork released regularly-timed puffs of smoke from amidst a cluster of smokestacks. The sign out front read: "Crossroads Dream Refinery." The refinery gave way to other buildings as they neared the center of town: shops, taverns, homes, markets.

Faeries moved among the buildings, going about their daily lives with the same air of routine as people in any other city. The women were small-statured and beautiful. Some had dragonfly wings like Sonia, while others had large butterfly wings, or heavy moth wings, or buzzing bee wings. None of them wore very much. The men were smaller, and held themselves in a hunched manner that made them seem even shorter than they were. Their wings were long and leathery, like bat wings, and their faces were narrow and pinched. There seemed to be five women for every man.

Some looked up as the carriage passed, but many just continued with whatever they were doing — chatting with each other, or sweeping out the entryway of their building, or locking up doors with heavy padlocks. Two hunched faerie men stood in the doorway of a shop, smoking pipes; the smoke curled over their heads in an alarming shade of green and formed shapes like thought bubbles over their heads.

The carriage shuddered to a halt. Once more it creaked, a terrific metallic groan that sliced through the air with an awful shriek, and then it set itself down hard on the ground. Adrian fumbled for the latch to open the door and spilled out, nearly falling over in his rush to put some distance between himself and the spidery carriage. He hugged his satchels to his chest, the way you're supposed to hug your seat cushion if your airplane crash-lands in water, and stumbled out onto the road. He stood in the shadow of a building that seemed to have been built predominantly out of river rocks and mud. A few twigs stuck out haphazardly from the mortar. Some still had leaves clinging to them. A sign over the door read *Depository of Illusions: Discount Used Dreams at Competitive Prices*. Across the street, a pink-haired faerie dropped the rug she had been shaking out and ogled him.

"Have a fun ride?" Lorelai asked. She shifted in her seat, looking down at him. Faint amusement tugged at the corners of her mouth.

"Thank you, Lorelai," Sonia said, climbing out of the cabin and standing —

purposely, Adrian thought — between them. "We'll be going, then. I'm sure you have business to attend to."

"I always do," she replied. "Say, you know where you're staying tonight? The Swaggering Spider's always got an open room." Her eyes flicked from Sonia to Adrian, where they lingered.

"I've made arrangements with friends," Sonia said. She started toward Adrian, taking slow steps backward as though unwilling to let Lorelai out of her sight. "But I do appreciate the hospitality."

Lorelai laughed. "I'm sure." She ran the tip of her tongue over her lips. "Well, anyway. I'd best get going myself. You let me know if you change your mind." She hesitated, then turned her eyes back to Sonia. Something fierce gleamed there. "You should stop in and give your poor old mother a visit, before you head out."

Sonia muttered her response, but it was drowned out by the nails-on-a-chalkboard shriek of the carriage legs coming back to life. Lorelai, once more facing forward on the driver's seat, snapped her fingers, and the carriage lurched forward and shambled down the path, its pointed feet leaving pockmarks on the dirt road in its wake.

"…What's the Swaggering Spider?" Adrian asked, when he was sure Lorelai had passed out of earshot. The faerie across the street had picked up her rug and was back to shaking it, but she continued to stare at Adrian as though not quite believing her eyes.

"Tavern," Sonia replied. "Just another of Lorelai's business ventures. At its best it's little more than a brothel. Folk come down, from the other cities, to…spend time…with the locals, and they pay Lorelai well for the privilege."

"Oh." He couldn't imagine a less appealing name for a brothel. "She said something about your mother…?"

Sonia was suddenly very interested in the pock-marked dirt road. Her wings sagged.

Apparently, awkward family relationships were the same no matter what world you lived in. Adrian found the thought oddly comforting. He glanced back up at the building, and wondered what exactly a "used dream" was, and why anyone would want to buy one.

Before he got the chance to ask, however, he was distracted by something coming up the path opposite the direction he and Sonia had come: two faeries, sitting astride two giant cats.

Not giant cats in the sense of lions or leopards — but regular, domestic housecats, blown to immense proportion. They padded silently over the pockmarked road, cats the size of ponies with huge round paws and long, twitching tails trailing at least three feet behind them. The right-most of the party was long-haired, steel-grey fur tipped in white across the toes, chest, and two dots above its eyes, which were enormous gleaming pools of bright yellow. To the left was a short-haired ginger tabby, its cream fur patterned with bands of orange; this one had amber-colored eyes.

Adrian stared at the spectacle, completely dumbfounded, and realized precisely what Sonia had meant when she had warned him about the effects of Irrational Beings on the reasoning mind of a human adult. Faeries wandering along a city street closing up shop for the night was one thing. Faeries riding into town like characters in a Western on the back of impossibly huge cats was something quite different. He gaped, and was too shocked to feel embarrassed for staring.

The grey-and-white cat halted a few feet away from Sonia, and its rider dismounted; the other followed suit, fluttering easily to the ground and moving to greet her fellow faerie. The cats, apparently recognizing that they had been discharged from service, wandered disinterestedly away from them. The ginger tabby flopped down in the middle of the street, rolling around in the dust. The gray one lifted its tail against the side of Depository of Illusions and marked its territory in a reeking wash of urine; it dripped down the side of the mud-and-stone walls as though the building had been hit by a sprinkler jet.

Reluctantly, Adrian tore his eyes from the giant cats, and, for the first time, took a good look at the faeries.

The one that had been riding the grey-and-white cat looked to be the bolder of the two, a self-appointed leader type; she was about Sonia's height, but thinner in build, tomboyish, and her hair was a shade of dark forest green that stood up at an odd angle, like a very thick, gently curving mohawk.

She wore a short skirt that seemed to be made of leaves, knee-high brown leather boots, and a very short dark green shirt that managed to cover very little of her body. Instead of Sonia's four gossamer dragonfly wings, this faerie had two translucent blue-green butterfly wings with long, trailing tails that ended at her mid-calf.

The faerie who had been riding the tabby stood next to the green-haired faerie, hanging back as if shy. She was built more like Sonia, curvaceous and buxom, but her curves were more pronounced, not as soft. Her wings were a pale pink in color, and shaped like the quintessential pixie wing Adrian was used to seeing in drugstores around Halloween time; she was wearing what looked to be a grass skirt crafted out of fine gold chain, and a white tube top that left the majority of her midriff bare, managing only to barely contain the swell of her breasts. Her hair tumbled around her shoulders in long, curling waves of pale blue. She wore a vague, dazed expression, as though she were daydreaming about something and not quite interested in the world around her.

"Are we late?" the blue-haired faerie asked.

"Doubt it," the one with the mohawk said. "We passed Lorelai's carriage on the way up, remember? The way that thing shambles along they probably could have walked here faster. Don't know why you made us ride all the way out here," she said, turning to Sonia. "Surely she wasn't too cheap to take you another half-mile?"

"I didn't want her knowing where he was staying," Sonia said, and then added something in that deep, lyrical faerie language that Adrian had heard her sing in once before. He guessed she was probably saying something about him that she didn't want him to hear.

The green-haired faerie said, looking up to set her eyes on Adrian with hawk-like intensity. "So you're him — the one who remembers."

Adrian nodded, dumbly, and thought that perhaps this would not validate their belief in the survival of his mental capacity.

"Adrian," Sonia said. She touched him on the back, a gentle pressure of fingertips on his far shoulder, her arm bridging his upper back. He thought he felt something protective, and possibly a bit possessive, in the way her fingers gripped his shoulder. "That's Laurel," she gestured first to the green-haired leader, then to the blue-haired, day-dreaming faerie, "and her life-companion, Evangeline." Adrian wondered if 'life companion' meant what he thought it did, but thought it might be rude to ask. "They both work for the Crossroads law enforcement."

"Hi," Adrian managed, feeling exceedingly foolish. He wondered what sort of faerie laws needed to be enforced, and whether there were faerie jails, and faerie handcuffs, and if they had a different uniform when they were on duty.

"Hello, hello," Laurel, the green-haired faerie said, pulling away from her companion to move near him, drawing rather closer to his personal space than he felt comfortable with. She examined him with gleaming, hungry eyes that looked, now that he thought of it, rather like the eyes of the grey cat she had been riding. "You *are* a fine specimen." She reached up a hand, running her fingertips down the line of his jaw, his neck, his chest; he shivered at her touch, and she smiled. "And so demure." She looked up at Sonia, who Adrian noticed — vaguely, peripherally — was staring back at Laurel with a look that was not altogether pleased. "Oh, Sonia, let's keep him!"

"Very funny," Sonia said, voice stern, her hand dropping to Adrian's waist and pulling him closer, her possessiveness now clearly manifested. "Come, ladies — night isn't far off, and we have a lot of preparations, if we want to avoid the Darkness."

Avoid the Darkness? Adrian thought, dimly; *what did she mean by that?* He didn't get the chance to ask before he was ushered forward, and he followed like a dumbstruck sheep being herded by a very forceful sheepdog.

Evangeline put two fingers in her mouth and whistled. The cats looked up, huge ears pivoting forward. One yawned, showing its massive pointy teeth and a long red tongue covered in barbs. Whiskers the size of arrows swept back against its cheeks and it rose lazily, taking a moment to stretch. Its scythe-like claws curled out of its huge paws and pierced the soft ground. It began to purr, and the sound reverberated through the ground, vibrating up Adrian's legs.

An inarticulate noise caught in his throat. "You're not going to make me ride that thing," he said. "Oh no. I've had my fill of weird transportation for the day."

"It'll be fine," Sonia said, still tugging him forward. Her hand caught him in a firm 'stay out of the traffic, little boy' vice grip that he knew there was no escaping. "It's only a half-mile. And much more comfortable than the carriage. You won't get sick, I promise."

Adrian gave her a wounded look, like a teenager whose mother has fatally embarrassed him in front of a hot girl, and muttered something under his breath.

"What was that?" Laurel asked.

"I said," he raised his voice, "that I'm not worried about being sick, I'm worried about that monster eating me."

Evangeline laughed. "You'll be fine. Here — you and Sonia can ride the ginger one. He's the gentlest cat in Dreamland. I'll ride with Laurel. She can sit up front." She winked at Laurel. Laurel grinned back.

Adrian looked desperately at Sonia, but she wouldn't meet his eyes. She tugged him forward to where the cat, apparently bored with the proceedings, had settled down onto its belly, all four legs folded up under its body and invisible in the mass of thick ginger fur. The tip of its massive tail twitched. Adrian closed his eyes and tried not to think of its dagger-sized teeth plunging into his chest. He tried not to think of it shaking its head with him in its jaws flopping uselessly like a ragdoll. He tried not to think of it pinning him down under the weight of its enormous paw...allowing him to escape...pouncing on him again and grinding him into the dirt, claws curling into his skin until he bled.

It didn't work.

Sonia snatched the satchels from his arms and gave him a hard push. He fell face-first into a furry vibrating wall. He heard Laurel snicker. Sighing, he climbed awkwardly up onto the cat's back. He buried his hands in the cat's neckfur. He felt Sonia leap up behind him; she sat side-saddle, one thigh pressed against his buttocks, one arm hooked around his waist, the satchels situated in her lap. She patted the cat's rump with her other hand, and it sprang to its paws and stood at attention.

Ahead of them, Laurel pulled Evangeline up onto the gray-and-white cat. They rode it around them in a slow circle, a bit like a cavalry general surveying his troops before the final charge, and stopped behind the ginger tabby. She called out something in faerie-language and the cats, as if on cue, started forward at an even, shambling pace.

Grudgingly, Adrian had to admit that Sonia had been right about the cat. It was much more comfortable than the carriage had been. The constant vibration of its purring was distracting, but not unpleasant, and it moved with a languid stride that seemed more like gliding than walking. Adrian hardly felt the paws touch the ground. After a few dozen steps he gradually began to loosen his death-grip on the cat's neck fur and sit up straight, digging his knees into the cat's sides for fear of sliding off. Sonia's hand stayed, calmly, on his side; her fingertips brushed his hip.

"Better?" She asked, leaning over so that her chin brushed his shoulder.

"Cats where I come from aren't nearly this well-behaved."

"They aren't always here, either," Sonia said. Her breath was warm in his ear. "Evangeline has a gift. Things listen to her."

At either side, the town center gave way to more farm-land. A sign at the edge of town read Swaggering Spider Inn. The building beyond the sign was a surprisingly normal-looking two-story white house. Light flickered from the inside in a rich orange glow that Adrian supposed was firelight, either from a fireplace or candle chandeliers. Maybe both. Outside, hanging paper lanterns lit up a courtyard furnished with maybe a dozen tables. The lanterns flickered different colors — blues, greens, purples — and cast their multi-hued light over the tables like a tiny, captive aurora borealis. Faeries sat at these tables, and other figures that Adrian couldn't quite make out from the distance. Many of the tables had bottles on them, and everyone seemed to be having a wonderful time. The Swaggering Spider was starting to look like a much better offer than it had sounded.

Evangeline clicked her tongue and the cats moved, turning away from the tavern and down a thin dirt trail. The trail wove its way past a pasture and into a small copse of trees. There, set away from the road at an angle that would make it invisible to anyone who wasn't really looking for it, was a small house. It, like some of the buildings in town, was built mostly of river rock and mud, with branches sticking out at odd angles from amidst the mortar. The whole structure leaned slightly to the left, and the roof seemed to have been shingled in sod dotted with wildflowers. A chimney rose up from the high end.

Laurel stopped her cat at the foot of the stone-lined walkway and hopped down, helping Evangeline down alongside her. Hands entwined, they made their way up to the front door — which was perfectly round, so it was hard to say whether it tilted to one side or the other — and after fidgeting with the knob a moment Laurel opened the door and the two of them stepped inside. Their cat jumped up onto the roof in one bound, curled itself around the chimney, and began to doze.

Sonia slid off of the cat and took Adrian's hand. He didn't climb off so much as ooze sideways until his feet found the ground. His eyes locked on the cat on the roof. Overhead, the sun burned fat and orange, coming dangerously close to the horizon.

"Come on," Sonia said, resuming her prior grip on his elbow. "Night's coming."

"Not if we hurry," Evangeline said, pushing the door closed behind them.

The house was small, cozy and sparsely furnished. It smelled woody and fragrant, some combination of herb smells that Adrian couldn't quite make out. Beds were built into the walls, little cubby-holes with lumpy mattresses and old, threadbare blankets. A round kitchen table, surrounded by three chairs, stood in one corner, and Sonia deposited their bags on top of it. A fireplace dominated most of the opposite wall; beside it, firewood sat in a neat pyramid on the floor, a bucket of kindling beside it. There were shelves on the walls, like in Sonia's cabin, but no jars of smoke on them. The floor in front of the fireplace was covered by a large, plush rug that looked like it had been woven together from braids of soft multi-colored fabric. There was a stack of pillows and blankets on the floor, as though someone had planned a sleep-over, and a number of bags rather like the ones he had packed for the journey.

Finally, Adrian found his voice. "You've all said something…about avoiding the Darkness, or something?" He said. "I…don't quite understand what that means."

"Well, we could all sit around in the dark and listen to you scream," Laurel replied, and knelt at the fireplace, feeding a bundle of kindling into it. "But that's more Sonia's deal than mine. So we figured we'd make you comfortable at least for the night."

Evangeline, standing beside her, rose up on her toes to pull what looked like a sprig of herbs from the mantle. She raised these to her nose and smiled, then handed a few to Laurel as she rose to her feet beside her, dusting off her bare knees.

"I don't —" he started, feeling very much like a broken record, for his tune hadn't changed much since his arrival in Dreamland. "How?"

"Balefire," Sonia explained, patiently, as the fire began to sputter to life in the fireplace. "Ritual fire, imbued with magic. Now, hush. We have to hurry."

The three faeries formed a circle around the fireplace, grasping hands; they recited an incantation, in their faerie-language, and each in turn threw a handful of herbs in the fire. They burned sweetly, like incense, and the fumes filled the cottage with thick, intoxicating odor, like the smell Adrian had first scented in the house magnified a hundredfold. Outside, the sun began to dip under the horizon. Adrian felt a thrill of uncertainty, fear for the upcoming night, the uncomfortable sensation of being an uninvited participant in a ceremony he had no place within.

The chanting broke off, suddenly, and the room was filled only with the sounds of the fire, the thick, woody smell of wildflowers and sandalwood. "Adrian, come on, inside the glow of the fire."

He did as he was told. The chain of hands broke as he entered, and everyone seated themselves in a lopsided circle, sprawling comfortably on the rug. He took a blanket and drew it close to him as he sat down, prepared to ward off the dark things in the night.

Outside, the darkness fell, swiftly and suddenly. The last vestiges of sunlight disappeared entirely from the surface of the earth as blackness blanketed everything, pouring through the window and through the cracks under the door, filling the house — filling everything, except for the ring of orange glow that surrounded the fire, protecting its inhabitants. Adrian, who had tensed preemptively for the onslaught of darkness, found himself cowering inside his blanket, wrapped like a huddling child, and his face burned with shame. He looked to Sonia, for some sort of explanation.

"Balefire," she said, again, and smiled, "is fed with wood and herbs — but also with creative energy. It has amazing protective abilities, but you must maintain it."

Evangeline spoke up. "For centuries, your kind have borrowed the properties of the Balefire, although they don't realize who it was that gave them the idea."

"You look confused." Laurel leaned back, comfortably, resting on her elbows and gazing thoughtfully at Adrian, inspecting him. "Let me see if I can explain. Imagine that you are primitive man. It's the middle of winter, and days are short, and nights are long and cold. The only thing that can keep you from dying of cold is the fire; it brings you warmth, and food, and light, and pretty soon the fire becomes central to your entire life, to your society. Your whole village gathers around it, huddled together in the warmth, and you make a celebration of it. You sing songs, and tell stories and jokes, and dance around the fire."

"It was the fae who introduced your kind to the idea." Evangeline picked up seamlessly from where Laurel had left off; she sat next to the green-haired faerie, and her fingers were absently stroking the other's hair back from her face. "When our worlds were closer, and there was free trade between the realms, and your kind was not so jaded by its cleverness — we taught your most primitive ancestors how to unlock the magical properties of fire, and it became the defining feature of your society. We borrowed your dreams and gave you some technology — fair trade."

Laurel sat up, digging around in a satchel beside her, pulling from it a large, squat bottle of honey-colored liquid and uncorked it. She held it in both hands, a gallon-sized glass jug, and regarded it thoughtfully before taking a swig. She held it out to Evangeline, and continued for her, "Rituals, celebrations, holidays — all were celebrated around a fire. Well…this is the same fire, although the stakes are raised a little."

"The Darkness," Sonia explained, because Adrian was looking bewildered, "is a form of primordial night, the original blackness from which everything is born, the heart of chaos. The thing that can combat the Darkness — the only thing — is dreamlight. Either harvested from humans, or created by Balefire. As long as you stay within the warmth and light of the fire, you are protected from the outside."

"Safe?" Adrian echoed, his voice empty. "You mean…there's…all this time, there's been a way to protect me, and you didn't tell —"

She held up her hand, placating, and smiled. There was pain in her smile, but understanding also. "It's not that simple, Adrian. It takes a concentrated effort on behalf of those involved. And…well, in big enough doses, it would be just as dangerous, if not a little worse, than the Darkness itself."

"How…?"

"Ever hear of too much of a good thing?" Evangeline said, simply, and took another swig of the drink before passing it over to Adrian. "Now, hush, and enjoy. It'll be a long while until you get to enjoy a night of firelight again."

BALEFIRE

"Normally, the fire would be a little larger." Evangeline pushed long strands of blue hair from her eyes, and looked around herself. "But we thought maybe a smaller fire would be easier to maintain, given that there's only four of us."

Adrian realized he was still holding a jug, and, to be polite, raised it to his lips and drank. A cool, sweet liquid trickled down his throat; it tasted like honey, and fruit, and wild flowers. It tasted like springtime would taste, if it were bottled. He swallowed it, and it burned all the way down his throat, hot, acidic, alcoholic. He grimaced, and passed the jug on.

"Faerie mead," Sonia explained, taking the jug. "You don't like it?"

"I'm not much of a drinker," he said.

Sonia shrugged, taking a long swallow. "Anyway. The way this works, is each of us take turns, providing an offering to the fire, to keep it burning."

"It's not very efficient," Laurel conceded. "But it is a whole lot of fun."

"Who's first?" Evangeline asked.

The others looked at each other. After a moment, Sonia shrugged. "I'll go."

"What are you going to tell?" Laurel asked, suddenly suspicious. "Not that awful ballad about the soldier and his wife, and that other lady's baby? Because, I know it's a classic and all, but every time I hear it I want to stab myself."

Sonia glared at her. "I like that song."

"I know you do," Laurel said. "That's the problem."

"Well, fine." Her gaze shifted to Adrian, and a slow smile curled the edges of her lips. "Here — I'll tell a story about dreams, for our guest."

Laurel wrinkled her nose, but did not complain, so Sonia started. When she spoke, her voice had a lyrical quality, as though she had a song in her heart that was straining to get out.

"When the world was young and all the races were new, fae and man lived in harmony. The faeries made their homes in the dark places, the unknown places, the forgotten places — where mysteries and dreams and hopes all dwelled. Mankind lived and worked alongside the faerie world, generally satisfied to leave them to their own devices. Sometimes a child would suffer from disease, or famine, or hardship, and the fae would feel its pain from the far side of the world and come to take them away to a place without such things. In their place they would leave a gift, sometimes — one of their own kind, or an item of faerie-make. But fae children are especially vulnerable to the pain and suffering of the rational world, and they rarely survived long under human care. Faerie gifts are too delicate a thing for the rough hands of men, and soon they would break.

"The practice of leaving changelings was abandoned, but the fae could never resist the cry of a child in pain. It rips through the very fabric of reality in Dreamland, and when a child's innocence is extinguished, it shakes the very earth we walk upon.

"As the world grew older, the children came to learn pain at younger ages. The magic that stayed alive in human thought was replaced by rationality, science, steel and plastic and batteries. Children's dreams grew weak, insubstantial. Fae kind suffered, and the Darkness came over Dreamland like a shroud. The fae fled to the cities and crowded around the few doors still open to the mundane world. The stragglers in the wild places — both fae and dream — suffered. Many died, many were twisted beyond recognition. Dreams became rare and valuable, and people began to steal them, hoard them. What was once the right of all folk became the privilege of those who could afford it.

"Misery overtook Dreamland, and it threatened to destroy it forever.

"But there was still a little hope. Children could still dream. Doorways to the human world remained open, and visitors would still come, and dreams would still be left, and the Balefires burned as best they could. There was still a little magic in the world, staving off the Darkness, and the fae clung to that magic and scraped a living in the glow of the fire for generations.

"Then he came.

"He was a dream, but he lived among the fae, and resembled them so closely, that most tended to forget what he was. He was powerful, more powerful than most dreams — vivid, but dark, born from nightmares, a dream forged from the pain of a child. He was handsome, once, and strong, and many believed that he would be a great hero for our people.

"He sought to cure the Darkness, forever. He hoarded the strongest dreams, and convinced them to follow him. They left for the edge of the world, where the Darkness festers, and during his absence the Darkness receded. The nights were not so long, the terror not so deep. A fire burned bright in the core of Darkness, fueled by the blood of dreams, but in the end the fire faltered. The Darkness twisted the survivors, perverted them into monsters.

"He still appears, sometimes, to steal away the dreams of children, to lead them to the end of the world, trying to rekindle the fire. They say he even creeps away to walk among the world of men, looking to steal children to dream for him, to fuel his fire."

"What's he look like?" Adrian asked, as soon as she had finished. The hair on his forearms stood on end. His heart leapt into his throat. "Where is he? What if that's where Nathaniel — "

"He's not real," Evangeline said, gently. "It's a ghost story, to teach us not to be so greedy."

"Are you sure…?"

Sonia gave his shoulder a little squeeze. "The story's been around for a really long time, anyway. We all learned it as kids, from others who had learned it when they were young. Just a…what's the word…fairy tale."

"Oh." Adrian couldn't tell if he was relieved or disappointed. He was, however, undeniably drunk. The mead had been passed in a continuous circle during the story, and each time it ended up in his hands he'd taken a bigger drink, feeling more fond of it with every swallow. His body was warm all over and slightly numb from the mead; a quiet, pleasant hum had taken refuge in his thoughts. The mead was already well over half gone, and he worried about what would happen if they drank all of it — but then another bottle had appeared, this one tall and thin and filled with some rich dark wine, and that was opened and passed around as well. Adrian realized he didn't care so much about The Nightmare Man. He didn't care much about anything, actually, and that felt very good.

"Well, Laurel?" Sonia asked, after everyone had drunk from the wine bottle. "I suppose you have something suitably crass, to liven our spirits?"

"Always." She leaned back, cradling a bottle of mulled faerie wine, and stared thoughtfully at the ceiling. Evangeline curled herself around Laurel's body, limbs and wings entangled with her, head rested against her bosom, rising and falling rhythmically as Laurel spoke. "Once, when Faerie and human worlds touched, there was a man who despised the fae, and found them untrustworthy. He was especially disturbed by the tendency of faeries to steal away human brides or husbands, and was keen to stop the activity in any way he could.

"Every year, the faeries held a riotous ball, a masked carnival of drink, song, and dancing, just inside the border of the human world — so that humans could visit, and enjoy the revelry, without succumbing to the madness in Dreamland. One year, the man, who was a very important merchant in his society, heard that the carnival would be coming to his town, and decided it would be worthwhile to investigate. He made excuses to all his family, and, so no one would suspect, left town a few days earlier than the fair, then rode out to stay in the town that would be hosting the event.

"Well, when the fair did come to town, he came inside and started to loosen up. He enjoyed good drink, and got a little drunker than he had planned. He found himself thrilled by the exotic food and music, and even humored one vendor by buying and wearing a very fine gold-embossed mask.

"As the night wore on, the party began to wind down, and the merchant started wandering among the tents of those staying the night on the grounds. He was stinking drunk and stumbling all over himself, and starting to feel maybe a little indignant that the party was ending just when he was starting to have fun — so, when he heard the sounds of two lovers in the bushes, he had to go investigate.

"There, in the bushes, was a tall, handsome faerie lad, young and supple and brown-skinned. And on her back, skirts pushed up around her hips, was a human woman, her face still covered by her mask. She was giggling like a school girl, and the sight of her made the merchant immediately hungry for her, and jealous of the faerie who was between her thighs. It wasn't the faerie's place, you see, to be cavorting with human women, and certainly not when the merchant wasn't getting any at all. So the merchant, who was after all a large and imposing sort of man, stepped forward and grabbed the faerie by the scruff of the neck, picked him up, and tossed him to the side. Then he knelt down in the faerie's place and picked up where the other had left off.

"Well, this went on for a little while, but as he knelt there with her legs around his hips he started to think that there was something a little familiar about this woman, and the more he heard her moans and screams the more he started to get suspicious. So he tore off her mask and, would you believe it? It was his own wife, piss-drunk on faerie wine and still muttering her faerie lover's name!

"Well, the merchant was so taken aback that he didn't know what to do for a minute. Before he could do anything at all, his wife — who was a quick-witted woman, and well aware that the tides had changed — had pushed him off and was halfway to her lover's side before the merchant could get himself untangled enough from his britches to follow after her. The two lovers took off into the night, and the merchant, too drunk to stand, recognized defeat and collapsed back into the grass, passing out cold.

"As luck would have it, the patch of bushes that had been private the night before weren't quite so private in the morning, and the merchant woke to find himself sprawled flat on his back, nethers bared for all the world, right in the middle of a whole circle of camp sites. And would you know it, while he was keeping busy with his wife in the dark, the faerie lad had nicked his wallet right out of his pocket?"

Laurel let loose a hearty laugh that was joined by everyone in the room, although Adrian's laughter was a bit reserved. The alcohol had started to draw him inside his own head, pulling him back into a pensive, quiet mood.

Apparently, Evangeline noticed his expression, because she lifted her head from Laurel's bosom and smiled. "Oh dear, Laurel, you seem to have offended our guest."

Adrian shook his head rapidly, eager to protest and defend whatever standing he had among the faeries, but the action made him feel a little dizzy and he ceased immediately. He tried to remember how much he'd had to drink, and how it happened that the jug being passed around was full again.

The fire roared at the grate, and for a while all of them fell silent, basking in its warmth. In the smoke, half-formed images seemed to materialize, shift, and disappear. He watched them for a moment, seeing horses and clouds and flickering, dancing people made of smoke — and then they were gone, as quickly as they had come. Adrian melted down into the floor, cuddling his blanket to his chest. Across from him, Laurel and Evangeline had begun kissing, passionately; he could no longer keep track of whose legs and hands were whose, and both of them seemed to be showing significantly more skin than he had remembered earlier.

"This is nice," Adrian remarked, sleepily.

Laurel looked up, pulling away from Evangeline, who — undisturbed — lowered her mouth to Laurel's collarbone; all Adrian could see was the tumbling wave of her curly blue hair. Laurel brushed her fingers through her lover's hair and smiled, slyly, at Adrian. "It's your turn."

"Pardon?" The word felt heavy in his mouth.

"Well, everybody shares something in order to strengthen the fire, don't they? So — it's your turn."

He felt rather hot, and in a way unrelated to the fire. "Why isn't it her turn?" He asked, gesturing to Evangeline, whose hands were busily engaged in places Adrian felt guilty for looking at. "She hasn't gone yet."

"This is her contribution," Laurel said, dismissively. "This is her favorite form of self-expression."

Adrian blinked, not sure if she was joking or not, and didn't say anything.

"…If you'd like, you could join in and…express yourself…." Evangeline offered, looking up to fixate her heavy-lidded eyes on him.

"Or you could tell a story," Sonia said, quickly, and Adrian found her hand on his shoulder, giving it a protective squeeze.

"I don't know any stories," he protested. "Not any good ones."

"A joke, then," Laurel said. "Surely you must know at least one joke?"

"I really don't —" He stopped, realizing that Laurel and Evangeline were looking at him with a decidedly hungry expression, and he looked down, heat rising in his cheeks. "Well, there is one joke," he said, tentatively. "That I learned at my wedding reception…" He looked up, and realized everyone was staring at him expectantly. He cleared his throat. "Er…"

"Well, go on," Evangeline said, looking only slightly disappointed at his chosen mode of self-expression. "Let's hear it, then."

"Alright. Um. Let's see." He looked around, and then, quickly, plunged in. His words seemed to ooze out of him twice as slowly as they should, as though the alcohol has turned his speech into some form of verbal molasses. "So there's this church — this big cathedral, actually, the kind that has a huge bell tower, that part's important because the joke doesn't make any sense if there isn't a bell tower. Anyway. And the bell ringer dies one day. So the bishop decides to start interviewing for a new guy to ring the bell, right?"

Everyone was watching him now with curious eyes, and he pressed on boldly.

"So the bishop interviews all kinds of guys. There's this weird hunchback Quasimodo guy, but he can't get up enough strength to really do it right. There's this really fat guy who rings the bell once and then he's sweating and panting so hard he can't even do it again. And a bunch more. But nobody's really what the bishop's looking for, so bell-ringing auditions go on for days."

Adrian smiled, sitting up straighter, his eyes shining in the light of the fire; he was starting, despite himself, to get into the story-telling mode.

"But finally this guy walks in who's got no arms. He walks up to the bishop and nods toward the bell — 'cause it's not like he can point, right? — and says, 'I want to be the new bell-ringer' and the bishop's like, 'um…I don't really see how that's gonna work' but he figures he might as well give him a fair shot. So the armless guy walks all the way up the stairs to the bell tower, leans out, and smacks the bell with his face! And the bishop's listening and he thinks, 'This is crazy, but that's the most beautiful bell-ringing I've ever heard.'

"Well, anyway, the bishop is just about to offer him the job — but then the guy without any arms leans forward to strike the bell again, slips, and falls to his death at the foot of the bell tower. The bishop runs out and there's this whole group of people standing around. They'd all heard the bells ring, see, and wanted to come see what it was because it sounded so beautiful. But anyway, somebody comes up to the bishop. 'Oh no! He's dead?' the guy says. 'That's terrible. Who is he, anyway?' and the bishop just shakes his head and shrugs and says, 'I don't know — but his face sure rings a bell.'"

Adrian giggled.

The others stared at him.

He raised his hands to silence them (although nobody was laughing) while he tried to stifle his giggles. "Wait — wait — it's not done yet." He jammed his hand into his mouth and bit down on it to stop his laughter before it totally consumed him. His head felt like it was attached to someone else's body. "So the next day, right, this other guy walks in. He looks just like the other dude, except he's got arms. He comes up to the bishop and he says, 'my brother applied to work here yesterday. He had no arms, but his whole life's passion was to be a bell-ringer. I wonder if you'd let me have the job, in his honor?' and the bishop by this point is starting to think that nobody will possibly ever get hired to do the job, so he says, 'well, sure, you can try anyway. Go up and give it your best shot. But be careful not to slip.'

"So the guy climbs up the stairs and he rings the bell and it's beautiful, and the bishop's about to breathe a sigh of relief that he's finally found a guy to hire — when the guy clutches his chest, cries out, and keels over dead on the spot.

"There's this group of people gathered around this time, too — the same people, probably, it's not that big of a town — but one guy comes up behind the bishop and claps his hand on his back. 'Such a tragedy,' he said, shaking his head. 'Who is this young man?' and the bishop just shook his head and shrugged. 'I don't know his name….but he's a dead-ringer for his brother.'"

Adrian wiped a tear from his eye. His belly ached from trying to contain his laughter.

The faeries blinked at him.

"How do you ring a bell with your face?" Sonia wondered. "They're so heavy, it must hurt a lot."

"It's…see, there's this expression, for when somebody looks familiar," he started, trying to explain. "So the joke, it's like…it's a shaggy dog story, see…"

"There weren't any shaggy dogs in it," Laurel said, reasonably.

Adrian thought perhaps it would be best to quit while he was ahead.

Outside, the earliest gleam of dawn was making itself apparent on the horizon, and Sonia smiled. "Light is coming," she said, with a glance over her shoulder. "It's safe to sleep, now. The fire will hold until the Darkness is gone."

"I'm not sleepy," Adrian protested, like a child, and betrayed himself with a massive yawn.

"Of course you're not," Sonia replied and brushed his hair from his eyes like his mother would, if his mother had ever treated him with that degree of tenderness, and before her touch had left his skin Adrian was snoring.

THE SWAGGERING SPIDER

In the small, square white room with its blank, white walls, a door opened.

The door hadn't been there earlier. Once it closed, it was gone again, and the walls were the same solid, boring white they had been since Nathaniel got there.

The Nightmare Man had to crouch to walk inside. He was too tall for the small room, and even when crouching his cloaked head brushed the ceiling. He carried a very old, weathered teddy bear in his skeletal hands. The bear was missing fur in places, and stained all over with mud. It looked like it had been sitting outside for a very long time, like a stuffed animal left at a grave.

"I'd like to go home now," Nathaniel said, wheeling around to face The Nightmare Man. "My mom is going to be really worried."

The Nightmare Man shook his head. He swept past Nathaniel, and his cloak felt like damp, rotting leaves when it brushed against him. He extended his hand, giving the teddy bear to the little girl. She held it at arm's length, looking at it appraisingly, before a wide grin spread over her features.

"New bear?" She asked, looking up at The Nightmare Man for confirmation, before hugging the bear to her chest. She petted it between its ears and set it down on top of the castle. It sagged, limply, to one side. Nathaniel noticed that it was missing an eye.

"I need to go home," Nathaniel repeated, louder. He stepped forward to tug at The Nightmare Man's cloak. "Please?"

The Nightmare Man pulled away, grabbing Nathaniel's wrist in his bony hands. His grip was hard and cold, like steel that's been left out in the snow, and the cold bit into Nathaniel's skin. The Nightmare Man made a quiet, low hissing noise in the back of his throat. His open mouth worked, as though trying to speak, and his sharp teeth flashed.

"You stay."

The words formed themselves in Nathaniel's head without being spoken. He heard them, the same way he heard the words of a book when he read it to himself.

The little girl looked up, holding her moldy bear protectively to her chest. "You don't go!" she said sharply. "You stay. You be my brother."

"I don't want —" Nathaniel started, but The Nightmare Man's cold fingers dug into the skin of his wrist and his insides went cold.

"You stay."

* * *

Adrian awoke with only a vague awareness of his body. He felt sluggish, still drunk. Everything seemed distant, muffled, as though he had woken up with his mind on the opposite side of the room as his body. He became aware of the intensity of the sun that streamed through the high windows and of the way his brain seemed to pulsate and throb. The time delay between his thoughts and senses grew shorter, and he struggled to get up. Managing to find his knees, he crouched on the hearth rug for a moment and looked around, getting his bearings.

Evangeline and Laurel were lying together in a tangled heap; he looked at them, tracing them with his eyes, trying to determine where one body ended and another began, and couldn't quite make sense of the pile. Someone's hand was in someone else's skirt. Laurel's bosom was hidden behind a tangle of curly blue hair.

Between the pile of winged free-love and Adrian, Sonia stretched out like a protective barrier, her head rested on her upper arm. Her eyes were closed, her lashes dark against her pale cheek. She looked small and vulnerable. He wondered if he looked that way to her when she watched him sleep and thought he probably did.

He glanced up at the window. Though he was sure he'd slept for at least a few hours, the sun outside was pale and new, early morning sun of the kind that managed to paint the sky pale gray rather than blue. It was probably around six, he thought. Just the time he'd normally wake up for a morning run. The idea was instantly appealing. He could run all the way up that hard-packed dirt path to the main road, and from there could go wherever he wanted. He glanced back at the sleeping faeries. They wouldn't even notice he was gone.

Yes. He'd go for a run. He'd make it quick, but it would be nice to blow off some steam before the journey properly got started. Especially if he'd be stuck in another godforsaken carriage, or riding on one of those monster cats. Adrian had never liked long car or airplane rides. And since there wasn't much chance of getting any Dramamine or Valium out here in faerie-land, tiring himself out seemed like as good an alternative as any.

Quietly, he crept away from the faeries and slid out through the door, closing it carefully shut behind him. Outside, one of the giant cats lay sprawled on its side in a patch of sunlight, its head and forepaws twisted upward and its maw gaping slightly open. Its sides rose and fell with steady, sleeping breath, and it paid no heed to him as he skirted carefully around it and onto the path. Although the cats had been plenty obedient with Evangeline telling them what to do, he wasn't sure he trusted it when she wasn't here. The image of being batted down into the turf by one dinner plate-sized paw planted itself firmly in his mind and he hurried onto the road.

He ran for a while, his thoughts a blissfully empty buzz. He counted his steps out of habit, listened to his breathing, focused on the steady rhythm of his footfalls on the packed dirt. The pleasant hum of emptiness folded over his thoughts like a blanket. He was peripherally aware of his surroundings, but he didn't pay much attention to where he was going. There were no cars to worry about, after all, and with only the single road to follow he was unlikely to get lost.

When he had counted off a mile in footsteps he stopped to catch his breath and realized he was in the shadow of the Swaggering Spider. He glanced around, a little guiltily, as though expecting Sonia to creep out of the shadow to chastise him at any moment. But she didn't, and he cast a furtive glance back at the building.

Last night, it had literally glowed with good cheer. This morning, it seemed not only empty but possibly abandoned, a building that sat back on the road like the discarded shell of a creature grown too big for its skin. Intrigued, Adrian took a tentative step forward, passing through the gate. The path was lined with stones and bordered on either side by grass. A pair of unicorns, one glowing pale blue and the other silvery-white, grazed absently on the far end of the grass. Adrian tried not to think about what they might be grazing on and looked the other way.

The tables he had seen the night before were littered now with all variety of trash: discarded plates and glasses, bottles and jugs (many of them broken), bits and scraps of food, cloth napkins, various articles of clothing, faerie wing-dust and bits of shimmery paper that looked like confetti. The hanging lanterns were all extinguished and drooped sadly over the path as he approached the door.

He hesitated at the door. He cast another nervous glance around, then twisted the knob.

The door opened out into an open room. The whole area was deserted, and in a similar state of disarray as the tables outside. The walls were paneled in dark wood, but rather than make the room seem tight and enclosed, it had the opposite effect: the dark corners of the room seemed to fade into shadow, giving the illusion of the area fading off into infinity. One side of the room was filled with tables. Beyond these, barely visible in the shadowy far wall, was a large fireplace. A set of stairs wound their way up into the dark second floor; the ceiling above had a hole in it, rimmed in wooden railing, so that people upstairs could look down at the ground floor. On the other side of the room was a dark wooden bar, the shelves behind it lined with bottles of various different sizes — some filled with alcohol, others with the swirling colored mist like the kind Sonia had sold to Lorelai.

These drew his eye and he made his way toward them.

As he came up to the bar he caught a flicker of movement in the corner of his eye — a gleam of silver that caught the dim light in the tavern. He jumped in his skin, reeling away from the bar, and nearly tripped over one of the stools.

Lorelai, who had been kneeling behind the counter to fuss with something in a low cabinet, stood. She shook her waist-length hair back over her shoulder. "Don't need to be so jumpy," she said, at a volume that seemed inappropriate in the hush that fell over the room. "Where's your babysitter, human?"

"The name is Adrian," he said, but he didn't feel much bravado. Maybe because it was accurate: Sonia *was* his babysitter, or surrogate, or at least his guide. He tried to think of something witty, or at least confident, to follow with, and came up short.

His eyes, moving without his permission, fixated again on the jars.

"Sonia hasn't told you what's in them, has she?" Lorelai asked, following his gaze. A smile touched on her lips. It was hard and cold, and her eyes glinted like burnished steel. "I'm not surprised."

"I don't know what you're talking about." But he thought back to the time in the carriage, when he had asked her about them and she had sidestepped the question. At the time, it hadn't seemed important — not when at any moment his stomach was going to do a barrel-roll — but now he thought back on it and was certain that she had changed the topic on purpose.

"Sure you do," Lorelai said casually. She ducked back down under the counter and returned with a damp cloth, which she began to absently smear over the top of the bar. Her eyes glanced up, just once, and she gave him the sort of hard, appraising look he had often seen on his grandmother's face during the months she came to stay with his mother after the divorce: the look that said "you're going to wear that, are you?" in a way that was both piercingly insightful and completely derogatory. "I imagine you were up all night keeping a balefire burning."

The statement — and it *was* a statement, not a question — caught him off-guard. "Well...yes."

"I hope you had fun." Lorelai's eyes dropped back down to the bar. She scrubbed at a sticky patch, scraping at it with a thumbnail through the damp cloth. "It's a waste of energy, but entertaining enough."

"You're not really explaining what's in the jars," Adrian said. "If that's what you meant to be getting at."

"Nothing gets past your notice," she replied, without looking up. "Dream-energy, is what it is. Dream-energy that your little Sonia siphons from the doomed and dying."

"…Dream-energy?"

"You're not so bright, one-who-remembers or not." Lorelai, finally satisfied with whatever stain she had been picking at, moved down to shine another part of the bar. Adrian's reflection stared up at him from the now-glossy surface. "Do I have to spell it out for you? Dream energy. A hundred times more powerful than balefire. A thousand, if you can get it from a child…but slim chances of that on this side of the lake."

He tried to make sense of this. He remembered the "Used Dreams" sign he had seen the day before. He could also swear he had heard something about dreams in a story, but for the life of him he couldn't remember; everything had jumbled and faded into a haze. A dream had slept with a merchant's wife, right? No, that wasn't it. But something like that. "So…in the jars. That's…a dream? Like, I-go-to-sleep dreams?"

Lorelai made an impatient noise. "Sometimes. Not always. Any strong, irrational thought forms a dream. The kind we get here," she gestured at the bottles of languid, viscous smoke, "are weak, torn out of the heads of grown-ups who hardly have anything left upstairs. Just vapors, really. Good for one use, maybe two. But the good stuff, the kind they keep for themselves in the Center Kingdom — that's quality dreamstuff. Dreams over there are strong enough to actually come alive. They walk and talk and live just like the rest of us, and you can milk one dream for years before it finally disappears. Of course, there's an embargo on corporeal dreams, nobody will dare trade them at market. They're too precious." Something like a snarl curled the corner of her lips, her face temporarily transfigured into something beastly, and then it was gone, her face once more an ageless mask. "But sometimes one… becomes available…through other means."

She looked up at him, then back at the rows of shelves behind the bar.

She reached out and took a small vial down, popping the cork off with her thumb. "Here," she said, nodding to him. "I'll just show you. It'll make more sense."

She tilted the vial and something poured out — a semi-viscous cloud of purple-blue smoke, about the size of a golf ball. It rolled in on itself like a tiny sun, wisps trailing off in all directions. Inside, Adrian thought he could make out a shape in its core, the faintest suggestion of a bird, its wings flared — but then the image was gone, and the smoke dissipated. It hung over the bar in a shimmering haze.

Without fully meaning to do it, Adrian reached out a hand to touch the smoke. His fingers brushed through it, and he felt a jolt run through him as though he had stuck his finger into a light socket. A sudden rush of energy washed over him, an electric buzz that spread through his body instantaneously. His fingertips tingled. His brain erupted with a sense of hyper-awareness. He had a single moment of brilliant, crystalline clarity where it felt that he could see the answers to every possible question, that everything in the universe was connected by thin filaments and he need only reach out his hand to pluck at the strings and he could play a harmony that united all of creation into one single beautiful song.

Then it was gone.

The sensation faded as quickly as it had come, and it left him feeling hollow and shaky, like too many coffees on an empty stomach. His hand trembled as he withdrew it.

"Like I said," Lorelai said, with a satisfied little smile. "That's the weak stuff. You can't burn it, not until it's refined. It won't ward off the Darkness or anything. But the pure stuff has its uses."

Adrian tried to sort out his thoughts. His hangover felt a thousand times worse, and now he was pretty sure there was no possible way to run this one off. "...Why not use your own dreams?" He managed. It wasn't the question he'd meant to ask, but it was the first that made it out of his jumbled, aching head.

"Sonia really *hasn't* told you much, has she?" Lorelai lifted her eyes to meet his. She shook her head. "Look, here's the thing. Faeries don't dream. Not like humans do, anyway. It's hard work to keep a balefire burning. Takes several people working at it and it leaves everybody exhausted within hours. We never could've crawled our way out of the Darkness if we hadn't figured out how to use humans for their dreams."

"…Crawled out of the Darkness?" He echoed. He leaned over the bar, suddenly intrigued. "I…I figured the Darkness was a new thing. Poison from the human world and all its rationalism or whatever."

She laughed. "You've got it backwards. The Darkness has always been here. It was here long, long before there were faeries or humans. It's the very essence of chaos. You humans have a folktale, I think? It starts, 'In the beginning, there was nothing'? Well — the Darkness is that nothing."

She turned back to the shelf behind the bar, withdrew a bottle of some pale rose-colored liquid and two glasses. She set the glasses on the bar and poured Adrian a glass, sliding it across to him. He took it without protest, although did not drink it. "Humans have a special capacity for refining chaos. Even your dreams, which can be completely ridiculous, have their own internal logic. And hope. There's no race in the universe — yours or ours — with a more limitless capacity for hope."

Adrian glanced down at the glass in his hands and sniffed it. He took a tentative sip. The taste wasn't alcoholic. It was, however, surprisingly bitter, and he grimaced and set it back on the bar. "So, alright. You use our dreams to…ward off Darkness."

"If you want to put it so simply. Yes." She knocked back a long swallow of the bitter rose-colored liquid.

"It affects you? The way it does me?"

"Well, I myself have worked rather hard to make sure I never have to experience it." A slight smile touched the corner of her lips. It was not a pleasant expression. "But, no. It won't kill us, or drive us crazy, like it does your kind. But it does affect us. If we live long enough in the dark places, we go back to being…well…wild. I'll put it that way. Uncivilized. You want to go up into the mountains, visit the dark places — you'll see all sort of kin like you'd never meet in the cities. Monsters, you'd probably call them."

Something bumped uneasily in Adrian's thoughts. At some point, he would have to address the fact that Sonia made a living by harvesting dreams from the insane people that fell into her woods. But he wasn't ready to deal with that yet, so he carefully wrapped it up and filed it away to consider later, when his head wasn't threatening to split open. "Sonia says this place is just a brothel," Adrian said, glancing around at it.

"Sonia lives alone in a cabin, listening to things scrabble around in the night. There are many things she does not understand, and all the better for her I suppose. But, myself…" Lorelai spread her arms, inclining her head in a "so what if it is" sort of gesture. "Lots of things make creative energy, help to keep the fires burning at night. Who am I to judge?" She nodded toward the glass in his hands. "But, never mind just now. You should drink up, it'll make you feel better, counteract the dream-withdrawal a bit. I imagine you've got a big journey ahead of you that you don't want to spend all day feeling as bad as you look just now."

He knocked back the bitter-tasting liquid in two hard swallows, and waited for it to kick in. Warmth spread over him, instantly soothing the pulsing ache in his head. His muscles relaxed. "So," he struggled to order his thoughts, which seemed suddenly more sluggish. "If all that dream-energy can keep Darkness away…why can't my dreams keep me safe? …And why can't Sonia, if she's been…?"

"Sonia doesn't have the technology to use what she harvests," Lorelai said. "But, something's keeping you safe, all the same." She finished wiping a table and crossed back to exchange her cloth for a broom. "You're not dead or insane, so that's something."

She snapped her fingers, and Adrian's glass replenished itself. She nodded at him to drink up, and he did so, swallowing it quickly. The bitterness coated the roof of his mouth, an alkaline residue that tasted like chewing alka seltzer tabs.

"Oh." Fuzziness crept in at the edges of his thoughts. His lips started to feel heavy, as though they'd been shot with novacaine. His fingers felt blunt and clumsy. He looked down at the empty glass in his hand. "You lying bit —" he started to say, but the words came out thick and jumbled, and before he could finish the thought the world swam away from him entirely.

* * *

When Sonia awoke, the sun was already fat and golden — a late-morning sort of sun, the kind that berates you as it streams through the windows, a sun that says, in the voice of your mother, you have wasted your day away, and nothing you do now will make up for all these lost hours. The sun illuminated a wide patch of floor, and Sonia lay stretched within the square as though a spotlight were shining upon her. A jolt of worry ran through her, sharp and jagged; the shock was visceral, like a rough rod rammed through her chest, dislodging her heart and replacing it with a sort of aching void.

She was worried about two things. The first, that the sun was much lower in the sky than it should have been, which meant she had certainly overslept. The second was that when she had fallen asleep, Adrian was laying directly in front of her; now he was gone, leaving a wide stretch of nothing between her and the door. This second realization caught her by surprise, and for a moment she was paralyzed, unable to force her body to catch up with her rushing, panicked thoughts.

Finally she managed to get her lungs and mouth and brain all working in tandem, and she let out a few unintelligible cries before forcing out the words, "Wake up! Wake up, he's gone!" She struggled to her feet, her wings fluttering haphazardly, her eyes darting around the room without taking in many of the details. All of this took up the expanse of a minute, probably less — but it felt like an eternity, the world far too slow to keep up with her thoughts which screamed and flew by in a blur.

He's gone, she thought, and her heart ached even as she thought this.

"I don't understand," she said, over and over, as the others found their feet and stretched and yawned and occupied an eternity with their waking. Sonia stood transfixed on the spot, battling with the desire to scream. "He stayed inside the light! He should have been fine!"

"I'm sure he's alright," Laurel said, stifling a yawn. She said this several times, but the words never seemed to get through. "He probably just wandered off. We'll catch up with him."

Sonia was inconsolable.

Evangeline, who had the most patience for emotion, laid her hand on her back and gently steered her out the door, murmuring something about how they would start looking for him straightaway, how he couldn't have gotten far, how he was probably a field over. Sonia barely heard her. In her mind, she could only picture Adrian being swarmed by the things that lived in the Darkness, the things which she heard scrabbling against the dirt floor of her cottage at night. She saw them clearly, like dark furry clouds, giant dust mites converging upon him from the feet up, gnawing and gnashing and biting until they had consumed him completely. She imagined the snickering voice that crept in the depths of the Darkness, the voice that sounded like the rasp of dry leaves in the wind. The voice was always there, at night, piercing through the blanket of Dark and speaking into her mind: *they're all doomed... there's no use in saving them...do the merciful thing...you've taken their dreams, just a little further and you can take their life...*

She had always pushed the voice aside. She would never — could never — do the things that it asked of her. But now she imagined that voice snickering with grim satisfaction at a job well done. *He's gone now,* the voice would say, the next time she heard it. *All your scheming and hoping, your fruitless rescue attempt — it was all for nothing. The humans belong to me. Every one of them comes to me in the end.*

"Sonia!" Laurel said, giving her a rough shake. "Did you hear her?"

"What?"

Exasperated, Laurel gripped her arm and twisted her around to look at something. She pointed. After a moment, Sonia realized that the ginger-and-white cat was curled up in the shade of a nearby tree. Evangeline, who had the gift of speaking to beasts, stood at its head, and conversed with it in the low rumbling language of felines.

"She said," Laurel continued, impatiently, "That the cat saw the human leave this morning. Running up the path, to the main road."

"...The Swaggering Spider," she said, realizing that if he had run up the path, he would have almost certainly ended up at the tavern. Her heart, which had been pounding away with the velocity of a hummingbird's wings, suddenly seized in her chest.

If Adrian had gone to Lorelai, he would have been better off consumed by the Darkness.

CONVERGING PATHS

Adrian dreamt about cats. Except they weren't really cats — they were cars. Fur-covered cars with glowing yellow headlights for eyes. Tabby-furred Buicks, their bodies large and muscular. Short, compact black-and-white patched Volkswagens. Dainty, slick-furred black Corvettes. Their engines rumbled like monstrous purring, the heavy idle of diesel engines, and they moved so fast that their tires were a dark blur under their crouching bodies. They circled around Adrian, whirling around him in a dizzying frenzy.

He watched, paralyzed, as they ran circles around him. At any moment, they might veer off course and collide with him. He wanted to get away from them, but there was no way out. He was surrounded, and any direction he stepped would lead him into their path. So he stood frozen and hoped that the cats would stop soon, or alter their course, so he could escape.

Something was wrong, though. They whirled around him at the same dizzying speed, but they seemed to fade, slightly, as though someone had turned down the saturation in a photograph. Vibrant oranges became dull, dusty tan. Slick glossy black became sooty charcoal. They looked more like cars than cats now. The fur retracted back. The slant of the headlights shifted.

They shimmered like a mirage. Adrian could see through them. The dizzying speed slowed. Highway speed. Neighborhood speed. School zone speed. Now they crept along on tired wheels, boring gray ghosts of cars that lumbered in slow-motion circles around him.

He heard something. Not the sound of engines or wheels on cement. A jumble of voices, from outside the dream. He reached for it, tried to make sense of it, and suddenly it broke through in perfect clarity as though he had surfaced from deep water.

"Is that…is that a human?" The voice originated somewhere over his head.

"Well he's sure not a bunny rabbit," another voice snapped back. "Stop staring at him like that. I've got a buyer lined up already."

"You're selling him?" The first voice sounded completely shocked. "For how much?"

"What for? So you can stand around and ogle him instead of working?" Something rattled, like heavy chains. "As if you could afford him. Stupid girl. Now, come over here and help me with this."

Adrian forced open his eyes. He lay on a dirty floor — or maybe a floor made of dirt — strewn over haphazardly with straw. Empty jugs and bottles lay scattered around the floor, littered among other junk he couldn't quite make out. His shoulder ached terribly. He suspected he might have fallen onto it. He saw two sets of bare legs near his head. He blinked, followed them up to their bodies.

Lorelai stood over him, arms crossed over her shoulders, her long hair hanging down nearly to her knees as she glared at another faerie standing a few feet away. The other faerie was shorter and had an up-turned nose and straight brown hair. Her wings were small and cream-colored, rounded like those of the small fluttering white butterflies he used to see in his backyard, the ones that looked like flying primrose blossoms.

She was dressed like a stereotypical barmaid, but the outfit didn't quite suit her figure, and she held herself in a slightly hunched way that suggested she was self-conscious in it. She was beautiful, but Adrian suspected she might be considered extremely unattractive by faerie standards; Lorelai was looking at her with open disdain, as though the insinuation that she might possibly try to buy a human was ludicrous and insulting.

The white-winged faerie looked down at him with an expression of open desire. Her wings fluttered and winked. Lorelai held a small glass vial in her hand, filled with lilac-colored dreamstuff. Adrian thought he saw a minute flicker of something cat-shaped in the swirling smoke, but it was gone immediately. She looked down at it and then, with a shrug, tossed it to the other faerie, who nearly dropped it. "Here. Take that as a consolation prize. A little something to keep you warm at night." The derision in her voice burned, and even though Adrian suspected the faerie who wanted to buy him would not be doing it with pure intentions, he couldn't help feeling sorry for her.

"You drugged me," Adrian said, finally, once he had found his voice. He struggled to sit up, rubbing his sore shoulder as he did so. "So you could… steal my dream."

"And the rest of you," Lorelai replied, without looking at him. "That's the plan, yes. Now, I'm no thief. I had every intention of buying you outright. But if Sonia is too much of a fool to see the value of her possessions, then that's her folly. I, for one, can't let a golden opportunity go to waste."

He was in a store room. As he sat up, he noticed the rows of casks lined up against the wall. A stack of empty lanterns stood beside these, and, just beyond, something shimmered. Adrian tried to get a clearer look. Something, now long dead, had been chained to the wall. At one time, it might have been man-shaped, but now it was impossible to tell precisely what it had been. The body was disfigured, as though large slices had been taken from it over time while it was alive: missing legs, hands, eyes. Its head lolled, its throat torn open, and its blood pooled around it, shimmering in rainbow colors like an oil slick. The corpse still glowed, faintly, like the last sunlight that clings to the horizon after the sun sets.

Adrian's stomach churned.

"Do you like it?" Lorelai asked, conversationally, following his gaze. "He was, before your arrival, the most interesting purchase I'd made in some time. A dream, you know. Wild-caught from the mountains. He had the sweetest little horns." She raised her hands to her forehead, extending the forefingers and waggling them. "I chopped those off and sold them as an aphrodisiac. You can sell just about anything to anyone, if you know how to market it right."

Adrian struggled to his feet, looking around for the door.

"Don't even try it," Lorelai said, extending a hand. She didn't touch him, but something like a rush of solid air shoved into his chest and crumpled him to the floor.

She turned a steely gaze back to the white-winged faerie, who had been inching closer as though if she just moved slowly enough she could sneak in a touch without anyone noticing. She froze on the spot and turned nervous eyes on Lorelai. She clutched the dream vial to her chest as though it were both fragile and extremely precious.

"Rosalie," Lorelai said, slowly, with the saccharine sweetness of someone asking for a very unpleasant and possibly illegal favor. She bent to dig among a pile of boxes in the corner of the room, ignoring the oozing blood of the dead dream, and rose with a length of dirty white rope. She tossed this to Rosalie. "Truss him up good and tight and get him out to the carriage. And, please try to hurry, won't you? I'd rather like to be out on the road before dark."

* * *

Sonia knew, the moment the cat's paw touched the gravel at the foot of the walk, that they were too late. It wasn't the fresh trail of pockmarks left behind by the carriage, or the "closed" sign posted on the door that tipped her off. She hardly noticed any of this. Instead, she felt Adrian's absence in her gut, the place of intuition. He had been here. He had dreamed. And now he was gone.

She slid off the cat's back, ignoring the call of the others who followed her, and walked up the path. The outer courtyard of The Swaggering Spider was in disarray, messy from the night before. Bottles lay broken in the grass, and dream-lanterns hung in sad, deflated tatters from the walls. "She must have left right away," she said, mostly to herself. She heard footsteps behind her, and knew the others were catching up, but she was already pressing through the door and into the tavern.

The bar was nearly empty. A handful of creatures sat at one table, heads bowed deep in discussion. An old, wrinkled faerie man with enormous drooping wings pushed a shop broom over the sticky floor, shoving dirt and debris into an already-swollen pile of broken glass, discarded bottles, and other trash.

"Where's Lorelai?" Sonia asked.

No one looked up. Someone muttered, "We're closed."

Behind her, Sonia heard the door open as the others entered. Evangeline broke away from the others and made her way to the bar, where rows and rows of dream-infused liquor lined the shelves. Sonia's heart hammered painfully in her chest, but she forced herself to stay calm.

"It's important," she said. "Do you know when she'll be back, or where she's gone?"

The wrinkled bar-man snorted. "As if she tells us anythin," he said, pausing to shake out the sticky bristles of his broom. "It's always 'Do this, do that,' with her, innit?" He grumbled, giving his broom an angry shove. "An' then she takes that maid with 'er, dumber'n a dead dog she is. They 'ead out to gods-know-where to do gods-know-what an' leave me 'ere to clean up this place an' put up with you lot."

"Yes, yes, it's all very sad," Laurel said. "But where *is* she? She stole something valuable from us, and we need to get it back."

"Valuable?" He glanced up again, brows raising. His eyes were large and watery brown, and they were filled with immeasurable sadness. "What kind of valuable?"

"The kind that's none of your damn business."

He shrugged. "Well. If she's in trouble wi' the law, I'd suggest lettin' the law handle it."

"Funny enough," Evangeline said, "We *are* the law." She parted her short gold-chain skirt over her thigh, flashing the branded mark of the Crossroads law enforcement that sat just below the bone of her hip.

Laurel did the same. "So I suggest, if you know more than you're letting on, that you start talking."

"I don't know nothin' about no dreams!" he said, and then his eyes widened with an 'I shouldn't have said that' look. He cleared his throat and averted his eyes and went back to sweeping.

"...Dreams?" Sonia ached to get away and start finding Adrian, but his words caught her off-guard. "What about dreams?"

"I told you, I don't know nothin'," he said, careful to keep his eyes trained on the floor. "What Lorelai does wi' the queen is her own business an' I got nothin' to do with it."

Laurel closed in on the man, gripping his shirt in her fist and tugging him upright. "What about the queen?"

"N-nothing," he stammered. "Just…I didn' have nothin' to do wi' it, alright? I don't watch what it is she's sellin' no more'n I go snoopin' 'round the back room for things don't belong to me, see?"

Evangeline's brows raised. "And what might you be snooping for, friend?"

He went stonily silent, pressing his lips together in a tight, thin line. Laurel shook him a little, but he refused to say any more.

"Well now," Laurel said, without releasing her grip on his shirt. "Things are starting to get interesting. What do you make of all this, Sonia? …Sonia?"

But Sonia was gone, the door to the tavern left open to throw a patch of sunlight across the dirty tavern floor.

UNDER A WATCHFUL EYE

Lorelai leaned back on the well-worn bench of her carriage, watching the trees along the path whip by at an impressive rate. Wind swept her hair back and tore at her face. Her eyes burned, but she didn't decrease her speed. She was carrying valuable cargo, and the longer it was in her possession, the greater chance of something going wrong with its delivery.

The mountains rose before her, forming an impenetrable wall, the barrier that divided Dreamland down its center. She rarely ventured into the mountains for trade. The folk that dwelt there had no use for dreamcraft, and no wealth to spend on any if they did. No, her destination was to the east, where the foothills cradled the great Center Kingdom and buyers practically begged to be divested of their prosperity. They had plenty of dreamstuff, certainly, but Lorelai didn't have any run-of-the-mill human in her grasp: she had a grown-up, one fully in possession of all of his faculties, and male to boot. Lorelai had never seen such a thing for sale in her life, and she had lived a long time. She *did* know exactly who would want him, though, had known since she saw him.

She has an appetite for dreams, she thought, imagining the pleased expression of her buyer once the goods had been delivered. *Just think what she'll do with this.*

As she thought this the carriage made minute adjustments, shifting to the right and scurrying forward with ever-increasing velocity down the road which would lead Lorelai to, among other things, the grandest market in all of Dreamland.

The carriage, like her tavern and much of the rest of Dreamland, obeyed her thoughts. This was not a normal power of faerie-folk, and she did not make a habit of announcing it. Wealth was best kept under a watchful eye, guarded and used with sense and discretion, or else it quickly found its way into the hands of thieves. This power didn't come to her for free, however, and its maintenance cost her more each day. Even now, the simple act of steering a carriage caused a dull ache to start in her heart, the echoing pain one feels in a rotting tooth, and she grimaced and clutched her chest.

With her other hand she felt around in the folds of the satchel next to her on the bench, and withdrew a small vial of dream-energy the precise texture and color of cotton candy. This she uncorked with her thumb and raised with a shaking hand it to her lips, draining its contents. It unfurled in her mouth, first blossoming and swelling, then melting down her throat and up her sinuses, burning and tingling as it dissipated into her blood stream. Her heart sped up, as though eager to pump the augmented blood through her veins, and her senses sharpened, skin tingling with sensitivity, mind buzzing with sudden clarity.

The pain evaporated. The world around her disappeared, and for a moment she felt as though she was flying, soaring among the clouds, bodiless and utterly free. The image disappeared as soon as it had come, the landscape re-materializing around her. It left the lingering taste of strawberries in the back of her throat.

She fell back against the bench, licking her lips. The dreams were getting weaker.

Well, never mind. Soon enough, you'll have more than enough, embargo be damned.

Cheered considerably by this thought, she replaced the now-empty vial into her satchel and allowed her eyes to flutter closed. No point worrying about anything more until she had arrived, she decided. The goods weren't going anywhere. Rosalie would make sure of that.

* * *

Inside the carriage compartment, Adrian tried very carefully to look anywhere but at Rosalie. It didn't make much difference: Her gaze was so intense that he could feel it no matter what he did. He didn't dare go to sleep, although the acid in his stomach kept rolling and bubbling like lava. He was desperately hungry, but also grateful he had not eaten anything. His throat burned from thirst and acid reflux, and his head and shoulder both ached terribly. His arms, tightly bound together, had begun to go numb. He flexed his fingers intermittently, making sure that they still worked, but any other movement was impossible.

Rosalie had not spoken to him since tying him up and frog-marching him out of the tavern and into the carriage. She kept opening her mouth, but all that came out was a sort of half-intelligible squeak. Then she would blush deeply and resume staring at him with an expression of open infatuation. Adrian had never been looked at that way by anyone, not even Jessica. *Especially* not by Jessica.

He kept the curtains drawn, which seemed to suit Rosalie just fine. In the semi-dark of the carriage it was impossible to tell exactly how much time had elapsed, but it seemed like it had worn on for hours already with no sign of stopping. He wondered what Sonia had thought, when she awoke to find him missing, and a terrible pang of loss stabbed through him. He pretended for a little while that she could find him, somehow, track his journey, and that once the carriage stopped Lorelai would find herself face-to-face with a small army of angry pixies who would fight valiantly for his independence. He noticed after a few minutes of fantasizing that pale, smoky tendrils had begun to rise like mist from his pores, and desisted immediately.

He glanced at Rosalie. She was staring at him with a glazed look that suggested she, too, was fabricating a daydream. "So, um. Where do you think we're headed?" he asked, finally, taking a stab at conversation.

"Huh?" Her eyes slid back into focus. She still held the vial of his stolen cat-car dream in her hand, and she rolled it around absently between her fingers. "Oh. Well. I don't know, exactly. The Center Kingdom market, I guess. Everybody trades there, if what they're trading is any good."

Silence settled between them, and Adrian decided he had asked the wrong question. He tried again. "I can give you my dreams," he offered, glancing down at the vial in her hand. "I mean, that's what she wants, right? I don't mind."

"That's so sweet of you!" Rosalie exclaimed, her eyes bulging and her face contorting into an expression of complete rapture, the way a young girl might fawn over a particularly adorable puppy when it yawns. "But it'll never do. You're far more valuable than any dreams you could give us. I wish you weren't! I'd buy you in a heartbeat if I could afford, but Lorelai doesn't really pay me enough, and…" she trailed off, here, a deep flush coloring her cheeks.

"Somebody told me that the inn was more like a brothel," he ventured, hoping to steer the conversation back on course.

Rosalie wrinkled her pug-like nose. "If you want to put it that way, I guess. I mean, that…that sort of stuff does happen, especially when the men come down from Center Kingdom, folk say they prefer our kind, but…" she trailed off, her blush deepening to scarlet. She didn't start up again.

When she didn't elaborate, Adrian decided not to pursue the topic further. "…Right." He thought about how to phrase his next question, although he was fairly certain he didn't want to know the answer. "Do you, um, know… who she's planning to sell me to?"

Rosalie shook her head. "No. Someone rich, I suppose." The bitterness in her voice was almost tangible. "Lorelai doesn't exactly share her plans with me. I was pretty surprised she's even letting me come along. I don't think she meant to, actually, but I got lucky I guess because I was there."

Silence fell between them again. Rosalie made no move to start up again. The slightly glazed look was returning to her eyes. The carriage creaked and groaned and shuddered and ambled on at a great rollicking speed.

"Hey, so," Adrian started, after a while, hoping to sound nonchalant rather than desperate. "Don't suppose you could untie me, could you? I promise I won't go anywhere. It's just that my arms are starting to hurt."

She jumped, as though startled from a dream. She looked down at his arms, as though noticing for the first time that they were tied together despite having done it herself, then looked back up at him. "You promise you won't try anything?"

"Cross my heart," he said, and smiled what he hoped was a trustworthy smile.

She glanced around the confines of the carriage, as though making sure no one was watching. She leaned across the carriage, reaching out a hand, her fingertips brushing the skin where the dreams had begun to creep from his pores. She jerked back as though electrocuted, eyes growing wide, and gave a small shudder. "No," she said, then, decisively as she sat back into her chair, rubbing her fingertips against the pad of her thumb as though feeling for residue. "No...I'd better not. She'll know."

"You can tie me back up when we slow down. She'll never have to find out."

She shook her head emphatically, her eyes wide and frightened. "She'll know. She always knows. She's...she know things," she finished, lamely. "Sorry."

Adrian sighed, resting his head against the curtained window, and started trying to formulate his plan B.

* * *

Sonia had lost the trail ages ago. The pock-marked earth, torn by the stabbing feet of Lorelai's carriage, had been blown smooth by the wind, or else covered up by wagon-wheels, pawprints, and hoof prints. Worse, she was lost. Sonia had never ventured this far north in her life, and it frightened her. She knew that there were none of the wild folk until the plains gave way to the foothills, but she kept expecting to see one slip out of the undergrowth anyway. She was also half certain that Lorelai would appear behind them, taking her by surprise. So far, at least, she had been fortunate. No one had crossed her path since she had broken away onto the side road, and she had been able to make good time.

Sonia had not visited the city since she was a child. Her mother had brought her here, once, when she was still too young to inherit the family trade. Sonia had never wanted to guard the doorway at the edge of the world.

She wanted to tend to the children and, even more, the dreams. She'd heard stories about the dreams of children, and she ached to see them. Not because she wanted the power, but because she knew they were beautiful — more beautiful than anything she had ever seen in her life.

"This is what your life would be," her mother had said, gesturing vaguely to the young faerie girls who milled around inside the castle walls. Their wings drooped. Their eyes wandered. They carried heavy loads, or washed soiled clothes, or watched with wistful eyes as carts traveled up the cobbled path to the castle. "Standing in arm's reach of the dreams, unable to feel their warmth. Laboring under others. Is this the life you're aching for?"

Sonia, then, barely eleven years old, felt tears sting at the back of her eyes. Something cold and clawed and miserable seized her heart, nesting in the hollow of her ribs like a tiny dragon made of ice. "But why?" She asked. "Why aren't they happy with so many dreams here?"

"Because it's not their job to be happy," her mother said, with a grimly satisfied smile. "And it's not ours, either."

For years, Sonia had believed it. She had never thought to question the bitter advice.

It wasn't until years later that she understood what her mother had been too jaded to say — or, perhaps, that her mother had thought it kinder not to say. Not until her relationship with her mother had been broken beyond repair. Not until she had found a human whose mind was beautiful and whole, a human whose dreams gleamed in the dark and warmed her like her own private sun. But she understood, then, about the look of longing and misery in the eyes of the servant girls in the queen's court.

She understood, finally, what the faeries of the court had always known: The children don't dream for the faeries. The dreams can never be yours to touch.

That proprietary urge…the desire to have, to hold, to consume. It was an urge that tore the likes of Lorelai apart….an urge that drove Dreamland to the maw of the Darkness. And knowing that, at any moment, she could reach out a hand and snatch the still-living dreams from his sleeping breath chilled Sonia to her core. Because it wouldn't be enough. It would *never* be enough.

And that's why all the faeries were so sad.

STIRRING IN THE DARK

After what seemed like an eternity, Adrian felt the carriage shudder to a halt. He had grown accustomed to the undulation and awful, deafening creaks; in the stillness that followed, his head reeled and ears rang as his senses struggled to adjust. His hands tingled, and when he tried to flex his fingers needles of pain stabbed up through his arms.

The door opened, allowing rich golden light to flood into the carriage. "We're stopping," Lorelai said, addressing neither of them in particular. She stepped back from the door to allow them to get out. She glanced up at Adrian, her expression inscrutable. "I'm going to untie you, so that you can eat. Wouldn't do to have you looking peaky when I delivered you."

"No, I'd imagine not," he replied, wearily. He tried to think if there was something he could offer her, some bargaining chip, but he came up blank. Lorelai leaned in close, her hair brushing over his arm as she loosened the rope around his wrists, then pushed him away. She gave Rosalie a significant, probing look, but said nothing further and disappeared into her carriage. She emerged a moment later to thrust a small package of cakes into Rosalie's arms, then disappeared once more. A lock clicked in the door from the inside, and after a few minutes Adrian saw a glow of colored light illuminate the curtains in the doorway, creeping out around the edges and spilling through the glass. The light danced and shimmered, the way sunlight plays on the surface of a creek.

Rosalie glared at the locked carriage door. "Well isn't that all well and good for you," she muttered. "Here. We'd better hurry up and eat. The sun will be down any minute." She turned back to Adrian, who had been edging slowly away from the carriage, and grabbed his arm in a vice grip. Not for the first time, he marveled at the strength of the faeries. He could feel his arm bruising under her fingertips.

They settled under a nearby tree to eat. Adrian supposed they might be at a higher elevation than they had been, as the trees were mostly evergreen. Overhead, a pair of brilliantly-colored jewel-toned birds had nestled themselves into the crook of a limb. One had its head beneath its wing. The other was pecking hopefully at a pine cone the size of a pineapple. Beyond the line of trees, Adrian saw a gentle ripple of foothills, rising up into mountains. Past these mountains was the great purple peak he had seen from Sonia's woods, a peak that seemed to be made of amethyst and gleamed in the sun.

Rosalie broke off a chunk of bread and handed it to Adrian, her hand lingering as he took it as though she were trying to sneak in another touch. He quickly withdrew the bread and began eating mechanically, hardly tasting it. It was some sort of fruit cake: a crumbly loaf folded through with nuts and chunks of dried fruit. It didn't taste nearly as good as any of Sonia's cooking.

They ate in silence, Rosalie occasionally glancing over at the locked carriage with a dour expression. Adrian took these opportunities to sneak furtive looks around the area, trying to formulate an escape route, but every time he did this she would look back at him with sudden sharpness that he wondered if she had somehow read his mind. When he was finished eating, Rosalie tied his hands back together.

Adrian gave up trying to escape for the night and settled back into a bed of pine needles, feeling exceedingly sorry for himself. Rosalie leaned back against a tree opposite him, carefully folding her wings so they wouldn't be crushed against the bark. She crossed her arms over her bosom and stared at him. Adrian had no doubts that if he tried to move she would be on him within the expanse of a second. Her eyes slid closed, but he could tell from her breathing that she was awake and alert. The sun traveled closer to the horizon, spreading a rich orange glow over the tops of the foothills. The carriage windows glowed like tiny nightlights, and Adrian rolled onto his side to keep them in view, drawing meager comfort from the light. He wondered if it would be enough to forestall the Darkness.

It wasn't.

As the light failed, the multi-colored dreamlight from the carriage receded, disappearing as though being sucked through a straw, whirling and shrinking until it was nothing but a pinprick in the distance, a tiny twinkling star. Then that, too, winked entirely out of sight, and the Darkness consumed the hollow where they camped. The night burst into life around them. Adrian realized he had never been outside when Darkness fell before, and now he knew why: It was a thousand times worse here in the open. Things moved among the trees, converging on him from every side. Some sounded small and insect-like; others sounded huge and heavy-footed, and he imagined inky black bears crashing through the undergrowth, coming for him.

Something skittered over his hand. He heard things, slimy and furry and scaly things, weave through the trunks of trees. Something breathed heavily near him, great rasping breaths that rustled the grass and caused gooseflesh to spread up his arms. He wanted to reach out, to grab hold even of Rosalie for some small comfort, but he was afraid that his hand might close around one of these unseen, shapeless horrors instead.

Memory tugged at the back of his thoughts, whispering an invitation down the dark corridors of his mind. He struggled, searching for some escape; in his mind, there were memories he desperately wanted to stay away from, but outside there were dark, slithering creatures that wanted to climb into him, destroy him. There was no shelter.

A door in his thoughts opened, and he walked in. He watched his memories through a distorted lens, like a camera smeared with vaseline, and people moved around in his thoughts like runaways from carnival mirrors. Slowly, though he struggled against it, the images cleared, and he eased down into them, engulfed by them, reliving them once more.

Adrian was the youngest person at the funeral. His mother had gone into a frenzy the day before, trying to find a suit small enough to fit. He'd outgrown last year's family-portrait suit (*a family portrait that had been taken off the wall and hidden away, the memory was too fresh, a curly-haired toddler smiling at the camera in her mother's lap, two sullen little boys tired and bored and itchy, the last photo of them all together, a moment frozen in time too difficult to bear)* and on short notice there was nothing stocked in the stores.

He remembered his mother dressing him in William's church clothes. They hung from him like loose skin, like wearing an elephant. William still fit in his last-year suit.

The morning of the funeral, she'd brushed his hair until it lay flat to his head, and straightened his collar, and smeared his cheek with her saliva-wet thumb. Then she burst into tears and hugged him to her chest and her hand pressed his face into her bosom and she cried for a long time. Then his hair was all messed up so she had to brush it all over again.

The casket was too small. It looked funny, like a toy — a coffin for a doll's funeral, not a person's. The lid was closed.

Adrian stood beside the toy-size coffin and stared at it with wide pale eyes. His hair was plastered to his head with gel and sweat and his sleeves went down to his fingertips. William was waiting in Grandmother's car; he'd been sent to time-out for making too much noise during the ceremony. Grandmother had dragged him outside and spanked him and everybody in the church could hear him screaming. Daddy looked embarrassed and Mommy cried some more.

But Adrian had sat the whole service in silence ("he's always been such a good boy," people commented and his ears burned with shame because he knew he wasn't a good boy, he was the worst boy of all) so he got to stand here at the coffin and say goodbye.

"You're not in there," Adrian whispered, just loud enough for the two of them in his very best make-a-wish whisper. "You're hiding. You're playing hide-and-seek with me and some day I'm going to find you."

He smiled then, a little bit, and he didn't ever cry about Samantha anymore except sometimes when he slept.

The edges of the memory began to blur, to fade. The colors faded, the way color had faded from his dream when Lorelai had stolen it, and suddenly he was no longer living the memory but watching it, no longer watching it but staring at a still photo, not a photo but a pen-and-ink drawing...

Outside of the dream, in the world where it was dark and cold, something screamed. It wasn't a human sound, or even an animal sound: It was unearthly and primal, the sound a soul would make if it could scream. Adrian jolted awake, shaking and shivering.

He could see nothing in the stifling darkness, but he could feel it: something many-legged and furry crouched on his chest, like the overgrown child of a cat and a tarantula. Tiny hair-like claws pricked his skin through his shirt. Hot, sour breath invaded his nostrils and Adrian realized the thing's face was inches from his own. He tried to call out, but realized he couldn't: The thing was crushing the breath out of his chest, and he couldn't get enough air. He flailed his arms, trying to push it away, and his hands brushed against the bulk of other creatures in the darkness. They seized onto him. Something long coiled itself around his arm, like an overgrown centipede, thousands of needle-sharp legs piercing his skin.

The thing on his chest hissed, a breathy sound of escaping air that rushed over Adrian's upturned face. It ran a long, scruffy feeler along Adrian's cheek, and clicked together what sounded like three sets of pincers.

Something else moved, treading on enormous, quiet paws. Adrian felt the air above him stir, felt the brush of fur against his face, and the weight lifted from his chest as the thing was knocked loose. The creature screamed, not the cry of elation that had woken Adrian but a cry of pain and terror that echoed inside of Adrian long after it cut off. The things on his arms released their hold, backing away from him. Adrian could make out the muffled sounds of what seemed like a hundred feet brushing and rattling over the undergrowth. He imagined a horde of cockroaches scattering away from a kitchen light, a dozen rats shuffling through the trash, a nest of snakes coiling and slithering away from a hand plunged into their midst.

Someone said something. The words didn't make any sense, or else Adrian's brain had lost its ability to understand. The creeping things in the dark did not return.

In the Dark, he couldn't see Rosalie standing over him, but he felt her proximity. He whimpered, despite himself, and she lowered herself to her knees beside him and groped for him until she caught his bound hands between her own fingers, and held them until he went back to sleep.

* * *

Sonia slept fitfully. She woke often, startled by noises in the dark, and had a difficult time settling back to sleep. Her cat left, slinking away into the Dark to hunt among the shadows, and she was cold and lonely without its company. Things crawled in the underbrush near her and rustled in the tree limbs overhead. In the distance, things without names called to each other in shrill, incessant screams. After waking several times in the night, she decided finally to sit up and wait out the Darkness.

It was then that she saw the light.

She disregarded it, at first, as a hopeful figment of imagination. Then, as it refused to disappear, she thought perhaps it was a unicorn: It glowed with the same incandescent radiance. It wasn't a unicorn, though. It was a dream.

She rose to her feet, following the trail of light as it wove through the Darkness. She wasn't sure why she followed the dream. She hadn't seen a corporeal dream since she was very young, and its presence filled her with simple elation — but that wasn't why she pursued it through the dark. She followed it because something about it felt familiar, like a person she had met in another life, like an old friend returning home after a long absence.

"Wait!" She whispered, urgently, as she ran through the dark, pursuing the retreating light. "Don't go yet!"

The dream turned a corner, and Sonia pursued, oblivious to the rising sun and the pale grey light that spread over the path. She followed it down the hill toward the castle.

* * *

In the white room, Nathaniel was having a hard time concealing his fatigue. He didn't know what time it was; the room was exactly as bright as it had ever been. But it felt late, and he was very tired, and extremely bored.

Nervously, he glanced at the smooth white wall, expecting it to open at any moment. The Nightmare Man was gone again. He kept coming and going, leaving at odd times only to return with some new source of amusement for the little girl.

If she was tired, she didn't show it. She seemed to play with boundless energy. When she grew bored of their make-believe at the castle, she had tugged Nathaniel away and forced the moldy teddy bear into his arms. She chattered some directions to him. He didn't understand much of it; she talked fast, with the heavy lisp of a small child, and he was fairly certain that some of the words were nonsense anyway. After a few minutes, when he just continued to stand stupidly with the bear in his arms, the girl had snatched it away from him and proceeded to start a new game.

Nathaniel was about to refuse — to explain that he really, desperately needed a rest — when the wall opened and The Nightmare Man entered. At his heels came a massive dog, unlike any Nathaniel had ever seen before.

The dog was the size of a bear, with shaggy fur the color and texture of moss. Tightly curled hair fell over its eyes, obscuring them from view, and a long purple tongue hung from its slack maw. The rear end of the dog was completely bald, its grey-green skin mottled with dark patches. A long, slender tail like a lion's swished behind it; there was a large tangle of curly green fur at its tip.

"Puppy!" The little girl squealed, delightedly dropping the moldy teddy bear and running to throw her arms around the dog's neck.

The dog nosed against her cheek, tail wagging behind.

Nathaniel had no desire to go near the thing. He felt The Nightmare Man's eyes on him and he was careful not to look up to meet them.

"More friends. They can stay forever, like you."

As before, The Nightmare Man's words formed directly into Nathaniel's thoughts. They sent a chill up his arms, and he wondered where the dog had come from, and what might come through the door next, and if he was really stuck here forever.

* * *

Lorelai woke before the others, and when Adrian opened his eyes he saw her standing over them both, hands on her hips. Her lip curled in a sneer. She looked older than she had when he first saw her: The wrinkles around her eyes and mouth were deeper. "Rosalie," she said, with a voice like ice, "What, precisely, are you doing?"

Rosalie, whose mouth had been slightly agape as she snored, jolted suddenly awake. She blinked up, unseeingly, at Lorelai, then let out a squeak like a frightened field mouse. "We didn't do anything!" she said, releasing Adrian's hand as if it burned her. "It just…it got dark, and these things were trying to get at him, so I…"

Lorelai's brow raised, cruel and ironic. She said nothing.

Adrian burned with shame. They ate breakfast and they turned their backs so he could use the bathroom behind a tree. When he was finished, Lorelai pushed him into the carriage once more. Rosalie followed, and they took care not to look at each other.

"So. Um. Thanks for saving me, last night," he said, finally, as the silence stretched between them. The carriage rattled and undulated and threatened to drown out his words.

She shifted in her seat. "You're welcome," she said without looking at him.

Adrian waited for her to say more, but she didn't. After a while, he tugged open the curtain, fighting back the nausea so he could look outside.

Ahead, there was a break in the trees, and through it Adrian could just make out a shallow valley that was cast completely in shadow by a giant building at the far end — a castle, he could see, now that they were drawing nearer. The castle filled up most of the visible horizon, blocking out the sky. It was like no building Adrian had ever seen before, although it held a certain familiarity for him, as though he *had* seen it somewhere. A children's storybook, perhaps, or an animated film — except that wasn't quite it. It resembled the large plastic Princess Doll castle that Samantha had gotten for her last birthday; Adrian could see it now, in his mind, the pink plastic bricks and the blue and white accents and the stable full of pure white smug-looking plastic horses. The building ahead of him looked exactly like that, only larger-than-lifesize.

It was made of some kind of stone, a shade of pink that he had never seen in nature. It was built in layers of walls, towers, and turrets, each accented in banners and flags, and even had a drawbridge over a moat. Adrian gaped at the castle as they approached it. It looked like an attraction at an amusement park, yet even from here he could sense a sort of gravity from it, an importance that radiated and hung tangible on the air.

Ahead, a ring of buildings had grown in the shadow of the castle, a village existing in the shallow valley. Small cottages lay on the outer rim, broken up with fields or pens of various animals; inside, arranged along the winding cobbled road, were stands and booths — merchant stalls.

From his vantage point, Adrian could see all manner of strange people selling stranger wares. Someone had a collection of brightly colored stones laid out on a soft cloth; another, a shelf full of odd-colored liquid and a large pot over open flame that occasionally emitted sparks. Another shopkeeper busily tended to what appeared to be extremely small sheep — or, at least, cottony white animals with four legs; the rest of them was obscured by fluff. Someone else was busy nailing up a sign that said, in very untidy lettering, "Buy Rats Here!"; at his feet was an enormous burlap bag that writhed and squeaked.

And, of course, there was dreamcraft. Adrian hadn't had the chance to consider the full scope of dream usage in Dreamland before, but now he was beginning to see that dreams were used to make nearly everything. He saw food and drink prepared from "100% dehydrated dreamstuff" that claimed to carry all sorts of medicinal properties from treating hangovers to curing impotence. A stall sold lights of all kinds: paper lanterns, candles, small glowing orbs that bathed everything in light ten times brighter than a halogen bulb. Many people sold dream-forge weapons, proclaiming them to be effective against "Imps, Sprites, Slivers and Jeepers" while others were marked with signs saying "Caution: Prolonged Exposure May Produce Euphoria and Poor Aim."

One stall held a variety of birds — small, large, bright, dull, singing and squawking. The shop-owner was a short, squat person of indiscernible gender who wore multiple layers of shabby clothing, like a homeless person.

Only the top of its head was visible over all the clothing, and this was topped with feathery hair that could, in fact, have belonged to an overgrown molting pigeon.

A shopper, a tall woman with pointed ears and large yellow eyes, stood before the rows of cages, looking between them indecisively. She licked her lips and — after a moment of hesitation — approached the owner of the bird stall.

They exchanged a few words in a language that Adrian didn't know, one that sounded different from Sonia's native tongue — something with a lot of rasping and clicking. Then the shopkeeper pulled down a cage of brightly-colored lovebirds and withdrew one. It handed this to the girl, who took it in both hands — her fingernails were long and sharp and curled, Adrian noticed — and inspected it thoroughly. Then she shoved the live bird into her mouth and Adrian could hear the crunch of bones and the muffled squawking. He looked away.

"Have you ever been here before?" he asked Rosalie, who was staring out of her own window with an overwhelmed expression that rivaled his own feelings.

She shook her head. "Never."

The castle, Adrian quickly discovered, was not so much a building as it was a massive gated community. It was much further away than he had expected it to be, and when they arrived the castle turned out to be substantially larger than Adrian had thought it was — large enough to fit a whole city into. They passed over a moat (Adrian spotted fat, lazy crocodiles swimming in it, cutting wide V's with their snouts) by way of drawbridge, then through a massive trellised doorway. The outer wall was at least three feet thick and built from solid gleaming pink stone, and the defense towers on either corner were each the size of grain silos.

Inside the walls, an eclectic hodgepodge of buildings made up the bulk of the city. They all seemed to have been built at different times, and from an unlikely variety of materials. Some looked like the houses in Crossroads: mud-and-twig, river rock, or little log cabins. Others seemed to have been woven together like baskets, or built entirely from glass. There were also wide patches of grass, and small pathways that broke away from the main cobblestone road. Small brown chickens pecked among the dirt along the roadway.

Small crowds milled outside of buildings, looking up curiously to watch as they passed. Most of them were tall, thin people with high cheekbones and long, pointed ears — more like elves than the pixie-like faeries Adrian had met so far. Here and there were other creatures: short, wrinkled goblins, tiny bearded leprechauns, and others that Adrian couldn't think of names for. The elf-like faeries tended to act as though the others didn't exist, and gave them a wide berth.

There were others, too, weaving among the crowds with ethereal grace, and Adrian could not help but stare at them. He had not fully appreciated what Lorelai meant when she'd talked about "corporeal dreams" but now he understood. The depleted corpse in the storeroom had not given a fair image of what they looked like when alive; they were stunning. Many of them looked human. Others were animals, or creatures that defied explanation. Quite a few seemed unable to maintain a single shape, and flowed seamlessly from one to another, features melting and reforming. All of them flickered around the edges, shimmering like mirages. Whenever one passed by, Adrian felt a sudden rush of energy wash over him, an infectious cheerfulness; the effects seemed cumulative, and by the time they reached the end of the cobblestone path he was grinning broadly although he had no reason to be happy.

"All of the dreams live here in the city," Rosalie said, her voice hushed with awe. "We're not allowed to buy them or take them back to Crossroads. They're so beautiful!"

A large building lay at the foot of the cobblestone path, a massive palace built from the same gleaming pink stone as the castle itself. It had many levels, all of them marked with large open windows, and the outer walls of it were decorated with carvings and statues and filigree.

The carriage shuddered to a halt, and the ensuing silence seemed to swallow them completely. Dreams and faeries milled around them, ignoring the carriage entirely, but a sentinel posted at the palace door swept forward to greet them. It was a knight, dressed in full plate armor that shone as though made of moonlight.

He stopped to exchange a word with Lorelai, before standing aside to allow her to jump down from the carriage. She swung the door open. "We're here," she said, simply. "Out."

"Huh?" Adrian tried to focus. Between the foggy, displaced happiness that had settled in his brain and the days of poor nutrition and interrupted sleep, he was feeling extremely sleepy. Somewhere, in the back of his mind, he vaguely remembered that he would be sold soon. It didn't seem particularly important.

Rosalie started forward, but Lorelai held up a hand. "Not you," she said. "You are staying out here until you're called for, and not a moment sooner."

She flicked her wrist, and Rosalie fell back against the bench, looking deflated.

The knight took Adrian's bound hands, helping him down from the carriage. His touch was electrifying, and Adrian's heart pounded in his chest as the armored fingers left his skin. A faint flicker of silver light danced around the knight, creeping through the chinks of his armor like sunlight through the cracks of a door.

Satisfied that Adrian could stand on his own legs, the knight turned smartly and walked into the palace. Adrian followed, Lorelai keeping close at his back as though waiting for him to try and run. The clanking of armor echoed from the stone walls around them, rattling and jangling like a box of loose keys. They made their way down the corridor; it was lit by torches whose fire burned bright blue and carpeted in a gold-embroidered purple carpet, and firelight danced and flicked on the walls. Between the torches, there were paintings and tapestries. Adrian peered at them, curiously, but didn't have a chance to linger over any as the knight walked quickly and it was all Adrian could do to limp after him at a steady pace. Lorelai jabbed him occasionally to remind him she was there.

Ahead, two ornate doors stood closed at the end of the hall.

"Look sharp," Lorelai growled in his ear, "or I'll have your head." She touched the ropes at his wrists and they fell away, disintegrating entirely before hitting the ground.

He swallowed, rubbing his fingertips over his wrists. The sleepy elation wavered, and he realized that lurking just below it was a terrible, seething horror.

The knight pushed open one massive palace door and held it open for them to enter.

THE DREAM PALACE

The corridor opened into a great hall, like a ball room. It was lit from above by chandeliers, but the ceiling was invisible, as though the candles were suspended in darkness or the ceiling were made of nighttime. At the far end of the room was a throne, upon which was seated a tall, willowy figure. She was very tall, with skin the color of caramel and large black eyes. The silver circlet she wore contrasted sharply with her raven-black hair. Flanking either side of the throne were two handmaidens who were probably twins; they were both pixie-like, with identical gold-and-black viceroy butterfly wings and hair a similar shade of red-gold. They wore shapeless white dresses which hung on them like sacks, and they ogled him curiously as he approached.

The knight led him to the throne and knelt at its base, taking off his helmet and holding it under his arm as he dropped to one knee. "My lady," he said. With his helmet removed, the knight looked insubstantial, as though without the armor to contain him he would simply blow away in the wind. His features were perfectly nondescript and seemed to blur together, as though his face were a vividly-imagined cloud.

"My message arrived in ample time, I hope?" Lorelai said, offering a small curtsy to the queen.

"Yes, yes. Ample enough, at any rate."

Adrian dropped to a knee alongside the dream-knight, because it seemed like the right thing to do.

This seemed to amuse the queen, as she laughed a quiet, haughty laugh. "You are a curious creature indeed," she said. "Stand, if you would. I'd like to get a look at you."

Adrian stood. He crossed his arms, feeling awkward. He uncrossed them, clasped them before himself, unclasped them, clasped them again in the small of his back. He rocked on the balls of his feet and tried not to look at the queen while she was looking at him. He could feel those cool, impassive black eyes boring into him.

"When I heard there was a grown-up in our midst, I thought it was just a story. A mere human-tale. We haven't seen your ilk in quite some time."

He smiled sheepishly, unsure of what he was supposed to say to that.

"From the state of you, you must be exhausted."

"He's in fine condition," Lorelai interjected. "Hardly a scratch on him."

"I have no doubt," the queen said, with a bemused smile. "You are always so gentle with your merchandise." She looked to the knight, then to her handmaids. "Valor, come, I have something that needs attending to. Ladies, if you will kindly show the human to his room?" She lifted her eyes to meet Lorelai's, and a smile tugged at the corner of her lips and flickered in her eyes. "And you, of course, may come if you wish. We shall discuss matters of payment once more pressing business has been addressed."

One faerie said something to the other, who giggled in the way that school girls giggle, and they came forward, each taking one of his arms and both looking as though Christmas had come a little early. He protested feebly that he could walk fine on his own, but they ignored him and chattered along happily in their own language. After making their way down a corridor and up a short flight of stairs, one released his arm to open the first door on the left. She held this open for him and gestured for him to go inside.

"Thanks," Adrian said, and the faerie blushed deeply and looked away, as though completely overwhelmed by his actually speaking to her. It took a moment to extract her from the door; after lots of 'I'll be fine from here's and a few 'can we shut this, please?'s, he finally managed to bid the faerie twins goodnight and closed the door behind them. He looked to see if the door had a lock on it, and realized with disappointment that the key locked it from the outside only. He tried the knob; it was already locked.

"This has been a very, very strange day," he said to the empty room. He made his way to the window, peering outside. It was barred, preventing his escape, but he could hardly muster the energy to consider escaping anyway. He wondered what price Lorelai was asking for. He wondered why the queen would want to buy him at all. The image of the whiskered woman in the market flooded into his thoughts, and he fought back the panic. *She's not going to swallow you whole,* he thought. *You're way too big for that.*

When they were kids, Adrian's great-aunt had given Samantha a book of fairy tales. It was a random gift; Great-Aunt Martha hadn't been in the habit of visiting them, and didn't really know when anyone's birthday was, or how old they were, or what they wanted for presents. So when gifts occasionally arrived in the mail, they were opened in trepidation; sometimes they were good, but more often they were strange or boring or vaguely unnerving.

The fairytale book wasn't very appropriate for a 3-year-old. It told the old stories, with all the blood and sex and incest, and used words that were too big. Adrian, who was an advanced reader, liked to steal the book sometimes and read the stories, although large parts of them made very little sense to him. Samantha always stole the book back, though. She didn't care about the stories, but she liked the pictures.

The book had been lovingly illustrated in full-page color prints showing castles and ogres and lonely towers and sleeping princesses. Samantha liked to open the book up to a picture and lay the book out flat as she played with her toys along the page, as though the illustration were the backdrop for whatever make-pretend game she were playing. Adrian tried to play with her, but she got impatient with him quickly. He was terrible at make-believe games, and when she sat cross-legged on the floor and chatted with herself, making conversation with whatever new invisible playmate she had made that week, Adrian would just sit awkwardly and wonder why he never had any imaginary friends.

I wonder what fairytale I'm in? Adrian wondered, as he gazed through the bars of his window. *Beauty and the Beast? Or Bluebeard?* He knew he should be afraid, but he was too tired for fear.

The exhaustion overtook him and he withdrew from the window. He stumbled his way with half-lidded eyes toward his bed, climbing into it, not even bothering to pull the blankets over him. He was asleep by the time his head hit the pillow.

* * *

The queen ran her fingers down the knight's breastplate, watching as his dreamlight crackled like electricity under her fingertips. She stood close to him, her head nestled in the hollow of his neck. His helmet lay on the floor, discarded, and the expression on his bland face was neutral as she ran a small, pink tongue the length of his throat.

"Are you sure you don't want to join?" she asked, her dark eyes darting toward Lorelai. "I have an extra knight I can spare. Honor or Glory or Duty or one of the others, if you don't feel like sharing."

"Courteous as your offer is, Isolde, I think I'll pass." Lorelai lounged in the window seat, her slender legs extended before her, her thin wasp wings beating idly. She examined her hands. Small wrinkles had begun to form, sagging skin around the knuckles, and faint dark spots began to show through the usual milky whiteness of her skin. "Now, if you'd like to offer one of your fine knights in payment for the human, that would be a whole other barrel of fish."

The queen took the knight's hands — the plated gauntlets, too, had been discarded — and laid them over her breasts through the thin fabric of her chemise Her own hand wandered down, exploring the gaps in his armor. "Knowing the sort of fate they would see in your hands?" she said, with a small laugh. "I've grown quite attached to them, I'm afraid."

"A dream from the gardens, then," Lorelai pressed. "That's more than fair to you. The human is a never-ending fountain of dreamstuff."

"But is it of high enough quality?" The queen made a low, pleased moan in her throat, and closed her mouth around the knight's. The light around him dimmed, slightly, the way a power surge dims a lightbulb. She pushed his face down to her throat, running her tongue over her lips. After a moment she continued as though there had been no interruption. "He's plenty handsome, I'll grant you, but will he provide?"

"He dreams well," Lorelai insisted. "He has the power to withstand the Darkness. I tell you, he's worth a dozen dreams, and I'm only asking for one."

The queen moved one of the knight's hands down below the hem of her chemise, between her bare legs. She closed her eyes and buried the fingers of one hand in his hair. Dreamlight crackled between her fingertips. It curled around her thighs. "Well enough. You may have your pick from the gardens," she said, at length. "But take care, would you? We're running low, of late. Thieves, you know." A moan caught her, then, breaking off any further conversation. She tugged the knight's head up, away from her collar bone, grinding her hips forward into his hand, and pressed her mouth against his. The light around him dimmed and flickered.

"Thieves?" Lorelai looked up from her examination of her hands. "How are they making it past your security?"

"We've caught one," she half-gasped, tossing her head back. She grabbed the knight's head in both hands and shoved him to his knees. She stood with her legs apart, hands on his head, fingers tangled in his hair. "Your kind — pixie folk — from…Crossroads."

Lorelai's brow rose. "You think a pixie is responsible for the dreams that have gone missing?"

The queen didn't respond for a moment. She tossed her head back, eyes closed, her skin alive with the electric tendrils of dreamlight. Her limbs trembled. She pushed the knight away, and he slumped against the wall, looking faded and spent. "No, I don't," she said, finally, rubbing her hands up and down her forearms, as though rubbing the excess dream energy into her skin. "But it feels good to have someone in the dungeons."

Lorelai shrugged. "I suppose."

The queen ran her fingers back through her own thick black hair, a soft smile on her full lips. "Now then. Run down and choose your payment. And bring in that poor servant girl from the stables." She met Lorelai's steel grey eyes. "I'm going to rest a bit, and then we'll see what this human of yours is capable of."

* * *

He had a strange dream.

In it he was sitting in Angela Weaver's kitchen. The walls were made of rocks and trees and strange things moved in the shadows, but the table and chairs and stove and cabinets were all Angela's. There were scuff marks on the tabletop, long scratches and grooves in the wood that almost, but didn't quite, spell out words.

She was smoking, taking long puffs of her cigarette through puckered lips. When she exhaled, the smoke was wispy and multi-colored and dreamlike. It gathered in a low-lying fog around the foot of the table, so thick that Adrian couldn't see past his knees.

"I can't stay here," Adrian said, but he didn't speak in words — he spoke in gesture and emotion and nuance. "I have to go. I have to find him — his sister is looking for him."

Angela shook her head and smoked and the curling blue smoke filled their strange room without walls. It was almost up to the tabletop now. It pinned Adrian in place, and he knew that if it got up over his head that it would suffocate him.

"Let me go, please." He wanted to get up, but he didn't, he couldn't. "I have to find him and say I'm sorry. His sister is looking for him."

"He never had a sister, Adrian," Angela said. Her voice was Sonia's voice, and it came from everywhere.

A giggle — a shriek of laughter.

A flash of golden curls in the shadows, among the slithering creatures.

"Wait!" Adrian cried.

The room dissolved and he was running. The golden curls bobbed ahead, out of reach. The laughter was everywhere and the air was thick with smoke. He brushed the smoke aside, swimming through it, but the more he ran the thicker it became. He realized he was not alone: There was another figure in the smoke, someone tall and thin and skeletal. The smoke around it shimmered and solidified into a long, tattered black cloak, and a pair of empty eyes stared out at Adrian from the gloom. Its gaze was terrible, full of loathing and accusation, and Adrian cried out and tried to get away but the smoke pressed in around him like a smothering blanket...

Adrian awoke, his body damp with sweat. He wrestled with his blanket, which had twisted itself around his lower body, and struggled to the basin of water at the foot of his bed to wash his face. A low fog of dreamlight curled around the foot of his bed, sparkling like fresh dew. It faded, soaking down into the floorboards or dissipating into the air, gone without a trace within moments.

Beside his bed, there was a change of clothes — fine clothes, not like the simple things Sonia had given him to wear — and a short note requesting his presence at dinner. He realized someone must have come in while he slept, to leave these for him and change out the water basin, and that they would have seen him wrestling with blankets as he wept in his sleep. He wondered why no one had bothered to steal his dreams.

The smell of spicy foreign food assailed his senses when he opened the door, and he followed his nose into the dining hall. Inside there was a long table, set with candles and platters of food; the candlelight danced and glinted off the platters and goblets, sending multi-colored flashes of light up onto the ceiling. Seated at the head of the table was the queen, dressed in a long gown. At either side of her stood the twin attendants. The knight stood at attention just inside the door. The table, though massive and covered in platters of food, was set for two.

The queen smiled encouragingly at Adrian, who hesitated before sitting down. He looked up the length of the table, staring past rows of serving platters. "Lorelai isn't coming?"

The queen laughed. "Lorelai has business to attend to, I'm sure."

Adrian glanced down at his place setting and was surprised to see that his soup bowl was filling itself. He blinked. The ladle hovered over his bowl and tipped out a creamy bisque before returning to the tureen, where it lay quite still.

"Help yourself," the queen said, with an air of amusement. She did not eat. "I imagine you must be starving."

His stomach gurgled. He looked again at the food. "Forgive me for being rude," he said, addressing his soup bowl as the intensity of the queen's gleaming black eyes made his stomach churn. "It's just, the last time someone I didn't know gave me something, I ended up being trussed up and carted halfway across the world."

She laughed. It was a throaty, good-natured laugh that didn't quite match the cold gleam of her eyes. "Apologies. You have every right to be suspicious." She raised her glass — a crystal goblet filled with something that might have been a sparkling white wine, or possibly a liquid form of moonlight — and tipped her head. "I promise you, I have no interest in either destroying you or re-selling you." The soup bowl levitated and crossed the table, the ladle spooning soup out into the queen's bowl. She took up a spoon and sipped it demurely. The twin faeries watched her with identical expressions of longing, but the queen did not look at them. "So, human. I imagine you must have quite a story."

"Adrian," he said, reluctantly. "My name is Adrian. And didn't Lorelai tell you all about me already?"

"I've known Lorelai for many years, so I know better than to trust her word about anything — and most especially a financial matter. I think it best to hear it from the source."

He took a tentative spoonful of soup. It tasted like tomatoes and opportunity and the first day of summer. He ate more, and, between mouthfuls, he began to tell his story. He hadn't intended to tell her anything, but as he ate he felt a comfortable warmth spread through him and the words began to tumble out faster until his brain no longer seemed to be in control of his mouth.

The soup bowls were cleared and a salad tossed itself and piled greens high onto his plate. It was assembled from a strange assortment of greens, many of which weren't even green but deep purple, or pale blue, and all of them leafy or spiny or wrinkly. The queen said nothing, but listened as Adrian poured out the story. He told her about Lorelai and Rosalie and his long journey tied up in their wagon. He told her how his dream had been stolen and he was taken captive, and the long-dead dream he had seen tied to the wall in the storeroom.

Subsequent courses filled themselves onto his plate. He ate roasted lamb and potatoes, tiny poached quail eggs over toast, ratatouille and cassoulet. Adrian talked about Sonia, and balefire, and how Zachariah had been destroyed by the Darkness. He talked about home, and the portal, and Nathaniel, and the Nightmare Man.

Adrian finished explaining all of this as he started tucking in to a rather large, steaming bread pudding dotted with dried fruit and glistening with butter. He stopped, realizing he had nothing more to say (he had managed, with some effort, to avoid bringing up any of the subjects he kept under locked doors in his mind, but only just) and peered past the now-empty serving platters to the queen. She had listened in silence while he spoke, but as soon as he had mentioned The Nightmare Man she leaned forward, eyes glittering with sudden, sharp interest.

"Well," she said, at length, when he didn't say anything further. "A thief, you have? An unfortunate coincidence. We have a thief of our own."

Adrian wasn't quite sure what she meant by this, but didn't ask. He cleaned his plate, and waited for her to continue.

The faeries at her elbows looked bored and quietly detached from the proceedings, but the knight at the door stood at sharper attention and kept stealing sidelong glances at Adrian. His expression was not entirely friendly.

The queen rose from her seat, delicately dabbing at the corners of her mouth with a napkin, and waved aside the attendants, gesturing toward the table. "I believe we have some business to discuss, then. If you will follow me?"

She nodded toward a doorway and Adrian rose from his seat, feeling the large quantity of food in his stomach shift a little as he did. He wanted very much to curl up for a nap.

The knight made to follow them outside as well, but she laid her hand on his chest to stop him. "No, Valor. Just the human. Don't worry — I rather doubt he would be able to kill me, even if that were his intent." She brushed her fingers along his breastplate, and dreamlight flickered and crackled like static electricity, curling around her fingers.

The knight looked dubious, but allowed them to pass, still standing firmly at attention. Adrian felt the electric crackle of his dream-energy as he passed, and shivered; the pale blue dreamlight peeking out from the gaps in his armor seemed to radiate cold rather than the usual warmth Adrian had come to associate with dreams.

"So. You've felt your share of Darkness," she said, as they stepped out into an empty corridor. The torches here burned low, casting long shadows along the hall. "And yet, here you stand. It's remarkable."

He shrugged, noncommittal. After talking all through dinner, he could think of nothing else to say. He certainly didn't feel particularly impressive for the achievement of surviving, especially as he had no idea how he had done it.

"Well, having seen it as you have, I'm sure you can appreciate the desire to avoid it whenever possible. A society has a difficult time thriving when it's being terrorized by long nights and chaos. Without our technology, we become…beastly. It doesn't forgive the way you have been abused, but it does explain it." She reached a doorway, set into the wall, and paused there. She turned to look at Adrian. "Our world, as you may have already learned, is powered by creative energy."

Adrian nodded. "You use human dreams, because they're more powerful," he said. "I know. Lorelai told me all about it."

She returned his nod, a slight smile tugging at the corners of her mouth. "Then you know about corporeal dreams."

"Enough to know that's what your knight is."

She laughed. "So he is. One of many — a dream of valor, of chivalry and nobility. He was born, I suppose, as someone's knight in shining armor. Now he's mine."

Something in the way she said this made the hair on the back of Adrian's neck prickle.

"But, getting to the point. There is a matter that needs attending, which I believe will ultimately benefit us both. But first, I think you need to see something, so that you can fully understand the way that our world functions."

She opened the door and swept through it without further explanation.

The doorway opened out onto a balcony overlooking a giant courtyard, a garden that seemed to stretch for miles, so far that Adrian could only barely make out the pink stone walls that contained it on all sides. Along the top of the wall, spread out at regular intervals, were strange crystal basins fitted with curving trumpets like those on an old gramophone.

Staring down at the courtyard from the balcony, Adrian thought that it defied description: As soon as he thought he had an idea of what it looked like, it twisted and shifted as though the reality of the area were fluid. Trees sprouted where they had not been before; buildings blossomed among the hollow places, then vanished; mountains erupted from the ground, then dissipated. In the very center was a tremendous fire, a bonfire larger than any Adrian had ever seen. It burned a strange shade, and from it great shafts of light rose up into the sky, shimmering and dancing like aurora borealis.

Around the fire — dancing, singing, playing hopscotch, jumping rope, giving chase — were at least a hundred children. As they played, the air around them shimmered and solidified, reality forming itself seamlessly as they imagined it into being. A little girl lay on her stomach, stretched in the shadow of a large tree; in her hand, she had a small stuffed rabbit. As Adrian watched, the rabbit shimmered and grew, becoming sleek and lean and real. It hopped away from her, then stopped, rising up to its haunches to sniff at the air before giving a thump of its hindpaw and dropping back to all-fours to scamper around the girl. Two young boys picked up sticks from the ground and began fencing with them. The sticks lengthened and flattened and glittered, a pair of swords that flashed and glinted in the light.

Adrian gaped.

The queen continued, as though conversation had never ceased. "My forebears devised an elegant solution to the Darkness problem."

"A balefire," Adrian said, voice hollow. "Large enough to light up a whole city."

"Yes," the queen said, looking satisfied.

They stood on the balcony, and Adrian stared down into it, feeling completely mindblown — but an odd feeling of elation swept over him, against his will. The energy emanating from the fire was different from the jittery rush of bottled dreams; it felt purer, cleaner, and filled him with warmth. "You kidnap children and enslave them here to power your city?"

"Human depression is destroying us — and them," the queen said, pointedly. "This is our only hope, for all of our sake." She raised a hand, gesturing to the far side of the corridor, where another doorway stood open. It was a tremendous door, arched and filigreed around the edges, the sort of door made only for castles and cathedrals and buildings of great importance. The view through the door was obscured with a twisting, shimmering blue-green mist. "Besides, they are free to come and go as they please."

Adrian leaned over the balcony, shrewdly scanning the sea of faces, searching for someone familiar within the crowd. A few girls, dressed as princesses with tall, pointed ribbon-trailing hats, sat around a table having high tea with what was unmistakably a shaggy brown-furred bear. It perched precariously onto its chair, one claw of a massive paw curled daintily around a teacup. They passed around trays of cookies and hors d'oeuvres and chatted animatedly among themselves, a low-lying multi-hued fog of dreams curling around their feet. Nearby, a boy drove through the clearing in a monster truck, buildings and trees crashing down in his wake, but no one paid him any heed and the rubble behind him shimmered and reformed, good as new.

"This Dreamland…isn't the same as the one you've been in," the queen said, her eyes trained on Adrian. "It's different, for them, than it is for us, or for grown-ups. They come and go through the doorway whenever they want. When they dream. When they play. When they hide beneath the covers of their bed and pretend to sleep. They find their way here, and go home when they've had their fill."

Below, a dream danced in circles around the fire. It was roughly human-shaped, but there was something animal about it as well, although Adrian couldn't pin down exactly what. It shifted and flickered and seemed oddly transparent and worn, like a threadbare blanket that allowed light to pass through. It wore layers of purple and black feathers and a headdress with wide, many-pronged antlers. Watching it dance filled Adrian with an immense, simple joy that he could not explain. It recalled images of running, of a light breeze scented with spring blossoms, of rolling in fresh grass and drinking from streams, and a dozen other things Adrian had never done, but suddenly felt as though he remembered.

The dancing figure turned a slow revolution and then, very suddenly, leapt into the fire.

The Balefire swelled, the flames turning a deep violet for a moment, and the smoke above flickered with images, half-formed thoughts that burst through the borealis and fluttered in the sky like so many birds. These images soared toward the trumpet-shaped bulbs along the stone wall, swirling through the pipes and settling into the basin as though they had been sucked up by a powerful vacuum.

Adrian jerked.

"A dream," the queen said. "Who had outlived its capacity to maintain a body. Nothing more." A wry smile touched her lips. "In other, less civilized corners of the world, dreams may meet a less dignified end. Those under royal control, however, sacrifice themselves thusly."

"I don't understand…" Adrian couldn't move his eyes from the courtyard. Below, no one seemed affected at all by the event. If anything, a certain uncontrollable joy seemed to have spread among the children. Many seemed to laugh for no reason, halting in their play to lean back their head and cry out in jubilation.

The queen followed his gaze. "When the children come here, to play… they can be whatever they want. They build this place, when they imagine it. Their thoughts, their wishes, their fantasies, it's all real here. They see what they wish to see. Most, I think, don't even realize that there is anyone around them. It's hard, as a human, but try to understand — Dreamland is created as it is experienced. It's different for everyone."

Adrian's brain hurt. He was too sleepy from the feast, and too bewildered by the immensity of the courtyard full of dreams, to wrap his head around any of this. "So, if I came here, and I was someone else, none of this would be the same."

"Probably." She shrugged. "The stuff they make, that they leave behind… it's their dreams."

"…Some kid dreamt that a person dressed as a purple bird would dance into a bonfire?"

"Dreams, once created, take on a life of their own," the queen said, her voice strained with barely-contained laughter. She came alongside Adrian on the balcony, standing very close to him. Now that she was near, he could see signs of age on her, slight wrinkles on her hands and about her eyes, slivers of grey among the fine dark strands of her hair. She touched his elbow, and her touch was cold, as though it were leeching the warmth from his skin. "When the children are long gone, back in the mundane world, or grown never to return…their dreams still linger here, living a life of their own. Many of the children you see down there, are their own dreams of themselves playing with them."

"You can make a dream of yourself?"

"You can make a dream of nearly anything, if you believe in it enough." The queen's fingers remained, feather light, on his elbow. The chill crept up his arm. She shifted her body closer to his, and Adrian caught a whiff of old-fashioned perfume, rosewater maybe. "The dreams grow, as the children grow. Their very presence in Dreamland helps to keep the Darkness at bay," the queen said. "And when the dream starts to feel used up…"

"…It throws itself into the fire," Adrian finished. His eyes flicked to the strange contraptions along the stone wall. "…And you…gather up whatever's left of them. To bottle and sell."

"Precisely." The queen smiled. Her fingertips curled around the curve of his arm, slid down his forearm as she entwined her arm with his. "It's always worked well enough, although in recent times we have suffered. Fewer children visit us, now, than they did in older times, and the Darkness is stronger. And the dreams are weaker."

"But you don't trade corporeal dreams to the other villages," he said, remembering Lorelai's wistfulness about powerful dreams. "They all live in Darkness, while the good dreams live here."

"Generosity can be taken to excess," she said, and her grip tightened. "Would you have me give dreams away to those who would mistreat them? Those who would destroy them for their own consumption, rather than cultivate them?" Something flickered in her eyes. "The lesser folk are not to be trusted. They are vulgar beggars and thieves."

Adrian wondered what made someone qualify as "lesser folk." He tried to ask this, but his mouth wouldn't cooperate. He felt the warmth in his side leech away, replaced by the icy coldness of her grasp. He tried to pull away. His brain would not give his arm or legs the signal, as though his body had fallen asleep as he stood here.

"You've met them. Would you trust your sacred treasures to the likes of Lorelai?" The queen asked. "And now, we come to the point. Come away with me from this place, I think we've seen enough for now."

He obeyed, as though his limbs responded to her orders rather than his. He wondered if he had been drugged again, but knew it was something else — something simpler. The word *thrall* formed itself in his thoughts. His heart began to speed up in his chest, tapping out a staccato rhythm that ached against his ribs, but his legs continued following the queen's orders rather than his own.

"Now." The queen entwined her fingers with his, leading him back into the palace, down the long deserted corridor. Torch light flickered and cast long shadows along the walls as they walked. She opened a door with a touch and led Adrian inside. It was a bedroom, rather larger than the guest chamber that he had slept in. The door shut behind them and she turned so that they were facing, her fingers still laced with his. Her eyes locked onto his, and though he tried to look away, he found he could not shift his gaze, or turn his head, or blink. His breath caught in his throat.

"Running a kingdom requires an immense amount of energy. You must understand. The dreams the children give are so weak...so fragile." The queen ran the fingertips of her free hand down his cheek. "But you. You can see us, touch us, survive the ravages of night...better even than the strongest dream, your mind could sustain us." She pressed her body against him, curling her hand around to bury her fingers in his hair, drawing him close as though for a kiss. His heart beat so quickly it threatened to break the wall of his chest, and a thought burst into his mind, a screaming panic that begged for him to run, but his legs refused.

"I've paid dearly for you, human," she whispered, breathily, into his ear.

"Now, it's time to see what I purchased."

A NIGHTMARE IS BORN

He felt her, then, inside his mind: an intrusive, hungry presence that rifled through his thoughts, accessing his brain as though he were nothing but a computer. He felt her hands on his body, fingertips brushing smooth flesh, but the sensation was distant, like his body was no longer his own. Her presence in his mind, though, was both intimate and invasive. She opened the doors, unlocked cabinets, overturned boxes.

Get out, he tried to say, screaming inside his head. His body, pressed down now on the bed, was completely paralyzed, but he hardly noticed. *Get out of my fucking head.*

The room around them dissolved. Adrian felt that his eyes were wide open and staring, but he could no longer see through them — he could only see inside. Or perhaps the memories had escaped his thoughts, somehow, and overshadowed reality. He could no longer feel the queen's touch on his skin, but he could feel her inside, the brush of fingertips against his thoughts. He struggled against them. She leafed through his memories like pages in a magazine, flickering past out of order, glimpses of time.

Adrian tried to think of other things, but his mind felt sluggish, disconnected. He counted, loudly, in his head: counting every step in a mile. He screamed the numbers in his thoughts, but they faded within seconds, the memories pouring out of all the hidden places.

There was little Nathaniel Weaver, tears drying on his cheeks as he peered out, frightened, from behind a motel bathroom door. There was Jessica, her brow creased, and the memory had no words but Adrian knew what she was telling him: *I've felt this way for a long time, but I didn't know how to say it without hurting you...we haven't been properly married for a long time...maybe we never were.* A gray-and-white, massive shaggy dog stood with its paws against the frame of the door, staring back over its shoulder expectantly, begging to be allowed outside. A cold night, children dressed in costume walking down the street, swinging plastic pumpkins or pillowcases full of candy.

The Nightmare Man.

Adrian stared into its wide, blank eyes and felt a chill of recognition that reached deeper and further than Nathaniel Weaver.

Samantha's funeral was the third week of October.

Adrian's parents, trying their best to maintain some sort of normalcy in a world that had been turned upside down, insisted that the boys not miss any school. The continued to take William to his Boys and Girls club basketball practices. And they insisted, although all the joy had gone out of it, that the boys go trick or treating on Halloween.

Adrian had saved up all of his allowance money since the start of September, when the Halloween store had opened up in the mall, in order to buy the best scary mask he could find. He didn't really like Halloween, but William did, and Adrian wanted to make sure he had a better costume than his brother. So he had bought the mask — a grayish-white skull with a wide, grinning mouth — and his daddy had let him borrow a big black overcoat that came down to his ankles.

But after the funeral, Adrian didn't want to be scary anymore. He didn't want to be scared ever again, not even for fun. His parents relented, buying him a new costume — Spiderman — and he had gone trick or treating with William, although it seemed very strange not to have Samantha with them, dressed up like a little pumpkin or witch. He had done alright, until they got to the house at the end of the block. It was a big, sprawling home, and every year it always had a spooky yard display with tombstones and fake fog. There was a skeleton exactly the same height as a little boy hanging from one of the trees in the yard. It rattled a little in the wind.

Adrian made his way nervously up the path, trying to remind himself that it could be fun to be scared if nothing was going to hurt you. He wouldn't ring the doorbell. William did it, rolling his eyes in exasperation (although, Adrian saw, he looked a little nervous too) and when the door opened the man inside seemed to take up the whole door frame. He wore a shabby suit and he was covered all over with red-black blood, all over his hands and chest, the way daddy had been covered in blood when he'd held Samantha's body, and Adrian started to scream and cry so hard that William had been forced to take him home.

That night he lay in a miserable ball in his covers, shivering and sobbing. This was before he had learned about making doors and file cabinets in his mind, and all of his thoughts tumbled around in his head without his control. He fell asleep, and in his sleep he imagined that his discarded Halloween costume had climbed out of the closet and stood over his bed. In his dream, the costume was more terrible than it ever had been in real life: the gaping mouth was full of needle-sharp teeth, the empty eye sockets were deep as pools, the overcoat was a billowing black cloak. It had bony skeleton hands and it pulled down the covers and pointed at Adrian, and its gaze was deep and accusatory. It didn't speak. It didn't need to. Adrian already knew why it was here.

He had done a bad thing, and now he was going to be taken away.

Adrian whimpered and cried and rolled in his sleep. He opened his eyes, and, for one terrible moment, the costume was still there. It stood over his bed, impossibly tall, as tall as the ceiling. It glared down at him with wide-open, empty eyes, its teeth gnashed in its empty mouth, and it extended a bony hand out for Adrian.

He screamed and stumbled out of his bed and fell on the floor, his legs tangled up in his blanket, and when he looked up again the Nightmare Man was gone. When his parents came in to ask what was wrong (a little exasperatedly, as Adrian had woken screaming nearly every night since the accident) he blubbered and gibbered and couldn't tell them. There weren't words to describe what he had seen. Weeks later, when his mother first taught him how to hide things in a box in his mind, The Nightmare Man was the first thing he locked up forever and resolved to never, ever think about again.

* * *

Lorelai sat across from Rosalie, neither looking at the other. The servants bustled around, without paying them much heed, and Lorelai's soup had gone cold while she examined the payment she had been offered. She had hoped for a corporeal dream; if not one of the knights, then at least an animal, a little dancing dog or a phoenix bird. But no. There were no dreams to be had, none harvested that lived long enough to be captured.

"Well, there have been a couple," the guards had said, nervously, shifting from foot to foot and refusing to meet Lorelai's eye; she tended to intimidate everyone she encountered. "But they've been stolen, see."

Lorelai counted her jars of dreamstuff again and sighed. She drummed her fingers on the table. The queen had agreed to pay the other half if her preliminary taste went well; in the meantime, Lorelai was stuck here, waiting. Lorelai hated waiting. She much preferred having others wait on her.

"How long do you think it will be?" Rosalie asked, stealing a sidelong look at Lorelai, the way a begging dog will sidle up to a person without making eye contact.

"As long as it needs to," she responded, rolling one jar of dreamstuff between her palms.

* * *

The memory shifted and Adrian watched a stream of images pour through his consciousness. A tiny pink hand clasped in a larger, skeletal one; a young red-haired boy sleeping in a motel bed; the entrance of a cave, tucked away in the depths of a forest, the cave depths glinting with dreamlight. The images were disjointed, nonsensical, and he had never seen them before — but the familiarity was undeniable, like memories of a dream he had forgotten upon waking.

Which, of course, they were.

AS ONE DOOR OPENS

The room materialized around them once again. Adrian realized he was on his knees beside the bed, breathing hard, shaking all over as the chill from the queen's touch faded from his skin. His body ached from falling, the sharp pain in his knees telling him how he had gotten here.

The queen lay curled in bed, writhing as though in terrible pain. She clutched her head, tugging at handfuls of raven-black hair and made a sound like an angry bird. He saw her as through a haze: Images from his mind still swam before his eyes, filling the room, and he had a terrible sinking feeling that anyone else who walked by would be able to see them, too.

"You — you lying — you're..." she sputtered, dragging herself over the bed to place it between them. She rolled off the bed but was unable to stand, and fell to her knees, head still clutched in her hands.

The door swung open.

Something shimmered in the hall, just outside the door; Valor stepped into the room, halting immediately as his eyes widened slightly in shock. He looked much less solid than he had at dinner. He still wore his armor, but he seemed almost transparent. He looked from the queen, to Adrian, then back at the queen, his brow creasing deeply along well-worn worry-lines. "My queen," he said, nervously. "I...apologies for interrupting..."

"Valor..." The queen said, climbing awkwardly to her feet. She swayed, slightly, and for a moment it looked as though she would collapse; the knight tensed, extending a hand as though to catch her, but she kept her feet. "Valor, please." She fell against him, burying her face in the hollow of his neck with hungry desperation. She trembled. "Dispose of the human. He is worthless to me. His dreams taste like ash and blood."

"What shall I do with him, my queen?"

"The dungeon," she said, withdrawing from him. She looked slightly more stable, but the color had drained from her face and her eyes were wild and glassy from pain. "With the thief."

He nodded, guiding her back to the bed. He touched her cheek almost tenderly before circling it, grasping Adrian's arm and tugging him roughly to his feet. The soft glow of dreamlight flickered along his skin, but his features shifted and blurred. He looked the way a person looks in an old memory: contorted, blank, nondescript. Adrian tried to remember if he had always looked this way, and realized he could no longer recall his face despite standing a few inches away. "Come, human."

Adrian swooned, his vision temporarily replaced by darkness and bursts of light. The blood had drained from his head, and his extremities buzzed with adrenaline — a fight or flight response with nowhere to run to. He could still feel the queen's touch inside his mind.

Valor said nothing more. His armored hands were cold and hard as they gripped Adrian's wrist, and Adrian struggled to keep up with his long stride as they left the bedchamber and walked down a series of hallways and stairs. Adrian couldn't keep track of the twists and turns. He was only tangentially aware of his body.

I created The Nightmare Man. He's my dream.

The thought came and went, unbidden, in his mind — ebbing and flowing like a tide.

She's here.

This thought was a constant, keening wail that played in his mind, repeating until it had lost all meaning: *She's here she's here she's here she's here here here.* The words meant nothing. The thought was too enormous to comprehend, like trying to see the universe all at once through the lens of a telescope.

He took her. She's here.

Valor opened a door and shoved Adrian inside. It was dark and damp and cold, but Adrian hardly noticed. The knight's faintly glowing dreamlight flickered, for a moment, before the door shut and drowned out the world in darkness.

She's here. He took her. She's here. She's here.

* * *

Valor's hands shook. The gauntlets rattled, the sound loud and jarring in the silence of the hall. Beneath the cool steel of his armor, his body pulled apart like wisps of cotton candy spinning in a machine, and the dreamlight wafted through the gaps in his armor, gathering around his feet like a glimmering fog.

Somewhere, someone was dreaming of another knight. Somewhere, Chivalry was being born, or Hero, or Gallantry. There would always be another knight to join the queen's army, just as there had always been

"Is it done?" the queen asked. She sounded weary, aged beyond her years from her ordeal in the bedchamber.

"He is in the dungeon," Valor agreed.

Her eyes flicked toward Lorelai, who stood near the doorway and clutched her chest as though in pain. "You seek to ruin me."

"I've done no such thing," Lorelai said. The fingers splayed over her chest curled, nails biting into her skin. Wrinkles deepened around her eyes and along the webbing of her fingers. "How was I to know what would happen?"

Out in the hall, Rosalie peeked through the doorway. She let out a quiet, frightened noise, like the sound of a trapped mouse, and ducked out of view once more.

"He is useless," the queen said. "You've wasted my time, Lorelai, and now you seek to rob me."

Something flashed in the witch's gaze; her lip curled with rage and loathing. "Rob you?" She repeated, scoffing. "Isolde, perhaps you forget how trades work. I give you goods. You give me goods in return. I earned what I own."

"And perhaps you forget your place," the queen shot back. She still cradled her head in her hand. "You only continue to exist because of my kindness. I could shut down your tavern. I could destroy your city. I could erase you from Dreamland entirely. I am your queen."

Lorelai hesitated a moment, sizing the other up.

Valor laid a trembling hand over his sword.

Lorelai looked away. "Yes," she said, and her tone was scathing. Her eyes drifted to the floor and stayed there, though the open loathing on her face betrayed her. "My queen."

Isolde's brows raised. "You are to return the dreams and gather your servant girl. I want you out of my sight by morning." She paused, and a smile touched the corner of her lips. "But, because I'm feeling charitable, you can have the human back. Consider it a refund."

The grey-haired faerie nodded, giving a short bow to the queen. Recognizing that she had been excused, she turned and made her way into the hall, her extremities trembling with rage. "Come, Rosalie. Let's gather our dignity and be gone from this place." She glanced around the hall, realizing that it was empty, and cursed. Where had the stupid girl run off to?

* * *

The dungeon felt a little like an old, musty basement. The floor was damp, and it smelled like mold. Adrian reached his hands out in front of him, groping around in the dark as he waited for his eyes to adjust. He could hear someone breathing, and he held his own breath to get an idea of where the sound was coming from.

"Hello?" a timid voice spoke from a far corner of the room.

The voice was familiar. "...Sonia?" he asked, disbelievingly. "Is that you?"

"Adrian!"

Something stirred. Adrian heard the flutter of wings and light footfalls, then felt the wind rush out of him as a body collided with his. Arms flung around him, and he was pulled into an embrace. He couldn't see her, but he could smell her. She smelled like lilacs.

"You're alive," Sonia said, into the hollow of his chest.

"You, too." Adrian's arms hung at his side.

157

The hug lingered, and overstayed its welcome. He remembered the feeling of the queen's fingertips against his flesh, of her probing touch in his thoughts.

Sonia pulled away. Her wings fluttered, buzzing quietly at her back, and Adrian felt the wind from them blow against his face. "How…"

"You first," he said. He felt behind him and felt a smooth stone wall. He lowered himself to the floor, leaning back against the wall. His eyes were beginning to adjust to the dark; he could just make out Sonia's silhouette. "What are you doing here?"

"I…" She hesitated, extending a hand to brush his shoulder. "Adrian, are you okay?"

"I'm fine." He shrugged away from her touch.

"…Okay." The buzzing of her wings grew in intensity. "I…well, I was out looking for you. And I saw — well, I felt — a dream. I followed it here. It felt familiar. I thought it might be yours."

"Was it?"

"I don't know. I never caught up with it. It disappeared before I could get a good look at it, and the next thing I know a bunch of guards were bearing down on me and calling me a thief." She paused, settling down beside him, careful now not to touch him.

"I'm sorry," he said.

"What?"

"I'm sorry. For wandering away, getting lost. Getting us both into this mess."

"It's not…it doesn't matter," she said. Her hand approached his, but she drew it back before their fingertips touched. "What's happened to you? Was it Lorelai?"

He nodded, then remembered she couldn't see him. "Yes." He took a deep breath, and explained — once more — everything that had happened. He came up to the point where the queen had taken him into her chamber, and hesitated. He couldn't find words to explain what happened. He wanted to explain about Samantha, and The Nightmare Man, and the way the queen's touch had torn apart the secret room in his thoughts. What he said was, "But the queen decided she couldn't use me, so she put me down here instead."

Sonia was silent, for awhile. It was a heavy, thoughtful silence. "We'll get you out," she said, finally, quietly. "We'll find a way to the Gatekeeper, still, and get you home."

Home. Right. It was so far away now, he had almost forgotten about it.

He said nothing, and leaned back against the wall, trying to make sense of his thoughts.

* * *

In the small white room, Nathaniel and his new friends played go-fish with a deck of tarot cards. Nathaniel didn't know what they were, but he had found them in the corner, hidden beneath the pile of leaves by the battered roller skates. They weren't very good for go-fish. But it was better than nothing.

"Got any…um…swords?" Nathaniel glanced back at his cards to make sure of what they were called.

"Go fish." The Nightmare Man's long, bony fingers held his cards too tightly, and they curled at the edges.

The little girl had little interest in the game. She kept laying her cards out on the floor, lining them up like tiles. She would flip them over, occasionally, then stack them all back into a pile. Nathaniel glanced over frequently, trying to get a glimpse of the cards in her hand. He suspected she probably had most of the cards he needed. She flipped over some cards from her jumbled stack: The Tower, The King of Cups, The Magician. Then she turned over the Knight of Swords.

"Ah!" Nathaniel said, pointing. "You have a sword."

She looked up at him, startled, then back down at her cards. She ignored him.

Nathaniel sighed. He wanted to ask to go home, but he knew there was no chance of it. He had asked already, dozens of times, and the answer was never "yes." He didn't really expect it to be.

"You're unhappy." The Nightmare Man laid down his own cards, face-up.

Nathaniel noticed that he did, in fact, have swords: the nine of swords, the seven of swords, the Queen of Swords. He started to say something about The Nightmare Man cheating, but decided there wasn't much point. He shrugged.

"*Are you lonely?*"

"I want to go home."

The Nightmare Man ignored him. "*I can bring you more friends. Both of you. Do you want more friends?*"

"I want my mom."

"*I can get more friends, for both of you. So you can stay and play.*"

Before Nathaniel could protest further, The Nightmare Man had risen to his feet and swept across the room. The shaggy green-furred dog looked up as he passed, tail thumping. The Nightmare Man laid his hand on the wall, opening the door with his touch. Then he slipped outside, sealing the door behind him before Nathaniel could even think to try and follow.

VALOR'S END

Rosalie glanced uneasily over her shoulder, making sure that no one was following her. She needn't have bothered. With Lorelai and the queen making a fuss in the great chamber and the guards prowling the garden searching for thieves, the castle was deserted. She hoped it would stay that way.

Her heart thudded heavily in her chest, pounding so hard against her ribs that she thought they might break. She had spent most of the time here in the city out in the stables, making conversation with the queen's servants. A dream would wander by, occasionally, and she enjoyed the jolt of energy from its presence, but the joy faded quickly when she remembered why she was here.

Adrian.

It was a ridiculous thing to think, but the thought welled up in her mind all the same: *If I can get to him before Lorelai, maybe we can escape together.*

She glanced over her shoulder, once more, before stopping at the door to the dungeon. It was a heavy iron door, without any windows, and too thick to hear through. She pressed her ear to it, trying to make out any sounds of life from the inside, but could hear only the blood rushing in her own ears. She withdrew, wondering how she could get hold of the key. The knight had the keys to the dungeon; she had seen them glittering at his waist in the great hall.

She extended her hand and touched the knob. It was warm, crackling with residual dream energy from the knight's touch, and she smiled faintly as her fingertips brushed the brass. Compulsively, she squeezed the knob and turned it.

The latch gave way with a click, and the heavy iron door cracked open.

"...Really?" She paused, hand on the open door, expecting a trap. "...He didn't even lock the door?" Not quite believing her fortune, Rosalie hesitated, the door open just a crack. Rather than allowing the light from the hall in, the opening seemed to let some of the darkness out. A long shadow spilled out onto the floor by Rosalie's feet.

Before she could push the door open any further, a sudden terrible sound broke out through the castle. A claxon wailed; people shouted; footsteps pounded from overhead. Rosalie jumped back from the door as though she had been burned.

What was happening? Had she set off an alarm by mistake?

Down the hall, near the lower entrance of the outer courtyard, she could barely make out a garbled mixture of shouts and cries. Most of it was lost in the general din of sound, but a few words managed to stick out: "Thief," "courtyard," and "alarm."

Not entirely sure what any of that meant, but completely certain that she didn't want to be found lingering here, she pulled away from the dungeon and ran back down the hall, hoping desperately that she would find Lorelai before her absence was missed.

* * *

Valor shook so violently that he rattled when he walked. He felt like he was coming undone beneath his armor. As a dream, he had never been hungry — but the pain in his body was like a hunger pang, like a terrible gnawing emptiness where his body tore itself apart and chewed through its own tissue. And yet, his shaking was not weakness from age and over-use.

Why had he left the dungeon unlocked?

It hadn't been a conscious decision at the time. He had merely done it, as if on impulse, and he was back in his queen's shadow before the full weight of the action had come crashing down upon him. The guilt tore through him, literally pulling him apart. He had not acted with valor. He had defied orders

— committed treason against his queen. His actions were his undoing, and now he was drawn toward the balefire and its relief like a moth pulled into a candle. Like all tired, worn-out dreams, he was ready to find peace in the flames.

He rattled his way through the doorway into the courtyard, crossing the garden toward the balefire. The children didn't look up. No one paid him any notice, and he pressed forward, walking as quickly as his trembling legs would allow.

Was it worth it, in the end?

He hoped so. He hoped the human found the way out, and quickly. He had felt it, the moment he had touched the human — the electric tingle of energy, the powerful realization that this human carried dreams more powerful than either the queen or the witch could handle, and more powerful than they deserved. Valor had seen right away what the queen had not learned until later: This human had created the dream thief. Perhaps he could be the one to destroy it.

In his exhaustion, the knight didn't see the thief's approach.

On the far side of the courtyard, the portal shimmered, twisting upon itself like a whirlpool. Its surface stretched, like a balloon expanding; for a moment, it struggled against its own surface tension, and then a figure broke through: tall and robed, with a gaping maw and wide blank eyes. The doorway closed behind him, sealing once more into a glassy smooth portal, and the dream-thief stepped soundlessly onto the grass.

It paid no heed to the children. Although the courtyard stretched on for miles, the cloaked figure crossed it in a few steps; it moved the way shadows move, darting and sliding without sound. It came behind the knight, and without a word it wrapped its long, thin arms around the armored dream.

* * *

In the total darkness of the dungeon, Adrian laid his head back against the rough stone wall and tried to sort out his thoughts. He could hear Sonia's wings rustling and the soft echo of her footsteps on the bare floor as she paced. Neither spoke. Adrian found that he had run out of words.

Something made a noise outside, muffled by the thick iron door, but he hardly registered it. It wasn't until Sonia's pacing had stopped and the dungeon had fallen into sudden, uneasy silence that he realized something was happening.

The latch clicked.

Adrian forced himself to his feet, fighting against the weakness in his legs brought on by exhaustion and confinement. Sonia's hand brushed his, and he didn't pull away.

"Who's there?" Sonia called.

No one responded.

No light spilled in from the cracked-open door, yet somehow the dungeon seemed to be growing lighter by the moment. Adrian could make out Sonia's outline, then a greyed-out and shadowy image of her features. Her eyes glistened in the semi-dark, shiny and reflective like a cat's.

"…We've been sitting in an unlocked dungeon." Adrian said flatly. "Why would…who doesn't lock their dungeon?"

Before either Sonia could respond, a great noise sounded out in the empty corridor — the brazen wail of an alarm, the sound of feet pounding the stone floor, armor rattling, angry and surprised shouts. All at once, the castle went from eerily silent to deafening, as though an explosion had gone off overhead.

Adrian strained to make out words among the cacophony, but only caught snatches of words. Many of the voices yelled in foreign languages. He made out "thief" and "here," but the rest was lost in the sea of yells.

Sonia stepped forward, hesitantly climbing the steps. She peered out through the open crack of the door. Adrian followed her onto the stairwell, crowding into the doorway. Their own hall was abandoned, but he could hear sounds above them and from either side, all converging to a single point somewhere to his left.

From somewhere far away, Adrian could just make out another voice — different from the others, yelling something else and coming closer. A woman's voice, and something about it made his skin tingle with familiarity and fear. He could make out no words, but it didn't matter; it was the queen's voice, and she sounded angry

Sonia slowly pushed the door open, poking her head outside. She looked up and down the corridor. "I…it's clear," she said, confusedly. "If we're going to go…we should go now." She pushed open the door the rest of the way and stepped out into the torch-lit hallway. The flickering light illuminated her pale skin, bounced off of her vibrant hair, cast long wavering shadows along the floor. The sound intensified and concentrated in a single location, coming clearly and deafeningly from the courtyard's lower door.

For a single moment, everything stopped. Sound, motion, sight, smell — everything came to a complete halt and Adrian froze in place. He was dimly aware of his surroundings; he knew that the castle was around him, he knew that Sonia was standing beside him. But his ears were filled with a rushing sound, and he could see — in his mind or in front of him, he couldn't really tell — a long corridor opening, a cloaked figure approaching, long fingers beckoning….

Sonia twined her fingers in Adrian's and tugged. "Come on! If the guards are distracted, we can slip out the servant's exit into the stables, and then…" she trailed off, realizing that Adrian wasn't following her or listening. He was firmly planted in place, staring down the hallway with the look of someone who had just realized something both nauseating and profound.

The dream-thief. The Nightmare Man.

"He's here," he said. He felt numb when he said it. The vision faded, but an overwhelming certainty settled in his heart, a knowledge beyond familiarity.

"Who?"

Adrian ignored her and started down the hall, brushing past her and moving toward the concentration of sound — and the door to the rear gardens.

"Adrian, what —" Sonia chased after him, grabbing his arm in both hands, stopping him in his tracks. He strained against her, trying to break free from her grasp, but it was like being caught in a web of iron. "What are you doing? We have to go!"

"The Nightmare Man!" Adrian yelled, finally breaking his silence as he struggled to break away from her grasp. Why wasn't she understanding this? He wheeled around to face her. "The person I've been looking for! The one who took Nathaniel! He's here." He made a choked, frustrated sound. "The dream-thief! He's a dream. He's been sneaking into the courtyard and stealing dreams — that's what everybody's going crazy about. It's the same guy."

"That doesn't make any sense! Nobody can break into that courtyard without going through the castle. Not unless they...." She stopped, eyes widening with sudden realization. "The portal. He comes and goes through the portal."

"I don't care if he sprouts wings and flies in, but he's here right now. We have to follow him!"

"You can't!" Her fingertips curled into his skin and she pulled, trying to tug him away. "There's too many guards. They'll see you. Even if you could… you can't go through that portal. It will kill you."

"You said that about the last one, too."

"Yeah, I know, but…" She gave him another mighty tug, forcing him to stumble forward and follow her a few steps down the corridor, away from the concentration of sound overhead. She heaved him forward another step, tugging on him like he was a very large and stubborn dog on a leash.

"I don't want to go home, I want —" Something clicked in his mind. "Wait a second. The Gatekeeper."

"That's what I'm saying. We have to get you out of Dreamland so that —"

"No. I mean — he has gates everywhere, right?"

"Yes…" She paused in her tugging, looking at him suspiciously.

He smiled. "So he could take me to…wherever The Nightmare Man is from?"

"I guess he could," she said, reluctantly, and then sighed. "Yes. I think so. Now come on before someone sees us!" She gave his hand another tug, but it was unnecessary this time. He followed her without complaint into the labyrinth of corridors beneath the castle's main floor.

"Do you know where you're going?" He asked, straining to hear, but the general din had died down and was just a single muted roar of distant sound.

"Sort of," she said, still gripping his hand as she ran as though afraid he might bolt if she let go.

"Oh. Well." The sound in the distance faded as they ran deep into the bowels of the castle's underbelly. It was darker here, too, the torches not as close together as they had been. The long shadows shifted as they ran and Adrian knew that nearly anything could be hiding there, concealed by the darkness. He tried not to think about it. "If we get out, how far away are we? From the mountain?"

"On foot? A couple of days. If we had some cats or something…" she trailed off, coming to a stop at a fork in the path. She lifted her head, sniffing, then tugged him to the right. The path had a slight downward slant to it and it smelled peculiar, like a combination of earth and spoiled fruit and over-cooked cabbage.

"Have you ever been there?"

"No."

"…Oh. But you're sure that he can send me…wherever The Nightmare Man is coming from?"

"He can send you anywhere." They came to another fork in the path, and this time Sonia tugged him left. The stone ground gave way to dirt, and the stone walls were damp and slimy. The smell intensified. "Adrian, are you sure about this whole Nightmare Man thing?"

"Before the queen…" he faltered, not wanting to go into any details about their interaction in her bedchamber. "…Anyway. She told me that someone had been stealing their dreams. That's why you were put into the dungeon, right? Dream-thieving?"

"Yes, but — "

"And if a kid gets lost in Dreamland — if he gets stolen — he'd get taken from that courtyard, right? Isn't that where all the kids are supposed to end up?"

"Well, yes, but —"

"So he must have taken him." He hesitated, not wanting to say any more, but added, "Besides. I felt it. Back in the hall."

"That doesn't make any sense." Sonia slowed down, glancing back at him.

Her brow furrowed, then a slow smile crept into her eyes. "But…it doesn't have to."

"Irrational beings, right?" he responded back, with a hollow grin. "…Where are we?"

The ground was damp. Their feet splashed in a thin layer of muddy water, and moisture dripped occasionally from the ceiling. The smell was overpowering — thick with sulphur and the sweetness of decay.

"This way," she said, giving his hand a tug. "I think…well, judging by smell anyway, I think we're in the sewer."

As if to prove her point, a pair of rats — each the size of small dogs and glowing faintly blue-green — scurried past them, tails dragging in the water. "We can get out this way?" He wondered what was going on above ground, in the courtyard. The terrible certainty that had settled into his heart had faded, somewhat, and he ached to get above ground and see what was happening. What if he was wrong? What if the Nightmare Man hadn't been there at all and he got to the Gatekeeper's mountain and all of this was pointless?

"Yes," Sonia said, interrupting his thoughts. "I think so. This should drain out near the stables. If everyone's still in the courtyard, we should be able to sneak out that way without being scene."

"That's a lot of ifs and shoulds."

Sonia shrugged. Her wings fluttered uneasily, but she said nothing else.

As she said, the tunnel did eventually open out into a large drain, but not before the water grew deeper and smellier. It flowed over the tops of Adrian's shoes and welled up between his toes and he tried hard not to think of where they were or what they were walking through. They climbed out of the drain and up a steep bank on the other side, coming out on the far side of the stable.

The stable wasn't exactly what Adrian had expected it to be. There were horses there, to be fair — tall white horses and fat grey ponies, lean black horses and stout Clydesdales. But there were a great number of other things there as well: cats of every color, giant birds that looked like ostriches mixed with llamas, enormous iguanas. And there, at the far end, crouched into a tight metallic ball, was a familiar spidery carriage.

Adrian walked toward it, glancing around to make sure that they were alone. They were. He couldn't see the courtyard from here because it was obscured by a massive stone wall, but he could still hear stirrings and mutterings on the other side. "Sonia," he asked, as he crept upon the spindle-legged carriage. "Do you know how to drive this thing?"

"What?"

"Lorelai's carriage. Can you drive it?" He stopped a few feet away. The carriage seemed to be sleeping; it sat very quietly and still, although it occasionally gave a small shudder as though snoring.

"Um. I don't know." Sonia came up beside him.

"You said the trip would take a couple of days by foot. How long by carriage?"

"Adrian, are you really trying to steal —"

"How long?"

"A day, maybe. Half a day if I can get it to go really fast." Her wings fluttered rapidly. "Adrian, we can't steal Lorelai's carriage!"

"Why not?" He stepped up to it, extending his hand to touch its side. As his fingertips brushed the polished black wood, the carriage sprang to sudden life, rising with a terrible creaking. It waved a spindly leg in front of it. "It'll be faster."

"But…" she trailed off. "Okay, fine. I'll try it. But I don't know if it'll actually work."

Adrian stepped out of the way, letting her climb up into the front seat. She looked around, searching for reins or pedals or anything else that might make it work, then sighed and crossed her hands in her lap.

The carriage twitched.

"What did you just do?"

"What?"

"You did something. And then the carriage moved."

"I don't know, I just was thinking about how we needed to get going, and —" The carriage moved again. It gave a tremendous screech and backed out of the stall. "…Seriously?"

"Is it…are you controlling it psychically?" Adrian asked, coming around to climb up into the front seat beside her. "You think and it...does what you ask?"

"I...think so?" Sonia adjusted her wings and smoothed her skirt before refolding her hands in her lap. She screwed up her face in concentration, and the carriage suddenly lurched forward.

Adrian thrust out a hand to grab hold of something — anything — for support. He gripped the bottom of the seat and gritted his teeth, feeling the absolute certainty that he would fall out at any minute.

Sonia glanced over her shoulder, casting a final look back at the castle. It was impossible to hear anything over the creaking and groaning of the carriage legs. Adrian wondered if anyone had noticed that they were gone yet.

"Faster would be better," Sonia muttered, and the carriage responded by surging forward at a nauseatingly brisk pace.

Adrian flattened himself against the back of the bench, hand clenched tightly around the seat, squeezing his eyes shut. At least it would be harder for Lorelai to catch up with them now.

TREASON

I t was nothing short of pandemonium. Rosalie pushed through the gathering crowd without notice. Guards and servants crowded around the door. Guards tried to shove through into the courtyard, forcing their way through the crowd, but no one seemed to know where they were going. Rosalie couldn't see outside over the heads of the milling crowd, and she didn't care to. If someone was stealing dreams from the queen, that wasn't any of her business; she just needed to find her way back to Lorelai before things got any worse.

"What's going on?"

"Did you see him?"

"It doesn't make any sense — it looked like a dream…"

"Why would a dream steal another dream?"

Rosalie picked up snippets of chatter and conjecture as she wove through the crowd at the door and made her way up toward the main chamber. She didn't know why she was going back there — Lorelai probably wasn't still there. But she didn't know where else to go.

"Valor's missing!"

"Did he go into the fire?"

"Somebody stole him!"

"I'm telling you, it was a dream."

"Dreams don't steal dreams!"

Rosalie broke through the crowd and took a deep breath. It felt like surfacing for air after swimming through a great distance. Her heart thudded up in her throat and her wings sagged at her back.

"Rosalie," a voice hissed nearby.

She jumped. A hand caught her, clutching her elbow, and tugged her into a shadowy area behind a large statue of a girl riding on a turtle. A pair of cold eyes bore into her, framed by a long curtain of silver-white hair. Lorelai had wrinkles at the corners of her eyes and mouth, and her skin had a translucent quality. She carried several small jars of dreamstuff in her arms — the payment they should have been given for Adrian.

"Where have you been, you worthless girl?" Before Rosalie could respond, Lorelai continued in a low, urgent whisper. She shoved the jars into Rosalie's arms unceremoniously. "Come on. While everyone's still distracted."

Rosalie didn't say anything. She held the jars awkwardly against her chest. Lorelai gave her a slight shove away from the statue and started down the hall, heading toward the store rooms. She was walking more briskly than usual, as though only barely containing herself from running. Her wasp-wings buzzed angrily at her shoulders.

"Um..." Rosalie finally said as they crossed a foyer and closed the distance to the next door. "What's going on?"

Lorelai made a disgusted noise. "The thief came and stole the queen's favorite toy, and now everyone's gone half insane trying to catch him."

"I...some people were talking. They said the thief was a dream."

"Give them a few hours and he'll be a chimera. Or a flying pumpkin." Lorelai snorted. She stopped, resting her hand against the heavy wooden store room door, and pushed it open. It creaked slightly, but opened easily, and a splash of multi-colored lights could be seen shimmering in the dark. "What use does a dream have of more dreams?"

"Maybe he's the dream from the old story — the one who took everyone to where the Darkness comes from," Rosalie suggested meekly. "Maybe he's real."

"That's ridiculous," Lorelai said, but something caught in her voice as she did. Her eyes narrowed.

"There's no reason it can't be true," Rosalie said.

"No...I suppose..." Lorelai extended her hand, curling her fingers around a jug filled with bright silvery-purple dreamstuff. She pulled it from the shelf and handed it to Rosalie, who tried to adjust her load to add it to the stack.

"Um…What are we doing?"

"The guards are all a bit…preoccupied," Lorelai said, laying another jug atop the stack in Rosalie's arms. "So we must pay ourselves what we're owed."

"So we're stealing?"

Lorelai clicked her tongue. "We're getting proper payment for our services." She laid another jug of dreams in Rosalie's arms. They sagged under the weight. Lorelai grabbed two more and tucked them beneath her own arms. "Now. Come along. We've tarried here long enough," she said, as though it had been Rosalie's idea to come in and spend time loading up on dreams.

Rosalie had a hard time following Lorelai out into the hall and toward the stables. The dreams were heavy and awkward, and the glass jugs kept sliding in her sweaty hands. Lorelai walked too fast and Rosalie struggled to keep up, barely able to see over the stack of jugs nestled in her arms.

The door to the stable loomed before them; Rosalie could just make it out above the jugs in her arms. She tried to shift the jugs in her arms so that she could see better, but realized immediately that was a mistake: one of the small jars slipped through her sweaty fingers and there was no way to catch it in time. It crashed against the hard stone floor, shattering instantly. The dreamstuff unfurled, twisting around Rosalie's ankles like an over-eager housecat.

Almost immediately, a voice sounded behind them.

"The store room door is open!"

"Did you hear that?"

Lorelai cursed under her breath and gave Rosalie a hard shove with her shoulder before taking off at a run for the stable. Rosalie followed awkwardly, unbalanced now. She could hear the clanging of armor and heavy footsteps coming closer behind her, and she struggled to run. More jars fell from her grasp, smashing to the ground and releasing their contents like sparkling, thick mist.

"Thief!"

Rosalie didn't turn to see who was yelling. It was a guard, that's all that mattered — and, from the sounds of it, he was coming up on her fast. She let out a strangled cry and threw herself forward, shoving through the door with one shoulder, not even bothering to hold on to the falling jugs as she struggled to get out into the open.

"Thief! In here! We've caught the thief!"

The door swung open under her weight and she stumbled out into the stable area, nearly falling as the path stepped down from stone to dirt. She clutched the surviving jug to her breast, only half realizing that she still carried it, and ran toward Lorelai. Her lungs burned.

Lorelai had stopped and was staring ahead with a cold, stony glint in her eye. Her jaw clenched. Both jugs under her arms were intact, but her hands were balled into fists at her side and her knuckles were white. Rosalie nearly crashed into her.

"What are you doing? Run! Guards!" Rosalie panted out, bent double and clutching the jug to her chest. The dreams inside shifted and jumped like an animal in a cage.

"It's gone."

"What?"

Lorelai pointed at the empty stall where the carriage had been.

The door opened behind them. "Stop! Both of you!"

"Fuck!" Lorelai spun around, extending her hand; the jug under her arm slipped, but she caught it with her elbow. The air rippled, and Rosalie felt a warm rush of air pass her cheek. The next moment, both guards crumpled. They lay in a tangled heap. "Come on!" Lorelai yelled, and started forward at a run again, shifting the jugs into her hands.

Rosalie wasn't sure how, but she followed, ignoring the burning in her chest. She clung to her dream jug as though it were the only thing keeping her tethered to the world and followed Lorelai into the cover of woods that grew alongside the courtyard's massive stone fence.

✳ ✳ ✳

In the white room, Nathaniel and the little girl were eating sandwiches. Nathaniel's peanut butter was dry and gritty in his mouth, and the crusts of the bread grated against his tongue like sandpaper. He tried to feed his sandwich to the dog, but the mossy-furred creature turned up its nose and refused to take it.

The little girl didn't seem to mind her sandwich. She happily munched away at it, humming to herself. She swung her legs back and forth under her chair, her elbows propped up on the table. Grape jelly oozed out from the edges of her sandwich and dripped down from the corners of her mouth.

Nathaniel wished there was a clock so he could tell what time it was. Not that it would help; he didn't know how long he had been here. It seemed like forever. He glanced toward the blank wall for the hundredth time, waiting for it to yawn open and the Nightmare Man to come in.

Whenever the door appeared this time, Nathaniel decided, he was going to run for it and try to get out. If he could just get out of this room, maybe he could go home.

The moss-colored dog lifted its shaggy head. Its ears perked forward, and a low whine caught in its throat. The little girl turned around in her seat and smiled widely; her mouth was stained purple from jelly. Nathaniel jumped to his feet.

The doorway appeared in the wall, gaping open like a hole in stretched-out play dough. The Nightmare Man appeared in the doorway, filling it with his cloak. Nathaniel ran for it, ducking his head low. A second figure came into view, stepping into the room; it was a tall knight, dressed in silver-colored armor. It flickered and glowed around the edges the way the little girl did.

The two figures stepped inside. The doorway was open and empty.

Nathaniel tried to make it through the door before it closed. A skeletal hand caught the collar of his t-shirt and held him back. He strained against it, uselessly, and watched as the door closed inches away from his face. He tried to squirm out of his shirt, but got tangled in the sleeves. The wall sealed itself, and once more the wall was smooth and white.

"I brought you a friend," The Nightmare Man said in Nathaniel's mind.

The knight stood awkwardly, staring down at Nathaniel. His hands shook a little, and his gauntlets rattled. Nathaniel looked up at him, peeking from within the collar of his shirt. He looked familiar and generic at the same time, like a drawing in a storybook.

The little girl shoved the last bite of her sandwich into her mouth and smiled. She waved at the knight with sticky purple fingers and climbed down from her chair.

"Where am I?" The knight said, finally, looking around at the empty room.

"Among new friends," The Nightmare Man said, and let go of Nathaniel's collar, letting him slump to the floor like a marionette with cut strings. *"Samantha...look. Meet your new friend."*

* * *

Adrian wanted to sleep so that he could ignore the terrible nausea that crept over him every time he opened his eyes, but he was terrified that he might somehow fall off the wagon if he did. He considered asking Sonia to stop so that he could climb inside of the carriage itself, but he didn't know if they were being followed.

They seemed to be moving quickly. He dozed, intermittently, but always jerked awake. Whenever he chanced to open his eyes, nothing around him made much sense. It should have been night time, he thought. He was sure they hadn't spent the night in the dungeon, and he was equally sure that he hadn't slept that long on the carriage. And yet, no matter how many times he dozed and awoke, no darkness fell, no moon crept up into the sky. The sky itself faded from blue to grey, a flat, lifeless color. There didn't seem to be any clouds, just a solid blanket of grey haze that covered the sun and muted it down to a pale disc.

As they journeyed north, the path became darker, and Adrian realized that he could no longer see the sun at all. It was light out, but light in the pale grey way of a sky before a snow storm. The creaking sound of the carriage sounded muted, as though all of the sound had been dampened or muffled. Adrian gave up trying to doze. Whenever he closed his eyes, half-formed memories crowded into his thoughts and he forced himself to open his eyes again. He thought about Nathaniel, and the Nightmare Man, and tried to think of what he would do if he couldn't find them after all. He thought about other things, too, things that had been shaken loose in his memories by the queen's invasive touch. He swallowed back his nausea and focused on the scenery as it passed by.

The carriage climbed up the jagged slope of foothills, climbing ever slowly higher as they approached the violet mountain peak. Although they were much closer to the mountain than they had been before, it still appeared as purple as it had from a great distance.

"We'll have to leave the carriage soon," Sonia said, glancing at him sideways to see if he was awake. In the distance up ahead, the path passed through an archway in a large stone wall that seemed to mark some sort of boundary. The opposite side was darker and shadowy. "And go the rest of the way on foot. It's too dangerous…we'll draw too much attention."

"Attention?"

"From the mountain folk," she said. "Hopefully we creep past them and make it to the gate by sundown." She glanced at the sky, looking where the sun should be if it weren't hidden behind a thick layer of cottony gray sky. "We should make it, I think."

He wondered how she could possibly know that the sun was going down or could even tell that it had, considering the strange quality of the sky overhead. Then again, Sonia had always been able to sense the oncoming Darkness despite the strangely arbitrary length of days in Dreamland. "Why are we avoiding the mountain folk?"

"They live on nightmare energy," she said. "Monsters, I guess you'd call them. Their dreams are dark and twisted and they live on fear. Faeries who try to use nightmare energy…it doesn't work right. It hurts them."

Adrian remembered the Queen, the way she had clutched her head as though it were splitting open when she had tasted his own nightmares. It served her right.

"Anyway. They're not…very friendly to intruders in their territory."

As they climbed the foothills, following the winding path up toward the purple peak, the tree cover became sparser but the atmosphere became darker. The sky was no longer the reflective white of fresh snow; it was thick and black and stormy, the angry sky that preceded tornado weather and hail. Mist seemed to curl up from the ground in places, wrapping in tendrils around stones, moving constantly despite the stillness of the air. Occasionally Adrian caught a flicker of something creeping out of the mist, but when he looked again it was gone.

"The Darkness is thick here," Sonia said. She followed his gaze over the misty landscape. "It never goes away completely."

Adrian nodded and reflexively scooted closer to her on the bench. It felt safe here, on the carriage. He was afraid of what would happen when they needed to abandon it and walk on the misty ground.

The gateway loomed ahead of them, set at the foot of the path: a massive twenty-foot stone archway that seemed to have been carved from a small mountain itself. Moss grew up its sides, and the stone was weathered and chipped away in places. No door or gate barred the passage through the arch, but the other side of the archway seemed dark and fuzzy, as though obfuscated by a thick fog.

"Well," Sonia said, bracingly, "this is it."

The carriage shuddered to a halt. It quivered, slightly, and Adrian wondered if it was afraid. He found that he didn't want to get off; he wanted to turn around and go somewhere else. Anywhere else. He couldn't explain exactly why, but the arch filled him with sudden and terrible dread. Sonia climbed down from the carriage, and Adrian reluctantly followed.

"Do we have to go through it?" There was no reason not to go around; no walls, no fences, no cliffs barring their progress. He could see the mountain clearly past the arch, but through the doorway he could only see the thick obfuscating fog. They stood together in its shadow, inches from the opening, and Adrian peered into the nothingness.

"We do," she said, grimly. "It's…just one of those things." She smiled apologetically and reached for his hand.

Her hand gave his a little squeeze, and he swallowed back the sudden fear that had crept up into his throat.

He squeezed her hand back and together they passed through the arch.

A MEMORY OF LEAVES

It was as though he had gone blind. His feet moved forward, stumbling blindly through the archway, but he saw none of the path before him. A cold dampness pressed all around him, a curtain of fog that seemed almost liquid as it washed over him. His breath caught in his lungs, and he heard his heart beating loudly in his ears. Sonia's hand clenched his, but his fingers felt as though they were a mile away, connected to another body.

Then, suddenly, the fog lifted and a world materialized around him in full, vibrant detail. But it wasn't a mountain path that he stepped out onto. It was a suburban lawn, more than twenty years ago, preserved in time. A white three-bedroom house, a lawn bisected by a narrow patch of driveway, a single-car garage, twin old trees rising up at the corners of the yard. The sun beat down overhead, rich golden afternoon light, and he could smell the damp, sweet odor of decaying leaves. He heard an echo of a child's laugh.

No, he thought. *No, please. Not this. I'm not ready yet.*

He wasn't asleep, so he couldn't awaken from the dream. He tried to cry out, but his throat tightened uselessly as though choking on the words. He tried to turn away, to twist out of Sonia's grasp and run back through the arch, but he had no control over his feet. They propelled him forward agonizingly slowly, moving at the speed of a moving sidewalk, thrusting him into the memory. It washed over him, consumed him. He watched it from above as well as from within, seeing it from every angle as though his own thoughts had been amplified and projected like a film onto the world.

He was seven years old.

William was nine. They were at home, playing in the front yard, enjoying the last lingering hours of sunlight of the late autumn afternoon. The shadows stretched long over the driveway, cast deep wells of blackness behind the shrubs. The lawn, which lay along either side of the driveway, had turned yellow-brown. The grass was yellower and browner on the right side, the side nearest the garage, because sometimes Daddy parked his truck there to keep the driveway clear. Each patch of lawn had a large pile of freshly-raked leaves piled in it, a small red-yellow-gold mountain that mouldered in the sun. The boys had helped their father rake them up that morning, but they didn't have any trash bags to put them in. "Doesn't matter," Daddy had said. "I'll go pick some up."

Then, because it made the boys laugh, he had made a point of backing out over the freshly-raked pile of leaves when he left. The leaves scattered, flying up into the air and falling like confetti to the grass. They fluttered slightly, and were still. William and Adrian both laughed, not least because they knew Mommy was watching with pursed lips, disapproving on principle of the undoing of hard work. Making a mess was rebellion. Daddy waved and smiled and pulled out into the road.

The boys raked the leaf-pile back up at their mother's orders. It stood now where it had before, maybe even better than it had been. They were pleased.

Samantha was outside with them. She was wore her new jumper and was busy picking up leaves that had strayed from the lawn-piles and placing them carefully on top of the pile. Each time she finished this, she would giggle unnecessarily and look back at the boys, as though seeking approval.

William sat in the Y of the large tree in their front yard. He leaned back against the rough bark of the tree, his feet against the opposite limb, lounging without care or concern, the utter image of composure. Adrian wanted up, too, and he stood at the foot of the tree and tried to find a way up. He was too small, and couldn't find a place to put his feet. His hands were sore and raw from constantly slipping on the rough bark. Samantha came to stand beside him and tried to climb up, too; she stood on her toes and jumped, miming her big brother's attempt to climb the tree. Her blonde curls tumbled around her cheeks. Adrian felt anger well up in him, anger that was too big for him, and it twisted and burned inside of his chest.

"Let's play a game," he said, pulling away from the tree. He felt a reckless, desperate need to prove himself. He needed to prove something to William, to the whole world, and although he couldn't find the words for what he needed to prove, he felt its necessity, and it was enough. The anger in him was dancing wildly with his shame, and made him want to do something impressive. "Come on, William. Come play with us."

"What do you want to play?" William sat up, pulling a twig closer to him. He snapped it from the tree and began to strip it of its bark with his fingers.

At the base of the tree, Samantha's eyes locked on the object in William's hands, and after a moment she knelt down and picked up a small, dry twig from the ground, and tried to peel the bark off of it. The twig snapped in half, but she didn't seem to care.

Adrian wanted to slap her. He wanted to push her, and make her fall down and get dirt all over her clean new jumper. He wanted to take the twig away from her. "Let's play hide and seek," he said. He looked up at William, and wondered if his brother could see the raging monster behind his eyes.

"Yah! Hide-go-seek!" Samantha wriggled in excitement, her face erupting into a wide, beautiful smile.

"You don't know how to play hide and seek," William said, matter-of-factly, to Samantha. He looked at Adrian, his eyes narrowed, shrewd, and Adrian was afraid that William could look straight through him, that he had seen through his plan already. William was, after all, the smartest person Adrian had ever met (except for their dad), and surely he would see right through him to the monster inside. But if he saw anything, he did not say it, and instead he frowned a little. "We can't play hide and seek with her. She's just a baby, she won't understand the rules."

"Am not!" Samantha protested. "Not a baby." She thrust out her lower lip in an aggravated pout, and held up three fingers. "I'm this many."

"We can teach her how to play," Adrian said. "It's easy. You want to play with us, right Samantha?"

She nodded enthusiastically.

"See? She wants to play."

William gave Adrian an uncertain, reproving look, and Adrian stood firm.

They stared at each other a moment and William shrugged, leaping down from his perch with all the cool suaveness of a cat. "Fine. But you have to teach her the rules. I'll be it, and you two can hide."

"Okay." Adrian nodded, and the beast in his chest purred. "Okay, yeah. Come on Samantha, let me show you."

William rested his forearms to the tree trunk, and buried his face in them, and started counting aloud. Adrian took Samantha by the hand; she dropped the stick she had been playing with, and he led her quietly to the hedge, whispering insistent directions to her.

"He's going to try to find us," he said, his voice low. "Because he's it."

"What's it?"

"It. The person who's it." Adrian's hand tightened around Samantha's, betraying his frustration. "You're stupid. It means the person who looks for everybody else. Understand?"

"Not stupid," Samantha replied, and tried to take her hand from his, but he tightened his grip and she stopped struggling.

"Whatever." Adrian flattened himself to the wall and squeezed in behind one of the thick hedges that grew along the side of the house, dragging Samantha in behind him. "So he's looking for us. And we have to hide. And the last person he finds — they get to be it, next time." He let go of Samantha's hand, and listened for William; he couldn't hear counting anymore. "You got it?"

"Okay."

She didn't understand, he thought; she couldn't possibly understand, because she was far too young and way too stupid. But it didn't matter, because he wanted her to be bad at the game. He wanted her to lose, over and over. Thinking about that made him smile, a fierce kind of smile full of teeth and anger.

They played a few rounds of hide-and-seek. Adrian discovered, quickly, that Samantha made her hiding places obvious by choosing to hide exactly where her brother had hidden last time: Wherever Adrian or William had been, the previous round, would be Samantha's hiding place this round, without fail. As Adrian had hoped, Samantha was terrible at hide-and-seek, but it didn't make him feel better at all. In fact, it made him feel worse.

"Hey, William," Adrian whispered, grabbing William's hand and pulling him close; Adrian was at the tree, where he would be "it" this turn, and Samantha had already toddled away to hide even though he hadn't started counting yet. "I have a fun idea."

"Yeah?" William looked skeptical. Adrian's fun ideas tended to be lame, and both of them knew it.

"Let's not find Samantha this time." Adrian's face was flush with excitement. It felt naughty, what he was about to do — it felt like a very bad thing to do, and that filled him with excitement. He didn't do Bad Things very often. Not nearly as often as he thought about them. "Let's leave her hiding."

"Why?" William asked, but there was a devilish hint of a smile on his lips and eyes.

"We'll pretend we don't know where she is. And we give up. And then she'll be there hiding, and then we won't have to play with her anymore. Because she'll still be hiding." He smiled. The monster in his chest purred louder.

"Sounds good," William said, and gave Adrian a high-five, and Adrian's heart swelled with pride and acceptance.

"She's in the leaf pile," Adrian said, out of the corner of his mouth. "I know she is, because I hid there last time."

William nodded, and the two parted ways and started searching everywhere else in the yard. They made a big show of it, peeking behind hedges, turning over rocks. The leaf pile giggled, and both boys ignored it.

"This is too hard," William said, in a loud stage voice as he stood in the middle of the driveway turning in a slow circle. "Samantha just disappeared!"

"She's not hiding *anywhere*," Adrian said, in an equally loud stage voice. "She's too good at hide and seek for us. We'd better give up."

The leaf pile giggled again, and shook a little.

Up the road, the rumbling of a diesel engine broke the sleepy silence of the neighborhood. A familiar silver truck appeared, coming around the corner, moving smoothly up the road to the house.

Daddy turned into the driveway.

Adrian realized, too late, what was about to happen. There was nothing he could do. He screamed, but Daddy couldn't hear him over the rumbling of his truck engine.

Daddy revved the engine. The truck jumped forward, over the driveway, driving at an angle toward the lawn nearest the garage. The engine purred. The truck bore forward.

The truck thrust its blunt nose into the leaf-pile.

William dove forward to stop their father, but it was too late — too late, because the truck had plowed over the mound of leaves. The truck rocked as though it were going over a speed bump at too high a speed. Gold and orange and red flew up in the air, fluttering down around like dying butterflies.

And under the insistent rumble of the truck engine, Adrian heard another sound, a wet crunching sound like a watermelon being smashed.

"Boys?" Their father was out of the truck. The engine was still running. His door hung open. "Boys, what is it? What's wrong?"

Adrian was screaming, incoherently. William was standing, struck utterly still and dumb, his eyes locked on the undercarriage of the truck.

Mommy burst out the front door, yelling at both boys to stop screaming. She stopped, suddenly, staring shrewdly around the yard. "Where's Samantha?"

Neither of them could answer.

Their father stood stiffly, like he'd been caught in a game of freeze-tag. His eyes darted between the boys. "Where is your fucking sister?" But he knew. Already, he knew.

He got to his knees. He crawled under the truck. It was still running, its engine still roaring. The truck trembled, just slightly. Their father disappeared under it, and Adrian imagined the truck roaring to life and rolling backwards, taking their father with it, and he choked on his terror.

Their father reappeared cradling something small and broken against his chest. Adrian could just make out a blood-smeared new jumper, and a rumpled shape of something that wasn't — could not be — his sister.

Their mother screamed.

Adrian sobbed.

William stood, utterly still, frozen, wide-eyed and firm-jawed like a statue.

And their father cradled the broken, bloody something to his chest. "Call 911!" he called, desperately. "Somebody call the goddamn ambulance!"

Nobody moved.

THROUGH THE ARCHWAY

drian felt a piercing cold, first — a cold that burned. It washed over him as though his body had been blasted with liquid nitrogen, and he was certain that if he moved, his body would shatter. Then, just as soon as the cold had come, it was gone, replaced by a fuzzy emptiness that spread over him, a numbness like the tingle of a sleeping limb. His vision faded, replaced first by darkness, and for a moment there was nothing: no pain, no sensation, no thought. Then he broke through the opposite side of the doorway, like breaking through water, and he fell forward, his legs suddenly refusing to hold him upright.

He felt the hard, rocky ground beneath his knees, the pebbles biting through the fabric of his trousers. His hand held the memory of something soft and warm, and he groped for it, aching for what had been lost. A rushing sound filled his ears, and nausea welled up in him. With effort, he forced it back. He wasn't sure if his eyes were open or closed: no matter what he could, he could see traces of memory, of fluttering leaves, golden ringlets matted with blood.

The rushing in his ears subsided, and he began to make out words from it. He tried to make sense of them. He felt something touch his arm. He reached for it, hoping for Sonia's hand, but his fingers brushed against something slimy and cold, like the inside of an oyster. He drew back his hands, repulsed, but felt the slime cling to his fingertips. Something many-legged skittered over his leg.

"Sonia?" He gasped. His arms shook. He retched.

Something slithered against him. He felt warm breath on the back of his neck.

A pale blue light flared, then, in the distance — as though coming at him from a very long tunnel. It moved forward, growing in size and intensity as it rushed forth. In the approaching blue light, Adrian could make out dim shapes of small, hunched creatures, but he couldn't make them out clearly in the gloom. They moved together, a seething mass, scampering away from the glowing light of the dream.

The dream galloped into view. It was a horse, a white horse with fur that was shiny like plastic; it circled him, its long mane and tail streaming behind. It looked exactly like a toy horse Samantha had, and he knew before he looked that she was sitting on its back, simultaneously three years old and older, grown-up, ageless.

The horse stopped, and Samantha looked down at Adrian, smiling. Her blue eyes glowed in the night, and light glinted off the golden hair that tumbled down her shoulders. The horse pawed at the ground with one great, plastic hoof, and then turned to gallop away, fading into the night. A dim blue haze hung over them, washing everything in faint light.

"Adrian?" Sonia stood, a few feet in front of him. She held an empty glass vial in her shaking hands. "Are you okay?"

He looked up at her, suddenly very aware that he was kneeling in his own vomit. His cheeks were damp with tears.

Sonia knelt across from him, green eyes burning with concern. "I'm so sorry. The Darkness fell just as we were crossing…and it's the thickest here… you always do so well, I didn't think —"

"It's okay," he said, thickly. Every word took effort. His arms trembled and threatened to give way, so he leaned back onto his heels. "I'm…fine." His eyes ticked to the vial she held in her hand.

"I took it from you," she said, guiltily. "I…it's the only one. I didn't sell any. It's just that this one…"

"So you knew," he said. "You've known, all along. About the dreams. About my sister."

"Not everything. But enough." She shrugged, grimacing as though expecting him to lash out at her. "You…you cry out. At night."

He keeled over sideways, then. Somehow, Sonia was beside him, catching him, holding him against her bosom. He didn't cry, but he shivered uncontrollably, and wondered what would have happened to him if Sonia hadn't kept his stolen dream.

* * *

Rosalie awoke with a start. She didn't know what had woken her; a sound, perhaps, or a sudden absence of sound. She hadn't remembered falling asleep, and she looked around, disoriented, trying to get her bearings. Where was she? Why was she outside? What was this warm jug of dreamstuff doing in her arms?

Then she remembered.

She sat up, her joints creaking from the cold of sleeping on the hard earth. No one had found them yet. That was a good sign, she guessed, but it disappointed her too. If they hadn't been caught, it meant that they would need to travel more today, and she wasn't sure she could handle any more running. Her legs ached. Her feet hurt. She had no idea where they were or where they were going or what Lorelai planned to do to her when they got there.

Nearby, resting in the shade of a towering elm, was a carriage with spindly legs and a dark, hunched body. Lorelai's carriage.

Rosalie's brow furrowed. Hadn't it been missing when they left? Had it run away?

The carriage lay quiet and still, and Rosalie crept to her feet, edging away from it, suddenly uneasy. Where was Lorelai? Rosalie didn't see her anywhere in the woods. She wondered if she was in the carriage, and decided she'd rather not find out.

If she left now, she thought, perhaps she could slip away before Lorelai found out. She would have to go into hiding, of course. Maybe she would live out on the border, tend to the addled-minded adults and harvest their dreams. Her mother had always wanted her to do that, anyway. Her mother had never approved of The Swaggering Spider, and until recently Rosalie had never been able to figure out exactly why. The patrons weren't so bad. Sure, occasionally one of the northern folk would get rough with her, but they paid well enough. Occasionally a feral dream — a real, corporeal dream — would arrive, and if Lorelai was feeling generous, everyone would get to enjoy it before she had her fill.

But when dreams entered Lorelai's private chambers, they never returned.

Rosalie started into the trees, still absently clutching the jug of dreams to her chest. Maybe she could catch up with the human, if he'd managed to escape, and she could apologize for helping Lorelai, and he could forgive her, and the two of them could go and live on the border. She'd take good care of him. She would have taken good care of the dreams, too, if she'd had the chance. Rosalie wasn't like Lorelai; she didn't ache for power or riches. She would never destroy something to consume it. She'd just have to show the human how gentle she could be. They'd gotten off on bad footing, but they could make it up. He would understand. She smiled, and stepped off the path.

She stopped, suddenly, caught fast as though the air around her had grown solid, as though she were a fly that had unwittingly flown directly into the invisible net of a large, hungry spider. She tried to move, to tug herself free, but she was completely immobilized. She trembled, deep inside, a feeling of cold dread spreading through her.

"Trying to sneak away?" Lorelai asked.

Rosalie whimpered. She hadn't heard the carriage door open, hadn't heard footsteps on the ground. "N-no," she stammered, and tried to pull herself out of the sticky air that had engulfed her.

"Evidence suggests otherwise," Lorelai said, and now her voice was in her ear, and her hand upon her back. Her face, inches away from Rosalie's, was contorted and beastly with rage. "Where did you think you would go, Rosalie?"

"I wasn't —" she stammered, and Lorelai gripped her right wing at the shoulder, twisting it painfully to the side. "I...I was looking for you!"

"You're lying!" Lorelai jerked, and the wing tore off in her hand.

Rosalie screamed. Blood spattered down her back, staining her blouse.

Her shoulder burned.

Lorelai held up the torn wing, limp and tattered like a bit of scrap fabric, and shook it in Rosalie's face. "Shall I take the other one?" She asked. There was nothing beautiful, or even faerie-like, in her features now; she looked like a harpy, or a gorgon, or one of the other nightmare tribes from the north. "What did you think? Were you going to creep away — run back to the castle, perhaps — try to sell me out for a pat on the head?"

Rosalie whimpered. "N-no, I swear! I didn't — I'd never —"

Lorelai tore off the other wing.

The pain seared through her, nauseating, burning, blinding. She felt the hot stickiness of blood drenching her back, soaking through her blouse, and she was powerless to do anything about it. She felt an awful vulnerability spread over her, as though all of her clothing had been torn off, as though she had been laid bare.

"Pathetic," Lorelai said, shaking her head. "After everything I've done for you — the job I gave you, the home I provided...."

Rosalie wanted to say something to defend herself, but she couldn't think through the searing white pain that had consumed her thoughts. The air around her began to shudder. The invisible web gave a great heave and threw her away from the trees; she stumbled, unable to keep her footing, and fell into a heap among a bed of pine needles. She curled into a ball, blood-stained and shivering, and sobbed.

Lorelai crossed the clearing and nudged Rosalie onto her back with the toe of one pointed boot, forcing her to look up into her face. Her skin, usually smooth and clear, hung loose and grey around her mouth and eyes. Her eyes widened, and she lifted a gnarled hand to clutch at her chest, clawing at her breast with yellowing nails. She made an awful choking sound, the sound of a vulture with a bone caught in its throat. Rosalie had one sick, hopeful thought that she was dying — that her heart had seized in her chest, that she would fall over and twitch and lay still and this nightmare would end — but then Lorelai recovered. She bent low over the bleeding faerie and extended a wrinkled old-lady's hand, prying apart Rosalie's hands.

Rosalie had almost forgotten about the dreamstuff still clutched in her arms.

"This is mine," Lorelai rasped. She snatched the jug away and withdrew, clawing it open with shaking fingers. She tipped her head back and poured the dream into her mouth, drinking it in, the whole jug in one long hungry gulp. As the dreamstuff poured into her it seemed also to swirl around her, to engulf her. She stood for a moment, utterly illuminated, and then the light faded. She was almost — but not quite — herself again. Her skin was still wrinkled at the corners of her eyes, and dark spots marred her skin. She looked down at the empty jug, curling her lip, and tossed it aside.

Her cold eyes darted to Rosalie, lying bloody and shivering in the pine needles. She raised her hand, extending it before her, and clenched it suddenly into a tight fist. Power flowed through her. Rosalie made a terrible wet choking sound, as though she were being crushed, and Lorelai turned without a word to climb back onto her carriage, leaving the bar-maid alone to die under the trees.

Lorelai climbed into the front seat of her carriage, seeking it out with her mind and the dream energy that flowed through her veins. She spoke to it, inside of her mind, and it spoke back in whispers and images and dreams — and what strange things it told her.

The human and the dream-harvester. The great purple peak. A doorway that would lead to every doorway. And a dream…a dream that had been stealing other dreams from the queen's own courtyard. Dreams that were, strictly speaking, no longer anyone's property.

A smile tugged at Lorelai's lips. Take me there, she whispered in her mind, and the carriage obeyed.

THE GATEKEEPER

By morning, Adrian had collected himself somewhat. He hadn't slept most of the night, but lay curled up in a shivering ball with his head in Sonia's lap, desperately ashamed of himself but unable to do anything about it. The pale glow of the dream-trail faded sometime around dawn, replaced by soft grey light as the sun began to rise around the curve of the peak at whose feet he lay. In the light, Adrian saw the full glory of the mountain. It was as vibrantly purple up close as it had been from a distance. It appeared to have been carved from an enormous chunk of amethyst, all smooth sides and sharp angles. A single path was carved in a jagged line up the mountainside, made up of thousands of stairs, each barely wide enough for two people to walk abreast.

"Can you walk?" Sonia asked him at last, looking at him gingerly the way one approaches the seriously ill. "We can wait, if you need, but…I think we'd best try to make it to the top by sundown. I don't want…"

He shook his head. He didn't want her to finish the thought. The idea of being clutched by the Darkness halfway up the mountainside was too terrible to consider. "I'm fine. Let's go."

Sonia bit her lower lip, her eyes glinting with concern, wings held high and nervous at her shoulders. He wasn't fine. That much was obvious. He still felt shaky and empty inside. He stank of fear and vomit and he was desperately ashamed. He wanted a shower more than he had ever wanted one in his life. But he could walk, and that would have to be good enough.

If they were right, it would all be over soon.

"If you want to talk about —" Sonia started, tentatively.

"I don't," he said, a little too quickly. "I just…it's a long walk." He followed the stairway with his eyes. It faded from sight, a hundred feet up, and continued to wind up forever to the very apex of the gleaming purple mountain. The smooth stone of the peak had been carved as though by giants into a building, a rough-hewn castle chiseled directly out of the stone. Grass grew in soil that must have been imported, the only living thing on the cold purple face of the mountain; stairs, uneven and crumbling in places, grew in a strange mismatch up the side of the building. At its pinnacle, thin white clouds covered a black, star-lit sky like scant hairs on a balding head; up there, the air was thin and it was night all the time. "…So, this Gatekeeper guy. What is he, anyway? A faerie, or a dream or…?"

"A little of both, maybe," Sonia said, shrugging. "If you use dreams enough, they poison you. You lose yourself in them. The power is great…but the consequences are irreversible."

As he made the laborious ascent up the mountain, Adrian was grateful for his years of running. Out of habit, he counted his steps and focused on his breathing. Normally this had the effect of clearing his mind, of sweeping stray thoughts into their associated mental file-cabinets and locked trunks so he could face his day. Today, it seemed to have the opposite effect. There were no more locked doors left anywhere in his mind. His thoughts and memories kept interrupting themselves, rolling over each other like waves in rough seas.

He thought about going home. He thought of the stacks of mail he would need to sort through from his overflowing mailbox.

Stacks of mail fluttering to the carpet like falling leaves.

He wondered if anyone was looking for him. Maybe there was a news story being circulated now: Social worker disappears while searching for missing child. *People would have a heyday with that, wouldn't they?*

Mom started drinking heavily around Christmas. He remembered the first time he found her passed out drunk on the couch, a hard crust of drool on her cheek. He'd thought she was dead, at first, dead like Samantha, and that too would have been his fault. That was the moment the realization hit him with unsettling force, like a sledgehammer to his gut: Everything bad that happened was his fault. Anything bad that happened from now on, that spun out from that one awful afternoon, would all be his responsibility, forever. He started to cry, and even after he saw her move, knew that she was alive, he couldn't stop.

He wondered if Jessica was worried about him. Maybe she came to his house, peeked in all of his windows, trying to see if he was okay.

"Who is she?" Jessica had asked, when he awoke one morning, shortly after they had started sleeping together.

"Who?"

"Samantha. You kept saying her name in your sleep."

He shrugged. "I don't know anybody named Samantha."

His legs burned. His breath came in fast, harsh pants. He chanced a glance down, over the edge of the stairs, and immediately regretted it: The world fell away beneath him in a sheer, steep drop. He couldn't see the ground anymore. Hurriedly, he looked back up, focused on Sonia's fluttering wings, on the path ahead of them.

The Nightmare Man, his eyes gaping pools of emptiness, his gnashing teeth. His long, bony finger curling back toward his skeletal palm, beckoning Adrian into the dark…

Maybe Nathaniel's been found, he thought, feebly. *Maybe he wasn't really taken here at all.*

"There's a difference between helping kids and wanting to be a superhero, Adrian!" Jessica said. "You have to accept that sometimes, you can't save them. That's just part of the job."

He thought about the Nightmare Man. He wondered why his own nightmare would kidnap a child, why he was stealing dreams. That was the part that still didn't make any sense to him. Yet he was so sure of it. He had felt him here, in the castle. Not the lingering residue of a relived memory, but the real thing. But why?

And why did he trust that feeling, anyway? Why, when he had been so deliriously certain of that other thing, the thought that he couldn't bear to hold because it burned him when he came too close? It couldn't be true. It couldn't be. People didn't come back from the dead.

And there weren't any faeries. Or unicorns.

He has her. She's here.

No sooner had he thought this than the stairs before him opened up onto a wide landing. Sonia stepped over onto it and glanced back at him, brows raised slightly, and he met her gaze with equal puzzlement. He could have sworn there were at least a hundred more stairs to go the last time he'd looked.

"Sonia…" he said, as he climbed onto the landing beside her, gazing at the castle's entry way. The door, fitted into a huge gash in the stone, seemed to have been carved from half of an entire redwood tree.

Sonia raised her hand at the door. There was no knocker, no embellished lion's heads with rings in their mouths. Instead, she reached up for a rope that hung at the door, and gripped it hard in two hands, and gave it a heavy pull.

A series of bells erupted from inside, echoing off the smooth walls, resounding deeply in the mountain. Deep, low brass bells and smaller, tinkling silver bells, all chiming in a cacophony of noise like a castle full of clocks all striking noon. After a while, the tolling of the bells subsided, and the castle, quite apart from being silent, was filled with another sound. Adrian recognized it, vaguely, tangentially, as the sound an old-fashioned music box makes, the sound inside clocktowers and old machines.

The door swung open and they stepped inside.

The inside was smooth-polished stone and decorated with brightly-woven tapestries and rugs. Torches burned in wrought-iron holders on the walls, and the light of the fire made the purple stone of the walls glow unnaturally, giving the room a violet haze. The rug under his feet was a single, impossibly long stretch of brightly-woven fabric that led him forward down a long corridor. Other halls branched away, small tunnels that led into dark passageways and, presumably, rooms beyond.

His eyes slid form one tapestry to the next, realizing that they told a story.

A figure, tall and skeletally thin with a mouth round and full of sharp teeth, stared down at him from the walls with wide white-blank eyes. Children, fair-haired and bright eyed, gathered around him, gazing up with expressions of adoration, or excitement, or hope. In successive tapestries, the figure led the children to a hidden place, in a mountainside, and they disappeared in the heart of a mountain and clustered in darkness — and then, in the next panel, emerged in the dazzling sunlight of another world, one filled with magic, and hope, and beauty. Perhaps it was the flickering of the torchlight, but they seemed to move, somehow; the subtle inclination of a head, the twitch of a finger, the bat of an eyelash.

"The Nightmare Man," he said, finally, tearing his eyes away from the tapestries. "He's…he's my dream. That's what the queen saw when she tried to do…whatever…to me. I…I made him."

"You weren't the only one."

"I — what?"

"He's your dream because you are the one in Dreamland," Sonia responded. Her voice sounded tired and strained. "If you were someone else, the dream would be different. The tapestry — the stories — the thief. They would be someone else's dreams."

"So if someone else came looking for Nathaniel…the Nightmare Man would be someone else."

She nodded. "Maybe. Or maybe no one else could have come looking at all, or they'd come looking for someone else." Her wings buzzed uncomfortably. "One thing…can be different things, also, to different people. Is it not that way where you come from?"

He thought he understood.

The hallway ended, coming abruptly upon another set of stairs.

As he climbed, he wasn't sure if it was weariness creeping into his legs, or the rapidly thinning atmosphere, or another factor entirely — but each successive step was harder, as though he were being pushed back, as though he were walking first through water and then, as he made it further up the staircase, through mud, and then tar. He realized his head was bent down and he was straining, with everything he had, to move at all, as the air around him pressed in heavily with a weight he could not attribute to any physical feature.

"Time," Sonia said, beside him, and her voice was both faraway and intimate, like a shout that had been robbed of its voice. "The collusion of time and space and pathways to Everywhere."

He wanted to ask exactly what that meant, but found he didn't have enough breath inside of him to do it.

Finally, after what could have been an eternity of struggle — but, Adrian realized, as he cast an unwise glance over his shoulder at the thousands of stairs he seemed to have climbed, it didn't seem like it had taken as long as it should — they reached a plateau He no longer felt as though he were swimming in tar. Instead, the air was alive and crackling with energy, like live electricity moving through the atmosphere, like he was on the inside of one of those lightning balls they sell at novelty stores on shelves alongside lava lamps and beaded curtains.

All around him, there were tiny paintings, each depicting a different scene in miniature. These were connected, like the spokes of a wheel, like the crossed lines of a massive spiderweb, by bridges to the enormous dais they now found themselves upon. He wondered why anyone would paint such tiny pictures, and why there were bridges to go see them, and then he realized that the pictures were moving, and — he squinted, to see clearer — that the pictures were, in truth, windows, doorways to different destinations. They weren't tiny; they were far away, distant by hundreds of yards, possibly miles, stretching out forever into infinity, and he realized, after he saw this, that the walls around him were no longer polished purple stone but empty, vast space. He realized that, all around him, stars were dancing and clouds were swirling in a fog of black and purple and dark blue.

He felt very dizzy, all of a sudden, and swayed on his feet. A delicate hand caught his arm and held him upright, and he could feel himself tremble now that he had a solid, stable body to compare himself to.

"I have foreseen your coming, as I see all things," a voice said, from everywhere at once, and Adrian jumped, "and I offer you whatever welcome I can."

Adrian's eyes landed, after a moment of searching, on the speaker, and he discovered that, after all he had seen, he was still capable of being surprised.

Adrian remembered how, when he was a child, there was a particular spider that had always fascinated him. It lived in the cracks and crevices of his bedroom walls, and had a peculiar appearance, both frightening and somehow loveable — it was a brownish grey color, as he remembered, and had a face with two large eyes and white hairs, like a bespectacled, blind old man with a beard.

Now he was staring into the face of a person who looked remarkably like that spider — or, perhaps, at a giant spider that looked exceptionally like a human. The figure was old and bent over, hunchbacked by time or disfigurement. His stomach hung, distended like the overlarge belly of a starving child, between two thin, spindling legs. The hunch in his back was large, and his head hung down against his chest, his thin shoulders rounded. His skin was a grayish brown color, and every fine hair on his body was white, standing out in glistening bristles against the darkness of his flesh. His head was totally bald, but he had a full, wiry beard of white bristles. His eyes were hidden behind thick black spectacles and Adrian wondered if he really had eyes at all.

"It's all right," Sonia said, reaching out to take Adrian's hand. "He's going to help us, remember?"

"My presence alarms you," the spider-man, the Gatekeeper, said in a voice that was neither deep nor booming but still somehow managed to fill the room — if a dais in the void of space could be considered a room. "I apologize."

Adrian wanted to tell him not to apologize, but he discovered he still had no words. Part of him believed that if he opened his mouth, whatever oxygen was in his lungs would escape and he would be depressurized and lost to the infinity of space.

"You have come to request something of me?" The Gatekeeper pressed, and he moved forward in an uncomfortable swaying, scuttling motion. He stopped before Adrian, and fixed black eyes on him, reaching out a thin hand with sagging, grey flesh to touch Adrian's cheek with one skeletal finger. His touch felt like the dried-out shell of a dead moth brushed against his skin. "Ask me your favor, so I might grant it."

"He wants to go home," Sonia said, quickly, before Adrian could speak.

The Gatekeeper smiled; his thin lips were barely visible through the scruff of his white beard. He stood uncomfortably close to Adrian, whose heart was thudding hard enough that he was afraid the Gatekeeper could hear him.

"I — what? No, I don't —"

The Gatekeeper withdrew his hand from Adrian's cheek and reached up, into the air, closing his fingertips around a small, invisible thread. He gave this a long pull, hand-over-hand, as though operating an invisible pulley crafted from spidersilk. With each pull, one of the doorways came closer.

The doorway sped through the darkness, growing brighter and larger as it approached, and Adrian stared at it with morbid fascination. It stopped, a few feet from him, giant and glowing. He could smell car exhaust and fresh-cut grass. He could see his own house, vacant and wonderfully inviting, and — through the contraction of time and space, the special effects of perception, he could see his workplace, and his desk, and Angela Weaver's dilapidated farm house, and the woods that had shown him a portal to some Otherworld an eternity ago.

He reached out, as if to touch it, but felt only air, grasped only smoke, and the image before him rippled; he looked up, seeking with his eyes where the image had come from, and saw it reprinted in miniature far from him, and he understood. It was a hologram, a simulation, a tempting view — not the doorway itself.

"Is that it?" Sonia asked.

He saw Angela Weaver, sitting at her kitchen table, smoldering cigarette in one hand, can of cheap beer in the other; she was staring out the sliding glass door into her backyard with a look of emptiness and resignation. Nathaniel's discarded toys were still on the floor, coated with a fine layer of grey dust.

Adrian could see Jessica. She was in the shower, exquisitely naked, rivulets of water rushing down her body, outlining the supple curves and lines of her form. A man Adrian didn't know was standing behind her, also naked, soapsuds gathering in the short black hairs on his chest. The man tenderly lifted the hair from the nape of Jessica's neck and kissed it, a hand reaching around her, touching, caressing.

Adrian saw his desk, the papers neatly arranged, pens gathered neatly in their holder, the handwriting on his legal pad small and immaculate. He could read the text on the legal pad, and made out the list of names, facts, coalesced data.

He could go home. He could walk through this door and it would all be over.

He shook his head and raised his eyes to meet the black spectacles of the Gatekeeper

"The tapestries, downstairs. The man in them — who is he?"

The Gatekeeper was silent for a moment, regarding Adrian with sightless, blank eyes, expressionless as buttons. He swayed back and forth on his spindling, improbable legs. He rubbed his beard, and it made the same dry rattling noise as dead leaves. "I do not answer questions," he said, at length. "I only open doors."

"You have to know who he is," Adrian pressed, and could hear a note of desperation in his voice. "You *have* to know."

"I open doors," the Gatekeeper repeated, firmly. "I can send you home. I am the only person who can."

"Adrian, please," Sonia said, beside him, in an insistent whisper; he heard the promise of tears just below the surface of her words. She groped for his hand. "They'll destroy you, Adrian. This place will tear you apart."

He looked back to his house in the door. After everything — all the nightmares — the Darkness — the cats and the journey and Lorelai and the queen and the impossibly long climb — he could go home.

He looked back at the Gatekeeper. He wished he could see what was behind the black glasses: the blank, expressionless face did not fill him with confidence. Legs shaking, he walked past the spiderlike old man, toward the bridge. He could just cross it, step through the door, and go home. It was that easy.

In the corner of his eye, something moved. It was another door, hung suspended in space. Although the image inside was small from distance, he could make it out with shocking clarity. There was a cave, rising up from the earth. Inside the mouth of the cave, he caught a flash of red hair…and a flash of gold. The sound of laughter pealed from the doorway, child's laughter, the kind that pierces and shrieks and carries across rooms. He ran for that bridge.

"Adrian, no!"

Sonia reached out for him, tried to stop him. Her fingers brushed his skin, but he didn't stop. Someone yelled something. His heart was thudding too loudly in his ears to make out what was said, and he didn't look back. He ran across the bridge. It creaked under his weight, swaying dangerously. For a moment, he thought it would flip over, throw him to his death on the stone floor a hundred feet below — but then he was over it, he was on solid ground again. He heard footsteps behind him, creaking on the suspended bridge, and felt someone approach from behind.

He threw himself through the open doorway.

THE WITCH

I f Lorelai never climbed another stair in her life, it would be too soon. The terrible ache in her chest, centered above her heart, grew in intensity with each step. It felt as though something were gaping and rotten within her. She trembled. Her wings fell, tired and limp, over her shoulders, and her long hair felt as though it weighed a thousand pounds.

The dreams were wearing off already. The more she ate, it seemed, the shorter they lasted. If she had been at full strength, she could have flown up the steps. *Oh well*, she thought, holding her head down and pulling herself forward out of sheer determination. *Soon enough, it won't matter. You'll have all the dreams you need.*

There were tapestries on the walls, but they were heavily moth-eaten and smoke-damaged. She paid them no heed and continued climbing.

At some point, the sky overhead opened into space. She stood, shaking, on the solid stone platform and sought out the Gatekeeper. He was crouched in the center of the stone, hunched up like a spider in its web, his distended belly sweeping the ground.

He lifted his head, staring at her from behind the glasses over his blank dark eyes. His bristly white beard twitched with a smile. "So you've finally come."

Lorelai was in no mood for games. "I'm looking for the human," she said, approaching the center of the dais. All around, a thousand rope bridges led to a thousand tiny, glowing doorways. More hung over her head, dotting the sky like stars.

"No," the Gatekeeper said, with a soft smile. He scuttled closer, still crouched low to the ground. His bony knees were bare and knobby and tiny wisps of wings still hung limp from his shoulder blades. He had been a faerie, once, but the power of dreams crackled around him; Lorelai could almost smell it in his veins. "You're looking for the *dreams*."

"So it's true? They're really there?"

"You will not find what you seek here," the Gatekeeper said, raising his hands. He pulled at something invisible, as though tugging a thin strand of web through his fingertips. "You will not find it anywhere. You would be best to abandon your quest."

Lorelai laughed. "I didn't come for advice, old man. Show me the door and I'll leave without any trouble."

"You walk a dangerous path, child," he said.

"Not as dangerous as yours," she growled, losing her patience. The throbbing pain in her heart was overwhelming. It spread to her head, dimming her vision; the world began to swim around her. She struggled forward, standing close to the Gatekeeper. "You're just the same as me," Lorelai rasped, groping for him. Her fingertips brushed his dry, papery skin and closed around his arm. She could feel the power of dream energy in his veins, flowing just beneath the surface of the skin. "Don't tell me you're not."

He said nothing.

It happened quickly. She plunged her hand into his swollen, distended belly. His blood, warm and filled with dreams, flowed over her hand. It shimmered like an oil slick, prismatic and gleaming in the semi-darkness.

He laughed. A dry, shaky laugh that sounded like the rustle of dead corn stalks.

She closed drew his shriveled old body toward her with her free hand and buried her teeth in his neck and the laughing stopped.

When she was finished, she dropped what was left of the body. It fell to the ground, mostly deflated, as empty as the shed skin of an insect. She wiped her lips with the back of her hand and felt the glow of power within her. It was warm and filled her, pouring beneath her skin like a protective coating. Not just power — knowledge as well. It felt as though everything that anyone had ever known had been deposited into her mind, as wholly and simply as if she had received a gift.

She licked her lips.

Now...some business to attend to, she thought, with a twisted smile, and pulled on an invisible thread, feeling for it with the new power that coursed through her veins. The doorway sped closer, hurtling through space to stop at her feet.

Around her, the mountain shook. Bridges rattled, and great stones broke free of the mountain and began to crumble. The Gatekeeper's magic had died with him, and doorways began to open and close at random. People and faeries and monsters ran, panicking, within the frames of the tiny windows to their worlds as the gates were torn asunder. Lorelai gave them no heed; it mattered little to her what happened now. The door she needed was open, and she entered even as the mountain crumbled behind her.

DARKNESS AT THE EDGE THE WORLD

Adrian stopped celebrating Halloween the year that Samantha died. He couldn't stomach scary movies or haunted houses. He didn't even like the candy. All of the joy had been leached out of the holiday for him and he mostly spent his Halloween nights holed up in his room.

Except for one time in college. He'd gone to a haunted house one Halloween, one that claimed to be the very image of Hell on earth. His friends had cajoled him into coming, and he had tried to be a good sport about it. Jessica had been there, before they'd started officially dating, and it was worth suffering through some stupid haunted house for the evening to be around her. He couldn't even really remember why he hated Halloween anymore, anyway.

At the time, he'd thought the execution was clever enough; if there were a Hell, he supposed, it would probably be something like that. The tour had led them through winding corridors set up in an old warehouse showing various scenes of costumed people being tortured. It was warm and smelled like gunpowder, and the crew that created it had built lots of clever special effects for fire and demonic laughter and anguished screaming.

Now, climbing to his feet on the other side of the portal, Adrian realized that the haunted house had been wrong. Hell wasn't like that at all.

This was Hell.

Sonia climbed to her feet beside him, dusting herself off. Her chest heaved with the effort of following him.

"You didn't have to follow me," Adrian said. "…But I'm glad you did."

She smiled shakily. "Where are we?"

It was strange having her be the one to ask him that question. It was stranger that he knew the answer to it. "The Darkness," he answered, starting forward. "Or…*my* Darkness, anyway."

It was dark, but bright also, as though the sun had been replaced by a giant blacklight bulb. Things flickered and glowed and shivered, shadows moving within shadows, blurs streaking through the sky. They were in a forest, but not *just* a forest. There were trees and asphalt and parts of living rooms and city parks and basements and cemeteries. There were filing cabinets and doorways and safes scattered among the trees. All of them were smashed and crumpled. It was like walking through the wreckage of the place he had once created for himself in his mind, the place that had been torn apart and laid bare.

"This is where you go? In the Dark?"

He nodded mutely. He started walking faster. He didn't want Sonia to see everything, but there was no way of shielding her from it. There was no way of shielding himself from it, either; it all seemed to be here whether his eyes were opened or closed.

People walked through the trees, sometimes clear and in-focus, sometimes blurry, sometimes mere flickering shadows. They spoke in voices like thunder and cracking twigs and screeching tires. It was like a dream, a hallucination — but it was real. Adrian knew that, if he knew nothing else: This was real, or at least as real as anything could be in Dreamland.

They walked down the path, or perhaps the path moved and they stood still, or maybe the world itself moved past them. Maybe all three at once. Pine needles and dead leaves crunched and whispered under his feet. The air smelled like diesel smoke and decay. The sky was black and empty and flickers of white smoke wound through trees and glowed in the sky and on the ground like low-lying fog.

William was there, standing in the middle of a patch of living room that stood between two trees. He was seventeen and his face was flushed with rage. He screamed at his stepfather, who stood behind a tree, just outside of Adrian's view. A few feet away, a young Adrian was sitting on a patch of cement in the hollow between the trees, clutching his knee; a young William stood next to him and jeered at his pain.

A truck ran, over and over, into a pile of leaves. Leaves rained down in a perpetual shower, fluttering in flashes of orange and gold.

Adrian's father, shirt soaked with blood, tears streaming down his cheeks, kneeled between the trees. He coddled a misshapen bundle in his arms that could never have been human.

A big shaggy dog ran across Adrian's path. It disappeared from view. Tires screeched, and a dog howled and screamed, and then it was silent.

Ahead, a truck — the same truck — drove into leaves — the same leaves.

Through all this Adrian walked, pulled unavoidably through his private house of horrors, his personal Hell on Earth. Dark things that were not memories or hallucinations crept through the undergrowth, hidden in the pale fog. He could hear them. They made a sound like termites chewing through a house, like rodents gnawing on wood.

Sonia said nothing. Tears fell, silently, down her cheeks, but she did not speak. She reached for Adrian's hand and he took it and gave it a squeeze. Gratitude surged through him — gratitude that she had followed him, that she could stand here now and ask nothing of him.

A creature scurried across the path. It looked like a rabbit, if rabbits had twelve legs and two mouths filled with teeth. It stopped, sitting back on gruesomely bloated haunches, and tilted its head at them. It had no eyes to speak of, but one mouth hung open with a long, mottled tongue lolling out; the other mouth chomped and slavered. It rubbed together three sets of clawed paws and its long ears swept forward, trained on the two of them.

Along the side of the road, more beasts turned their eyes toward them. They slithered out from logs and climbed down from trees and lined the path. They hissed and chittered and growled, but did not come any closer — not yet.

"Enough," Adrian said, moving to stand between Sonia and the creature in the path. His words sounded dull and muted, like the air was too thick to carry sound. His heart hammered in his chest, but he swallowed back his fear. All around him, his memories and nightmares played like the backdrop of some twisted play, but they didn't matter anymore. He was done being afraid of things he couldn't change. "The Darkness hasn't killed me yet," he said, more loudly. "And it won't."

The creatures laughed. They circled them, creeping up toward the edge of the path, but they did not approach him. The rabbit-beast before him snarled with both slavering mouths, but it did not come near.

Adrian squeezed Sonia's hand in his and took a bold step forward. "I've figured you little bastards out," Adrian said, with more bravado than he really felt, his fingers tightly laced with Sonia's. "You're not so scary. You just *want* me to be scared. You can't get close to me if I'm not, and if you can't get close then you can't do anything to me."

Behind him, Sonia let out an unintelligible whimper, but he didn't release her hand and didn't allow himself to share her fear. Rosalie had saved him from a creature in the Darkness, once, so he knew it wasn't impossible to do it again.

The creatures hissed. Adrian was just a few feet from the rabbit-beast now. He could see the pale things that writhed beneath its shadowy black fur — worms or maggots or something else entirely. It stood its ground, and Adrian held his breath against the stench as he came upon it without veering off course. Moments before impact, the creature vanished, dissipating into smoke with a screeching cry that echoed inside of Adrian's mind.

The world flickered and disappeared around him and it was only blackness and emptiness and, rising from the earth before him, the mouth of a cave.

Some primitive origin stories tell of great caves at the beginning of the world, a dark rocky womb from which the first people of history crawled from the earth. Standing there, Adrian thought this was exactly that kind of cave.

"I don't like this," Sonia said, quietly, but she didn't release his hand.

"Me, neither," he said, and walked toward it anyway.

The mouth stood above ground, turning a gaping maw towards the sky. It was at least eight feet tall at the opening. The inside was dark and black and a cold noxious wind blew out of it. It smelled like mildew and disease, like the sick-sweet smell of infection; it smelled like sour breath and dried blood and rotting fruit.

Hundreds of thousands of shadowy slimy things poured from it. They seethed and trembled and crawled and crept away from the cave, disappearing into the crevices of the world. Adrian hesitated just a moment, standing between a gaping, spewing crater and the sum total of all the misery in his life.

He went into the crater.

THE NIGHTMARE MAN REVISITED

Inside, the cave was damp and slimy.

Skittering creatures moved all around him, brushing him they spewed out into the world. He recoiled from their touch, but they didn't seem to care about him, continuing forth to crawl out of the cave entrance to infest the dark places of Dreamland. The cave walls were warm and wet, as though coated in blood; it felt like he was crawling into the body of something that was alive.

He tried to avoid the walls on every side, but he still found himself quickly coated in slime, like amniotic fluid from hell. He heard Sonia behind him; she was breathing heavily, her breath coming in short, frightened gasps that might have been sobs. He wanted to say something to her that would make her feel better, but there was nothing he could say that could make this any less horrifying than it was.

The climb down was mercifully short, and he felt a cool draft touch his face before the tunnel opened up on a wide, empty space. He slid forward and dropped down into a crouch, taking in deep breaths of the sweet, open air. Sonia dropped down beside him. He heard the heavy flutter of damp wings; muck splattered him as the wings shook off the film of grime that laid over them.

It was bright inside. That was the first thing he saw — it was brighter than it should have been, brighter than the inside of a cave could ever be. It took a moment for his eyes to adjust. At first, all he could see was white. It was as though he had fallen through the end of the world and landed on a blank sheet of paper that stretched out infinitely in each direction.

As his eyes adjusted, the room became visible. Or, perhaps, it was forming itself; perhaps some artist was sketching in the details of the room around him. The room around him grew more cluttered and crowded; it was too small to comfortably hold all of the things that it did. A table. Some chairs. An exact replica of the queen's castle in miniature. A huge dog with shaggy green fur.

A knight. A figure dressed in robes.

A wide-eyed, red-haired little boy.

And Samantha.

She wore her jumper. It was new and clean. Her mouth was stained purple from something — jello, maybe, or grape jelly. She was solid and beautiful, three-years-old and whole. She tilted her head, staring across the room at him.

"…Samantha?" At that moment, nothing mattered. The rest of the room was inconsequential. Nathaniel, The Nightmare Man, Valor the knight — he hardly realized they were there. He felt his heartbeat up in his throat and his chest ached as though something inside were straining to get out; his ears filled with a rushing sound. He couldn't think.

Samantha drew back shyly, hiding her face. The Nightmare Man extended his thin, skeletal arm and she ran to him, clutching to his legs and burying her face in the folds of his cloak. The knight stood perfectly still in the corner, like a decorative suit of armor, the shaggy dog at his feet.

She doesn't recognize me, Adrian thought, with tears burning the back of his eyes. *Why would she? It's been twenty-five years. .*

"…Mr. Montgomery?" Nathaniel said, uncertainly. He glanced between Adrian, who was soaked through in mud and slime, and Samantha, who was half-hiding behind The Nightmare Man and peering out at them with one large blue eye, then to Sonia. "Are you real? Or is this still make-believe?"

Adrian couldn't answer. His eyes were pinned on Samantha. She still clutched a handful of black robes in her small fists, but her eyes were fixed on him now with curiosity.

"I was wondering when you would come," The Nightmare Man said in a voice that made no sound but echoed in his mind. *"We've been waiting for you for*

so long."

"Are you new friend?" she asked, finally, uncertainly.

"We'll be your friends," Sonia said, kindly. She dropped down to her knees, so that she would be at eye level with her, and smiled. "You don't have to be frightened. What's your name?"

Adrian tried to make his brain work. *This isn't real,* he thought. *She's dead.*

"Samantha," she said, shyly, without loosening her grasp on The Nightmare Man's cloak.

Unicorns aren't real, either. Faeries aren't real. Monsters aren't real.

Sonia's brows raised. "I see." She fell silent, still crouched on the floor.

She's not dead she's just hiding the body wasn't even real she was hiding she's not dead.

"Mr. Montgomery?" Nathaniel said, again, uncertainly. He folded his arms around his chest. "Are...we going home now?"

"It's been very lonely," The Nightmare Man said, as though responding to Adrian's thoughts. *"We kept waiting for you. When you didn't come, I tried to find you. But you were older."* He ran long, skeletal fingers fondly through Samantha's hair as she nuzzled against his side. She flickered around the edges, like the glow around Christmas lights.

"So you grabbed the wrong kid," Adrian said aloud. "Thinking it was me."

The Nightmare Man nodded, closing his wide, blank eyes. *"When I realized I was wrong, I thought maybe you would come anyway. If I kept the child, you would come here to look for him."*

"I'm here," Adrian said, and his voice cracked. He wanted to go on, to say something more, but he couldn't find his voice.

The ground rumbled.

The walls shook; the floor trembled. Valor's armor rattled, and he looked up, peering through his visor in alarm. The dog jumped to his paws, growling.

Sonia stood. "What was that?"

"She's coming," Valor said, dully, from within his armor.

"What? Who's coming?"

But Adrian didn't have to ask. He felt it, moments after Valor had.

The wall shimmered and twisted and bulged, and someone stepped out —
someone tall and thin, with sagging gray skin and large bloodshot eyes and
a curtain of silver hair.

"Aww. Am I interrupting something?" Lorelai's voice was cold. She looked
monstrous now, contorted. Her skin hung in loose folds along her cheeks
and elbows, the way a snake's skin becomes loose before shedding. She held
one hand out before her, fingers clenched, and the room fell utterly still.

Adrian, like the others, stood frozen, immobilized — as though caught in
a spider's web.

"Nice trick, stealing my carriage," Lorelai said, walking closer. Something
moved and writhed under her skin, casting pale shadows against her
complexion as though something inside were yearning to escape. "Too
bad it came back and told me everything."

"Lorelai, what are you talking about?" Sonia struggled against the invisible
bonds that held her in place.

"*Dreams*, Sonia, you silly girl." Lorelai licked her lips, shaking the long
curtain of silver hair over her shoulder as she stalked forward. She looked
around, her eyes sliding from The Nightmare Man to Valor, lingering the
longest on Samantha. "Stolen dreams. That's why you're here, isn't it? So
that you can find all of the stolen dreams for yourself — you and your pet
human?"

Adrian let out a hoarse cry, struggling to move. "Get away from them!"

She ignored him. "A little greedy of you, isn't it? I'm especially disappointed in you, Sonia. With a human to share your bed, you hardly need all
the dreams. Oh, he wouldn't give anything of quality to *me*, of course, or
that fool Isolde. But I'm sure, given the proper motivation, that he could
have served you just fine…"

Nearby, Nathaniel's wide eyes were leaking tears. He let out a low,
miserable whimper. Samantha merely stared up at Lorelai, wide-eyed and
confused. The glow that surrounded her died down like a flashlight that's
run out of batteries.

"And another human — a child, even." Lorelai clapped her hands together,
looking positively delighted. The things beneath her skin seethed and

writhed and strained against her flesh. "Well, isn't that convenient."

"Keep your filthy hands off of him!" Adrian yelled.

"Lorelai —" Sonia said, straining forward against the invisible bindings. "Please, stop this. You can't…the dreams are killing you. Look at you! Look what they're doing to you!"

"They're keeping me alive, stupid girl!" Lorelai slashed her hand through the air, and four gashes like claw marks appeared in Sonia's cheek. "Look at me? Yes, look at me! I need them!"

Sonia grimaced. Her skin sizzled where it had been sliced open. Light tendrils of smoke curled away from the flesh. "You don't. I know what's happening to you. We can stop it. I'll help you."

Lorelai circled Sonia, stopping to stand between her and The Nightmare Man. The things beneath her skin writhed so it looked like her skin was bubbling like water in a cauldron. "Help me?" she responded, laughing a hard cold laugh. "And how do you plan to do that? Tuck me away in bed with some warm tea? Do you really think there is anything you can do that can reverse *this*?" She raised her arm, holding it inches from Sonia's face. The dark things under the skin writhed and bulged, like bugs crawling under the flesh. The skin itself was mottled and pale, like damp paper.

"It's not too late," Sonia said.

Across the room, the spell's effects seemed to waver. Valor lifted an arm, slowly, painstakingly; his armor creaked. Something broke, and he stumbled forward, suddenly freed of his bindings. He lunged across the room, drawing a sword from its scabbard as he did so.

Lorelai caught his wrist as he lifted the sword over his head. She twisted, and he let out an anguished cry. He flailed, clawing at her with his other arm, but it was useless. She lifted him easily, and his feet waved in the air like a bug that's been caught by its shell. Lorelai squeezed, and he crumpled in on himself like a discarded can, dreamstuff oozing from the cracks of the ruined armor. His sword clattered uselessly to the ground and disintegrated.

"What a waste," Lorelai said. "There was hardly a drop left in him. The queen saw to that, I suppose. No matter — the rest of you look quite fresh." She smiled a cold, ruthless smile and turned her eyes back to Samantha.

Adrian struggled. He was still caught in the bindings; his shoulders ached with the strain of fighting. "Stop it! Leave her alone!"

She lifted a hand, the fingers now curled and sharp like claws, and held it over her head.

Sonia screamed.

The Nightmare Man broke free; he clumsily whirled around, throwing his body fully between Lorelai and Samantha. He outstretched his arms, hiding her behind the smoky folds of his cloak.

Lorelai plunged her hand into his chest.

The enchantment that had caught them all released. Sonia fell to the ground on her hands and knees. Adrian stumbled forward; he met with Nathaniel, who clutched at him in a sort of desperate terror. Sonia struggled forward, crawling toward Samantha, who had backed away from Lorelai and now sat huddled in a corner. Everything happened too fast.

The Nightmare Man said nothing. Blood poured from his chest — blood saturated with dreams, a gleaming prismatic substance that shimmered like starlight, but there were long strands of Darkness in it as well, ribbons of black that gleamed like oil. It engulfed Lorelai's arm, and everywhere that it touched sizzled and popped. The skin tightened.

Lorelai pulled him closer with her free hand, the one not buried in his belly. Dreamstuff oozed from his eyes like tears. She bent over his throat and opened her mouth wide. It was all over within seconds.

Sonia hunched, curling protectively over Samantha. Samantha buried her face in the hollow of Sonia's neck. The dog whimpered and huddled close to them.

Adrian pressed Nathaniel's head to his torso, trying to cover his eyes and ears. He looked away. But he could not block out the sound from his own ears — the same wet gulping sound that unicorns made when they ate flesh. He tried to find the strength to run, or fight, or do something but he was shaking too hard.

No — wait. *He* wasn't shaking.

The ground was shaking.

A deep, low rumble sounded from above, the sound of the earth giving way, of rocks cracking. The sound of a mountain being torn asunder. The dreams that had held the place together were dying along with The Nightmare Man.

Lorelai dropped what was left of The Nightmare Man and stumbled backward, clutching her chest. Her skin was clear and tight and young again, but things still writhed beneath her flesh and she made a desperate choking sound.

The room dissolved around them. The cave melted, the memory-filled forest flickered and faded like a rear projection that had been shut off. They huddled together on a small island of stone surrounded by stars and vast stretches of blackness: What had once been a platform at the top of the Gatekeeper's mountain, though now it was crumbling and diminished. Nearby, the center raised dais sat cold and empty, with a crumpled body leaking dreamlight over the floor.

Lorelai doubled over, trembling. She clawed at her chest and her face, and her silver hair fell over her face and hid it from view. She collapsed to her knees, throwing out her hands to catch herself. The ground continued to tremble. Doorways shook and revolved; overhead, all of the portals had faded into a bright blur.

Lorelai made a terrible sound, sputtering and trembling.

Sonia started to stand, but the ground was shaking so badly now that she couldn't get to her feet. "Lorelai...?"

In response, Lorelai's body gave a full shudder. She made a noise like a wet, strangled scream. Her skin bulged as the things inside of her pressed outward. Then, with a sudden wet tearing sound, the skin burst open. Blood, prismatic and shining, dripped down from a hundred small gashes along Lorelai's arms and shoulders. And things began to crawl out of her.

Shapeless, wet, slimy, furry, skittering things. Things that poured out of her like roaches scattering away from light. Things that broke through the skin and slithered like centipedes. Things that oozed and dripped like blood.

They seethed out of Lorelai's body, engulfing it. Her body was covered in shadow, a dark mask that held only a hint of its old shape. The dream-infused blood pooled away and smoke curled up from it as the dreams separated out and escaped into the atmosphere. Lorelai screamed, but not for long.

FLIGHT

The world was crumbling.

The mountain cracked with a sound like thunder, and the ground beneath them shivered and rumbled. The bridge that had once connected this platform to the center dais swung broken and useless over the side; it rattled and cracked against the trembling, floating stone. Other platforms shifted, breaking apart and raining down into nothingness below. Doorways collapsed.

"Sonia!"

"We're okay!" Sonia held Samantha to her chest, struggling up to her feet. She stood in a half-crouch, wings buzzing in an attempt to counter-balance against the violently shaking ground. "You have to get out of here!"

"We *all* do!"

Nathaniel cling to his arm. He cried in quiet, low sobs that were nearly drowned out by the explosive noise that surrounded them. Samantha leaned against Sonia's leg, clutching the dog to her chest, her eyes wide and terrified — but they were locked on The Nightmare Man's body on the shuddering ground.

A door, Adrian thought desperately. *If this is still my dream, then I dream of a goddamn door.*

A shaft of light tore through the vast emptiness beside him. It stretched, spreading and forming a small circular hole in the air. The hole expanded, agonizingly slowly. The portal was green and black, like the symbol for poison, and the surface rolled and boiled.

Adrian inched toward it, gripping Nathaniel's hand in his; he could hardly walk, the ground was shaking so badly. The ground cracked; a long, wide chasm opened in the floor between where Adrian and Sonia now stood. The Nightmare Man's body slipped through it; the inky black shape that had consumed Lorelai followed, both sliding away from view as they plummeted into nothingness.

Smoke curled up from the chasm, thick and smelling of sulfur.

"Adrian, you have to go!"

"I can't leave you two! Come on!" He realized as he said it how futile it was. The chasm yawned between them, now several feet wide and spewing yellowish smoke. He could barely see them through the smog.

"We can't!" Sonia yelled. "We'll never make it."

The portal began to shrink. Nathaniel tugged at the hem of Adrian's shirt.

"We'll be fine! We'll find another way out," Sonia said. "Just go!"

Feeling like something was coming loose inside of him, Adrian nodded mutely. There were so many things he wanted to say to Sonia — and to Samantha — but there wasn't any time. The chasm in the floor opened wider. The portal swirled and shrank.

Another door, he pleaded in his mind. *Anything. Just — please. Keep them safe.*

The smog was so thick that he could no longer see them, and he couldn't hear anything over the roar of the crumbling mountain. He stumbled toward the shrinking doorway, Nathaniel beside him.

Adrian squeezed Nathaniel's hand in his, and together they crossed through the portal.

It felt like walking through a waterfall. There was no tumbling, no end-over-end falling. Only a shocking, drenching sensation of pressure and cold, followed by a period of senselessness as the world turned itself around.

GOOD DREAMS

"Mr. Montgomery?" Nathaniel's voice broke through his consciousness. He nudged him.

Adrian groaned and opened his eyes.

He was on his back in a patch of woods. He heard cars honking and dogs barking in the distance. Through the trees, he saw a smog-colored sky and a partially-obscured Stop'n'Go sign in the distance. He was wearing a suit, his tie askew. Nathaniel was on his knees next to him. Neither of them were soaked in black primordial goo, but Nathaniel's cheeks were smudged with dirt and he had a small scrape on his forehead.

They lay near a hole in the ground, and Adrian craned his neck to peer over at it. It was some kind of fallen-in space — an old cellar, a mineshaft, a long-buried sunken building that had broken through. He looked back up at Nathaniel. His insides shook.

"Nathaniel…" he started, feeling very confused and disoriented, like waking up from a dream. There was something very important that had happened, but he couldn't remember exactly what it was.

Nathaniel grabbed both of Adrian's hands in his and tugged, trying to help him stand. "It's okay Mr. Montgomery," he said, giving him a knowing look. "We're back home. See?" He cast a glance back over his shoulder, toward the fence of his backyard. "It's time to go home now, I think. I miss my mommy."

"Back home," Adrian echoed. He rose to his feet, looking again between Nathaniel and the half-buried cavernous space. Nothing made any sense. He remembered faeries and unicorns and giant cats, and he remembered a dark slimy place filled with things that slithered. Someone had died —

someone important to him — but he couldn't remember who, or why, or if it had really happened or if it had been a dream, or why he was here in the woods.

Everything jumbled together in his head and the details blurred around the edges. His eyes felt like he'd been crying. His legs ached, as though he had climbed a thousand stairs. But he followed Nathaniel home, walking unsteadily back to Angela Weaver's dilapidated house, coming back to himself slowly. The fuzzy ringing in his ears subsided, although the fog in his mind persisted.

Angela stood on the back porch, leaning over the railing. She smoked a cigarette and stared narrow-eyed at the world, the crow's feet at the corner of her eyes making her look older than she was. She squinted, as Adrian and Nathaniel came into view, and she hesitated a moment as though uncertain of her senses. Then she screamed in joy and jumped over the rail — tripping, nearly falling in the planter box below — and ran across the yard. She dropped her cigarette and screamed again and swooped down on Nathaniel, picking him up and hugging him to her chest, kissing him all over. "My baby!" She yelled, and tears sprang in her eyes and her voice caught with a sob. "My baby, oh Jesus my baby."

Adrian stood there, a little awkwardly, and tried to make sense of everything.

Angela looked up, after a long time, after Nathaniel's squirming finally made her set him down. She looked up at Adrian — ruffled, wrinkled, dirty, hair going in all directions — and her eyes widened and softened and she looked at him in a way she'd never looked at him before. "You found him," she said, breathlessly, and flung herself at him, wrapping her arms around him and sobbing into his shirt. "You found my baby! Oh God bless you, Adrian! God fucking bless you."

He patted her awkwardly on the back. "Where's..." he groped around for the name. "Zachariah? The psychic?"

Angela withdrew from him, narrowing her eyes. "Who?"

"The psychic detective —" he started, and then changed his mind. *Time works differently here,* he thought, but didn't know what that meant. "Never mind."

She pulled away from him and scooped up her son in her arms. Nathaniel smiled sympathetically over his mother's shoulder, and the three of them went back into the house.

* * *

The rest of the day went by in a blur.

Lots of people called Adrian, from the police department, from the media. They wanted to talk to him — the heroic social worker who had single-handedly rescued a missing child from the caved-in cellar where he had spent nearly two days. It was a big story, much bigger than the disappearance itself had been.

He mostly ignored the calls. He locked all the doors in his house and took a long, hot shower. He stood in the shower until the water ran cold, and then he leaned against the cool tile wall and felt the water hit his back like rain. He was shivering when he got out, but he didn't care.

When he got out of the shower, he saw that he'd missed a phone call. He didn't recognize the number, but he checked the message anyway. It was from William.

"Hey little brother," he said to Adrian's voicemail. "Saw you on the news. Pretty crazy shit. They were saying something about an old cellar caving in? Call me."

And Adrian did, for the first time since his wedding.

He bought himself a six pack and called his brother and they talked and he drank and they talked some more, and they reminisced and cried and laughed and Adrian got a little drunk and the battery on his phone wore down. He went to sleep late at night — too late to even consider waking up for a 6 AM run — and slept clumsily and boozily.

He woke up early anyway. The sky outside was pale grey tinged with pink and gold, but the sun wasn't up yet.

Someone was in his room.

He jolted awake, bolting upright in bed, clutching his covers to his chest.

Sitting at the foot of his bed was the most beautiful woman he'd ever seen, like the best parts of every girl he'd ever loved put together into one person. She had short purple hair and transparent dragonfly wings. There was a golden-haired little girl on her lap, slumbering peacefully against her chest.

"...Sonia?"

She smiled. "You made it. I wasn't sure you would. I couldn't see anything, when the door opened I didn't know...I'm so happy for you, Adrian."

"Sonia, how..." he rubbed his eyes. He blinked. They were still there, both of them, in his bed. He could feel the warmth and weight of their bodies through the covers. "Am I still drunk?"

"A little. Listen, I can't stay long. Daylight, in your world — it's like the Darkness in ours. I just wanted to let you know — we're okay. All of us. Some of the doors are gone, but..." she shrugged. Her wings hummed. "I'm keeping an eye on her for you. So you don't have to worry about anything happening. I promise."

His eyes dropped to the Samantha and his heart thudded heavily in his chest.

"I always wanted to be with the children," she said, and reached out a hand to grasp his. "But I like taking care of the dreams even better. Thank you."

"Can..." he started, but his voice faltered. "Could I come back? If I wanted?"

She smiled, a heartbreaking smile. "The doorways are different. They might not lead to the same place, they might not even exist anymore. But... well, it's not impossible. Nothing's really impossible in Dreamland, is it?"

She shifted, rising to leave.

"Sonia, please don't go," he said, twining his fingers around hers, pulling her back to him. "Please stay. Both of you." He looked up at her, pleading, childlike. "At least for a minute?"

"Alright," she said, and crawled up next to him on the bed, curling her body around his, Samantha between them.

He wrapped his arms around them both. Samantha slept, her thumb in her mouth. She flickered, casting a pale glow along the walls like light caught in a suncatcher. He didn't wake her.

Sonia laid her head on his chest. "Go back to sleep, Adrian."

His eyes drooped.

He slept, and when he woke again the sun was orange and bright and high in the sky and his head hurt a little. His bed was empty, but his covers smelled like lilacs and he smiled and snuggled back into his pillow.

He went back to sleep and dreamed good dreams.

About the Author

T.L. Bodine writes dark fantasy and horror of all kinds, from the zombie novel RIVER OF SOULS to the Wattpad-exclusive gothic, THE HOUND. She's interested in uncanny, fantastic things, and the way real people with real problems interact with them.

When not writing, she can usually be found watching horror movies, playing story-heavy video games, or experimenting in the kitchen.

She lives in New Mexico with her husband, David, and two small dogs.

You can connect with me on:

🌐 http://www.tlbodine.com

🐦 https://twitter.com/glassratmedia

Subscribe to my newsletter:

✉ https://tlbodine.substack.com

Also by T.L. Bodine

River of Souls

Undeath is a manageable condition.

That's what the media says, anyway: with the help of the miracle life-extension drug, Lazarus, the Undead can retain their humanity and live normal, happy lives. Without it, they become violent, mindless walking corpses.

Davin Montoya was eager to believe all of that. Forced to drop out of college to take care of his teenage sister, Zoe, after their father drank himself to death, he was more than happy to sign the no-good alcoholic over to the government's Lazarus House for treatment. That was one less thing for him to worry about.

Until an accident left him joining the ranks of the freshly deceased himself.

Now, keeping his death a secret is the only way to keep his sister out of foster care. But to do so, he must venture into the underground society of Unregistered Undead - a dangerous world of drug deals and government resistance. But when their access to Lazarus begins to run dry, the truth starts to unravel…and it's not what anyone expected.

The Beast in the Bedchamber

A goddess, disguised as a cat, chooses a man to be her slave…

A girl is sold into marriage to pay off her father's debts, but her husband is nothing like she could have expected…

A man is cursed to wander for eternity unless he finds true love - and he must do it as a dog…

The Beast in the Bedchamber features seven modern fairy tales about beastly bridegrooms.

Insomnia: Stories to Read with the Lights Turned On

Reading horror stories late at night when you're home alone is never a good idea, but that hasn't stopped you before.

One night, clicking through links, you find yourself on a strange site filled with spooky stories. Inspired, you even try writing one of your own. You didn't think anything bad would come of it.

You were wrong.

Insomnia is a short story collection and a story in its own right, incorporating 15 original short horror stories set into a broader narrative. Read it in order…and read it with the lights turned on.